M

Reunions Can Be Murder

A CHARLIE PARKER MYSTERY

Connie Shelton

INTRIGUE
P R E S S

DENVER

ISBN 1-890768-46-4

First Printing, December 2002

This book is a work of fiction. Names, characters, places and incidents are either the product of the author's imagination or are used fictitiously. Any resemblance to actual events or locales or persons, living or dead, is entirely coincidental. Although the author and publisher have made every effort to ensure the accuracy and completeness of information contained in this book, we assume no responsibility for errors, inaccuracies, omissions, or any inconsistency herein. Any slights of people, places or organizations are unintentional.

Library of Congress Cataloging-in-Publication Data
Shelton, Connie.
    Reunions Can Be Murder : the Seventh Charlie Parker Mystery / by Connie Shelton.
        p. cm.
    ISBN 1-890768-46-4 (alk. paper)
    1. Parker, Charlie (Fictitious character)--Fiction. 2. Women private investigators--New Mexico--Fiction. 3. Women dog owners--Fiction. 4. Missing persons--Fiction. 5. Family reunions--Fiction. 6. New Mexico--Fiction. I. Title.

PS3569.H393637 R48 2002
813'.54--dc21
                                        2001052511

10 9 8 7 6 5 4 3 2 1

To L.—we miss you.

Acknowledgements:

The author wishes to acknowledge the following people for their help, encouragement and contributions to this book: Dan Shelton, as always, my aviation expert and partner in all things; Susan Slater and Peggy Smith, first readers who helped make this book much better than it started out; to the real Keith Randel, the inspiration for a memorable character, and to his lovely bride, Gretchen, who keeps him in line. Last, but certainly not least, thanks to Robert Leslie of White Oaks, NM, who gave me a tour of the old schoolhouse and museum, and shared his memories of growing up. And to the people of White Oaks, I beg your indulgence in allowing me artistic license with your town. While the basic layout I've described is reasonably accurate, all people, events, and details are strictly out of my own imagination.

Oh, and last (really)—thanks to my cousins in the Ellison clan who suggested the title for this book at one of our family reunions where, thankfully, no one died.

ALSO BY CONNIE SHELTON

THE CHARLIE PARKER SERIES
Deadly Gamble
Vacations Can be Murder
Partnerships Can Kill
Small Towns Can be Murder
Memories Can be Murder
Honeymoons Can be Murder

NONFICTION
Publish Your Own Novel

ONE

The fire was apparently set sometime in the early morning hours and by the time our phone rang at four P.M., the vicious April winds had whipped a thousand acres of pristine forest into a raging inferno.

"I'll call you when I get there, hon," Drake said, hefting his flight bag. "It may be late." He checked his watch.

"Two and a half hours flight time, right?" I asked, calculating roughly the distance to the fire base camp in southern New Mexico.

"I'll try to give you a buzz on my cell phone, but you know how it is once I get on scene. The crew will bombard me, and if there's any daylight left the fire boss will probably want to do a quick recon."

"If I haven't heard from you in three hours, I'll call," I told him. I wasn't merely being a nagging wife, it was an FAA requirement that he either file a flight plan with them or we provide our own flight following. Experience had taught us that doing it ourselves was better.

"Love you," he whispered, through a soft, lingering kiss. He gave my ponytail two quick tugs before we parted.

I watched him walk across the tarmac—his body trim in his khaki flight suit, and that enticing bit of gray showing at his temples beneath a black cap and dark aviator sunglasses—to our blue and white JetRanger, which airport personnel had pulled out of the hangar and fueled for his flight. Although I'm now a licensed pilot myself, I've spent the past few months building up my hours and am not yet at the point where I'm qualified to take on government work. Not that I'd want to—fighting forest fires is some of the most dangerous and hair-raising work a helicopter pilot can perform.

Drake methodically circled the helicopter, performing his preflight routine, then stowed his bag in the rear compartment and climbed into the right hand seat. I watched as he began his startup checklist, then fastened his harness and adjusted his flight helmet while the rotor blades slowly spun up. He blew me a kiss, then lifted the craft gently off the ground; within a couple of minutes it was just a small speck to the south of the airport.

I took a deep breath. "Okay, kid, let's go," I said to Rusty, our big reddish Lab. I noticed the dog seemed to have put on a few pounds and suspected Drake of sneaking him extra treats in the six months we'd been married.

Rusty hopped into the backseat of my Jeep and I settled into the front, already feeling that stab of loneliness that came over me whenever Drake left on a job. Especially these types of jobs, where we didn't know how long he'd be gone and nothing was definite, including his return. I was learning to adjust to the reality of having a husband with a hazardous job, but it wasn't easy.

I pulled away from Double Eagle Airport on Albuquerque's west side, taking the long stretch of two-lane road that appeared to go nowhere but eventually led to Interstate 40. Hitting that busy thoroughfare fed me into the stream of eighteen-wheeler traffic rolling into town. I joined the stream, knowing it was fruitless to try to move ahead. By the time I reached the North Valley, traffic had slowed to a complete clog.

A two-year construction project to revamp the interchange linking the two major interstate highways that quarter the city had thrown everyone into a tizzy, especially those poor out-of-towners who innocently wandered into it. I exited at Rio Grande Boulevard, knowing that the city stop-and-go would be quicker than the freeway, especially during the five-thirty rush hour. Continuing east on Central, I pulled into the parking area behind the Victorian-housed offices of RJP Investigations twenty minutes later.

I'm a partner with my brother, Ron, at RJP. Although I've cut back on the number of hours I spend here now that Drake and I have the helicopter service, Ron's out of town this week so I offered to check in each day. Which means I have to stop by and lock up by six o'clock so Tammy, our part-time afternoon help, can go home.

As soon as I opened the door Rusty leaped out of the car and proceeded to roam the fence line of the backyard parking area. I entered the gray and white converted Victorian house through the back door into the kitchen and immediately heard raised voices coming from the reception area.

"Problem?" I asked Tammy, who was seated at her desk looking about ready to cry.

"I've been trying to tell this lady that Ron is out of town," she said in a voice just barely over a whisper.

I turned to the woman who hovered over Tammy's

desk. She was close to six feet tall with broad shoulders and an even broader torso. She wore a polyester pantsuit of chocolate brown with an orange and white scarf twined at the neckline and attached at one shoulder with a gold circle pin. Her gray hair suffered from a bad perm that hadn't been refreshed in awhile. Despite the fact that her wardrobe hadn't been updated in twenty-five years or so, she had an intimidating presence and I didn't blame Tammy for cringing. I turned to the woman.

"Perhaps I can help?"

"I doubt it. I need a private investigator and I need him now." Her voice came out like sludge, harsh and forceful but with a slur to the words. I wondered if she was drunk, but the black eyes that bored into me were sharp.

"Well, as Tammy explained, Ron is the licensed private investigator and he's out of town for the next week."

"What about you? What's your position here?"

"I'm Ron's partner, Charlie Parker. I'm the accountant who handles financial matters for the firm."

She latched onto only one word. "Well, if you're a partner, you can help me." She hiked a huge brown purse into the crook of her arm. "You can take the information and get started."

Her manner made me grit my teeth but I take credit for having a little intelligence. When someone half a foot taller than me, who outweighs me by sixty or seventy pounds, tells me to take some information, okay, I'll take it. I ushered her into the conference room and carried a yellow pad and pen in with me. Under my breath I told Tammy she could leave at six, just to be sure she let Rusty in first.

"My father's missing," the woman began, plopping herself into one of the leather chairs around the table.

"Let's start at the beginning." I wasn't going to let her take complete charge. "Give me your names and addresses."

"My name is Dorothy Schwartzman. My father's name is William McBride." She recited both their addresses. Hers was midtown, in a neighborhood of two- and three-bedroom homes built in the late fifties. His was in the north valley, off Rio Grande Boulevard, in an area that could go either direction on the economic spectrum. Recently trendy, the north valley area could just as easily contain a run-down adobe hovel or a fifteen thousand square foot villa. "We think he's becoming senile. He's eighty-four years old."

"When was the last time you saw your father?"

"Late February."

"That's nearly two months," I said. "Have you reported this to the police?"

"Yes, I did." She acted like I'd asked an imbecilic question. "They said they couldn't treat it as a missing persons case because Dad was probably right where he said he'd be."

"He told you where he was going?"

"Sent me a note. Said he was going prospecting."

"Prospecting. Did he say where?"

"Not in the note, no. But he has two or three favorite places and I told the police about those."

"And those would be . . . ?" Why did I feel like I was pulling teeth here? I glanced at my watch, wondering whether Drake might have reached his destination.

"Am I keeping you?" she asked, sarcasm dripping from the words.

"No, ma'am." I gritted my teeth but bent over my notepad. "Go on."

"Well," she shifted in her chair, settling in for the long haul. "One of his favorite spots has always been White Oaks. And of course he's had this lifelong enchantment with the stories of the Lost Dutchman Mine in Arizona."

I wrote down both names. "Where is White Oaks?" I asked.

"Down south."

"South . . . in New Mexico?"

"Well, *yes*. Just a few miles out of Carrizozo." She must have caught the impatient look that crossed my face. "I know, not many people have heard of it, but it was quite well-known at one time. They found a bit of gold and silver around there. They quit regular mining some years ago. I'm not sure if anyone still lives there."

"And your father went there prospecting? What would he hope to find—gold and silver?"

"Of course there's no real sizeable amount of gold or silver there anymore," she said, almost smiling. "You have to know my father to understand why he'd do this. He's a man who has desperately wanted, his entire life, to be rich. He's completely wrapped up in the idea. His greatest dream would be to find the mother lode, the big deal, win the lottery. It has never once crossed his mind that he might get rich by working hard and investing wisely. That just isn't in his makeup."

"So he went on these prospecting trips regularly?"

"Oh yes. I suspect he'll do it as long as he's physically able to pull himself over the rocks."

"And what's different about this time? As the police

said, why don't you believe he's right where he said he'd be? Would he normally stay in contact with you?"

"My son, Roger, drove down to White Oaks a couple of weeks ago. Didn't find any sign of his grandpa. Dad never was one for staying in touch, just went on his merry way and the heck with the rest of us."

"Maybe he just wants some time alone and doesn't want to be bothered," I suggested.

"Hmmph."

"Well, I've taken all the information," I said. "I'll hand it over to Ron next Monday and he'll get back to you."

"Oh, that won't do at all," she insisted in her nasal slur. "I'm telling you, young lady, you need to get started on this right away."

"He's been gone two months already and the police don't feel there's any reason to treat it as a missing persons case, so why will one more week make a big difference?"

She pulled out her wallet and laid five one-hundred dollar bills on the table, along with a set of keys and a five by seven photo of a weathered man who looked out of place in a gray suit and blue-striped tie. "I'm worried that he may forget where he is or that someone may take advantage of him. That's him," she said indicating the photo, "and those are my spare keys to his house and pick-up truck. Please find him. Our family reunion is coming up in a week. He *must* be there."

TWO

"Excuse me?" I wasn't sure I'd heard her correctly. "This is all about a family reunion?"

She gave me a pointed stare.

"You haven't given us much time."

"Just start looking for him." She'd risen from her chair and towered over me, speaking in a tone that left no room for argument.

I watched her wide backside retreat just before the front door closed with a firm clunk. What a strange woman, I thought. Actually, it sounded like a strange family. I glanced at the money on the conference table. Guess we had ourselves a client.

Tammy's desk was clear, the night lamp on her credenza turned on. Rusty whimpered impatiently from behind the kitchen door. Thank goodness Tammy'd been smart enough to contain him before he could do something as uncouth as slobbering on Dorothy Schwartzman. I freed him and he followed me upstairs to my office where I laid the yellow notepad on my desk and locked the cash into the small safe concealed beneath the seat at the bay window. I checked the answering machine—nothing there— and locked the front door before heading back to the kitchen, where I unplugged the coffee maker and locked the door behind me.

A chill wind came out of the east, raising instant goose-bumps on my arms. Our April weather can best be described as unsettled. Gorgeous, sunny spring days can easily alternate with dreary, rainy ones and the winds can be fearsome. Sometimes we get all this in one day. I rushed to the car and grabbed the light jacket I keep in there. A couple of minutes with the heater running full blast, and a pleasant warmth began to spread through the vehicle.

The dashboard clock told me that it had been two hours since Drake left on his flight. With any luck, by the time I got home he'd be calling to let me know he'd arrived safely. Resisting the desire for some of Pedro's green chile chicken enchiladas, I drove straight home.

I unlocked the heavy door and switched on some lights. The house felt cool, dark and abandoned in the last of the day's fading light. The smell of new paint and dry-wall still hung in the air. We'd only been back in our recently remodeled abode for about six weeks and I was still adjusting to the newness of things. After a fire last October had partially gutted the house, we'd decided to update the '50s style ranch home with a few modern con-veniences, like a large master suite with exercise room and Jacuzzi, new guest quarters, and a made-to-order home office for Drake's business. As a last-minute afterthought, we'd also updated the kitchen cabinetry and appliances figuring—after all, while the place was torn up we might as well do everything.

I hung my jacket and purse on the coat rack just inside the front door, thinking tonight might be a good time to get around to unpacking the boxes of dishes and knick-knacks that belonged in the china cabinet. Luckily, the fire hadn't touched either the living or dining rooms, and we'd been able to clean and store my mother's family keepsakes during the remodeling. It was high time I got busy and put them away, and it would help fill the hours while Drake was gone.

The answering machine light in the kitchen glowed at me steadily. No word from Drake yet. I busied myself by nuking a frozen dinner for seven minutes and scooping doggy nuggets into Rusty's bowl. The phone rang just as I was pouring a glass of iced tea to go with my sumptuous dinner and I sloshed some onto the counter-top.

"Hi, sweetheart, just letting you know I made it to my destination just fine," Drake said.

"They didn't have you fly any recon tonight?" I asked.

"Nope. I landed within the very last of my legal day-light limit. Guess they'll have me out here at the crack of dawn tomorrow, though."

He told me what little he knew about the progress of the forest fire and I told him about the new case that had walked into the office. There wasn't much more to say and I hung up feeling kind of empty. Spent the rest of the evening arranging china in the cabinet while an old Ingrid Bergman movie played on the set in the living room. By nine o'clock I decided I was tired.

Five A.M. found me wide-awake. The early bedtime and the unfamiliarity of Drake being gone conspired to waken me without hope of drifting back off again. I puttered around, letting Rusty out, making coffee, taking a long shower, and I was still ready to leave for the office by seven. Once there, I puttered some more—making more coffee, opening my mail from the previous day, and entering a few billing records on the computer. I found my eyes trailing to the yellow pad with Dorothy Schwartzman's information on it. I drummed my fingers on the desk. I made a couple of doodles on the pad.

Face it, I was bored. Must have been, to seriously consider beginning the investigation for Dorothy. The woman had rubbed me the wrong way in nearly every way possible, yet I was seriously thinking about working the case. Plus, I just had the feeling she'd be calling in a day or two for a progress report. The thought of dealing with her again didn't set well.

The sound of the back door opening perked Rusty's ears and he rose from his position on the Oriental rug in my office and raced down the stairs.

"Hey, boy," came Sally's voice from the kitchen. I could picture her reaching for the tin of dog treats on the counter and sneaking one to him.

"Anything exciting going on?" she asked as I entered the room, empty coffee mug in hand. Her wide smile greeted me, and I noticed her shaggy blond hair had been freshly trimmed.

"Drake's on the fire near Ruidoso," I told her.

"Oh, gosh, I heard about that one on the news this morning. Doesn't sound good. They said it was man-made!"

"That's what I heard too. Guess I'll know a little more this evening when he calls in. Meanwhile, we got a new case yesterday afternoon. An abrasive woman who insists that we get started on it now, even though I told her Ron was gone."

"An emergency?" she asked as she put her lunch sack into the fridge.

"Hard to tell. An elderly man, who went off on his own, left the family a note telling them where he was going, hasn't been heard from since. The police won't take it as a missing persons case because they say he's probably right where he said he'd be."

She grinned at me, a wide smile on her freckled face. "And you just aren't satisfied with that, huh? And you're just thinking you might follow up on it."

"Well . . ." I didn't want to let on that Dorothy Schwartzman had basically bullied me into doing it. "I might just make a few phone calls."

"Uh-huh." Sally poured herself a mug of coffee and headed toward her desk. "Well, I've got several letters to get done before the morning's over. Chrissie smiled today." She flashed one of those doting-mommy smiles.

Sally's daughter, Chrissie, had been born in February while Drake and I were still away on our honeymoon. Sally and Ross had arranged their schedules so one of them was always home with the baby. Since Sally had always worked mornings for us anyway, we kept that schedule; Tammy was really here in the afternoons to take more of my workload so I could help Drake with his business. Logistics are always so much fun.

I carried my refilled mug back to my office and considered what I might do for starters to locate the missing William McBride. Figuring that simplicity is always the best method, I first dialed his home phone number here in

Albuquerque. It sounds overly basic, but it's amazing how many times people make things much more complicated than they are. There was always the chance he'd come home in the past day or so and he'd simply pick up the phone. Of course, then I'd have to give Dorothy most of her money back—but at least I'd be rid of her. The phone rang and rang, ending that little fantasy.

"I'm going out for awhile," I told Sally.

Rusty trotted eagerly beside me so I told him he could come too.

THREE

McBride's home was pretty much what I expected from the outside. Built in the days before the rural north valley had any tight zoning, the structure was a ramshackle collection of rooms that looked like they'd been tacked onto something that used to be a house trailer. The outside walls had been stuccoed in a variety of colors, ranging from pale pink to light coral to dark adobe brown. I tried to see a theme there but couldn't quite spot it.

The property, which I judged to be about an acre in size, started level with the elevation of the lane it bordered then dropped off into a dip near the same area where the third addition to the house began, so that room sat cocked at a slight downward angle. A couple of huge, old cottonwoods stood at the western edge of the property, flanked by thickets of mesquite and scrub oak, creating a wall of green between McBride's place and the neighboring one.

I parked in the flattened dirt area in front of the house where years of vehicle traffic had beaten out a turn-around spot. There were no vehicles in sight, nor any fresh tracks. Obviously, no one had driven in here within the past week or so.

Rusty whimpered as I pulled to a stop. Not seeing anything he could harm, I let him out to perform his own inspection of the place. He immediately thrust his nose to the ground and began checking the driveway and path leading to the front door, paying particular attention to a couple of scraggly shrubs along the way.

I inserted the key Dorothy had given me into the wobbly doorknob lock and it turned easily. The stench in the place almost knocked me backward and I began to fear that I might have located William McBride much more quickly than I wanted to. My throat clamped shut and I placed one hand over my nose and mouth.

Rusty pushed past me and trotted into the first room he came to, a small, square living room. He sniffed the air with no particular foreboding, and proceeded toward the kitchen. Fearful of what he might find, I followed.

I caught a strong whiff of gas as I passed the oven and automatically reached for the dials to be sure McBride hadn't left them on. He hadn't. Everything was tightly in the "off" position. I crossed a linoleum floor tacky with grease residue to the room's only window and strained against it to get it open. It finally raised with a groan of old wood against wood and I went back into the living room to do the same in there. With two windows and a door open, the smell emanating from a back room somewhere was drawn past me with some force, and I gagged again.

I stepped out to the small concrete porch and grabbed a couple of lungfuls of fresh air before venturing back inside. Rusty had disappeared into another room beyond the kitchen and I walked again across the floor, which sucked at my shoes, to find him. Down a short hall, I found the source of the stench—an unflushed toilet, full of dark brown water that had congealed through evaporation into something unmentionable. Ugh.

I ran some water in the sink, testing to be sure the home's system was operational, before taking my chances on flushing the commode. Ready to flee if it overflowed, I pressed the handle. Luckily it worked. The brown muck flushed away and fresh water rushed in. Now why would someone leave home for a planned trip without flushing the toilet?

Could McBride be so senile, as Dorothy had implied, that he'd forget something so basic? Or could there be a more sinister reason? Perhaps he'd been interrupted and kidnapped. But how would that explain the note he'd sent?

I gave the room a good dousing from a rusty-looking can of room freshener, then opened another window. A canine yip from elsewhere in the house grabbed my attention.

"Rusty! Where are you?" I stepped back into the hall, trying to figure out where he'd gone. The short hall led to a bedroom. Rusty stood pointing beside a dresser, to a corner of the floor. I stepped behind him. A dead rat lay on its side—its body a good eight or ten inches long and its tail perhaps double that. Was there to be no end to the sensory delights this house held?

"Uck! Get away from that," I told the dog, pulling at his collar.

He turned to me, as if to say, *What? What's the matter with this?*

"C'mon, you." I yanked him away from the dead rat and looked a little closer. The body was already beginning to show significant decay and its odor had obviously contributed to the overall ambiance of the house. I glanced around the room. The bed was neatly made, the dresser top clear of bric-a-brac. I'd get back to it later. I led Rusty from the room and closed the door behind us.

Back in the living room the air had cleared somewhat. I gazed over the layout. A faded gold velvet sofa sat against the far wall, with an end table piled high with papers. I flipped through them, finding mostly pieces of unopened junk mail and a few bills. The postmark date on the phone bill was February. Surprising that the phone company hadn't shut him off yet. Likewise with an electric bill. No water bill—perhaps he had his own well. I picked out the bills and left the junk. I'd have to ask Dorothy whether she wanted to take care of them.

Checking the other furniture in the room, I found there wasn't much of interest. A small bookcase held a TV set, a little thing probably made in the '60s with a white metal case with red trim, and a few books. I flipped through the books. Most of them were about mines, ghost towns, and gold strikes. Here and there, I came across notes and maps drawn on lined notebook paper, presumably in McBride's handwriting. I put the books and notes in a small stack with the mail I planned to take with me. They would make some interesting reading tonight at home.

A bedroom on the other end of the living room appeared to be the one he used. The bed was made, the covers neat and smooth, but the dresser top contained a collection of the kind of things we all accumulate in everyday life—a good-sized handful of change, two small pocket knives, some crumpled receipts, and a wrapped Starlight mint. The receipts were unimportant, meals at Furr's Cafeteria dated over a year earlier. All this was coated in a neat layer of undisturbed dust.

I made a quick run through the dresser drawers but found nothing more interesting than two copies of *Playboy* from 1973. The adjoining bathroom's vanity drawers yielded an unusual system of filing his financial records—two drawers jammed full of check duplicates on an account at First Albuquerque Bank. None of them were dated within the past six months, so I wasn't sure they'd be of any help. I left them in place.

There were no prescription drugs in the medicine cabinet, unusual for a person in his eighties, I thought. But then, if he'd taken a planned trip, he'd have packed his regular medications with him. The clothes in the closet were simple and few—Levi's, plaid flannel shirts, a light down jacket, and two pair of worn hiking boots with mud in the treads. The gray suit, shirt, and tie from his portrait hung together on one hanger at the far right-hand side of the closet. His one suit of dress-up clothes. For some reason, the odd thought that McBride would probably end up being buried in that suit flitted through my mind.

I turned away from the closet and scanned the room once more. Nothing jumped out at me.

"C'mon kid," I told Rusty, who had settled on the matted carpet, head on paws. He was obviously miffed that I'd pulled him away from his great find in the other bedroom, and he'd not found any more treasures.

Near the front door, the smell of gas was fainter but still present. I made myself a mental note to call Dorothy as soon as I got back to the office and suggest that she have the gas shut off or get a repairman out here. I locked the front door and decided to have a look around the yard.

Behind the house sat a small toolshed built of warped gray planks. A rusted hasp attempted to keep the door closed but it was pretty much a losing battle. A Master padlock was looped through the ring on the hasp, but the screws holding the device to the shed were barely holding their own. I found a short piece of rebar on the ground behind the shed and pried. Two quick pulls and the screws came away as if they'd been mounted in modeling clay. At my insistence, the door swung outward with a groan.

I was disappointed to see that the shed was nearly empty. What kind of man was this, anyway? Where was the clutter they all collect? In one corner stood a cardboard box about four feet tall by a foot square. According to the labeling, it had contained a metal detector but it was empty now. A few garden tools hung from nails on the opposite wall and a bunch more nails jutted outward in a haphazard row to the right of them. I imagined picks, shovels, and other mining implements hanging there, but had no actual proof of that. A dented wok-like pan lay on the ground near the cardboard box. I turned it over and saw by the series of concentric ridges inside that it was a gold pan. It was pretty beat up and I guessed that McBride probably had a newer one that he'd taken with him. Admittedly, I was filling in a few blanks but I hadn't found anything that disproved the theory that the old man had simply packed up some tools and a few clothes and headed for the mines.

I was drawing a blank on what to do next and, as the

police had, I wanted to conclude that he went where he said he was going. Somehow, that wasn't going to be good enough for Dorothy Schwartzman though, and I wasn't keen on the idea of facing her without some better news. She was definitely set on the idea that her father attend that family reunion, whether he wanted to or not.

I stepped out of the shed and glanced around. A stiff breeze rustled the leaves on the cottonwoods with a sound like decks of cards being gently shuffled. The wind blew on through quickly, leaving the air still again. I whistled to Rusty, who by this time had his nose aimed at a woodpile at the back of the house, and motioned him to get himself back to the car. We pulled out and headed south on Rio Grande. Back at the office I called Dorothy's number and was grateful when I got an answering machine. I left her a message about the gas leak in her father's house and told her I'd found some unpaid bills and would forward them to her. I stuck the bills into a large brown envelope, addressed it, and stuck on some stamps.

"Want some lunch?" Sally asked when I took the envelope down to her desk to be added to the day's outgoing mail.

A system had evolved within the office where Tammy called in to take lunch orders, which she would pick up on her way in. It was nearly twelve-thirty and she was apparently on the phone now. I decided on a turkey and Swiss on whole wheat from Bob's Deli.

Sally filled me in on a couple of messages that had come in while I was gone and I trekked back up to my office to begin returning phone calls and taking care of my standard workload. By five o'clock I'd paid the month-end bills, sent out statements to our regular clients—mainly law firms and insurance companies—and entered most of the monthly expenses into the computer. I'd updated the system the previous month and was still getting used to the new way of doing things. I was just pulling my jacket on when the phone rang.

"Charlie, it's Dorothy Schwartzman on line one," came Tammy's voice over the intercom.

Goody.

"Have you located my father?" Dorothy's nasal whine came over the line without so much as a hello first.

"Well, not yet." I felt an edge creep into my voice.

"I got your message," she said. "Is that all you've done?"

"Investigation is always a process of elimination. We try to start at the beginning, with the closest and most logical premise."

"And that is—?"

"And that is to find out whether he left any clues at home. Whether there might be signs of foul play, forced entry, or just a simple clue about where he might have gone." Why was I explaining my every move to her?

"Well, he *told* me where he'd gone," she reminded me sarcastically.

"I *know* that." I felt my teeth clenching. "Our job is to find out whether he actually *did* what he told you he was going to."

"And did he?"

"Dorothy, I've only been on this case for half a day. If you'd rather find a different investigator, feel free. Otherwise, I'll report to you when I have some new information."

I said goodbye and hung up before she had the chance to grill me further. Pushing away from the desk, I leaned back in my chair and remembered to unclench my fists. In the past I'd only become involved in cases when the person needing my help was a friend, or when a genuinely nice person was unfairly accused. I wasn't sure how long I'd hang in there for a nasty-tempered person like Dorothy.

"Dammit, Ron," I railed, "why'd you leave me stuck with this?"

"Everything okay?" Tammy asked from the doorway.

I opened my eyes. "Yeah. I'm just trying to get my blood pressure to come back down."

She looked skeptical. "Okay, if you're sure. I . . . um . . . wanted to ask you. Would it be okay if I left a few minutes early today?"

"Sure." I didn't even ask for a reason. I was plenty ready to get out of there myself, although I wasn't sure why. There certainly wasn't anything exciting waiting for me at home.

An hour later, with an order of Pedro's take-out enchiladas in front of me at the kitchen table, I spread William McBride's books and papers out to take a look. One of the items caught my attention. It was a single sheet of paper, folded intricately into a packet about four inches square, the edges tacked down with sealing wax. McBride's shaky writing covered one side in oversized letters. MAP-L.D.M.

L.D.M.? Lost Dutchman Mine? Surely not.

FOUR

Every miner, dreamer and speculator for the past hundred years or more has fantasized about the possibility of finding the Lost Dutchman Mine. I'd heard the legends all my life, about Jacob Waltz's amazing gold treasure. But the more stories one heard, the more confusing and convoluted they became. I pried one edge of the sealing wax loose.

The paper was obviously old—yellowed and crisp—but not a hundred years old. Could be thirty or forty, though. I flattened it out and looked more closely. The map was hand drawn in black ink from a fountain pen. It was a water-based ink, definitely, because in one spot a drop of water had blurred one of the lines. The drawing showed lines veering off in several directions, a series of tent-shaped triangles—they might depict mountains or tents or most anything else—and a variety of squiggles and tiny circles. I didn't see anything to identify a town or highway. I wondered whether McBride had drawn the map of his own knowledge or if it had been given to him.

Judging by the condition of the paper, I guessed that he hadn't opened the map in many years, and it certainly hadn't been folded and refolded a lot, as I'd expect if he'd carried it with him and tried to follow it to a destination.

I set it aside and picked up one of the books.

I was well into the story of the old German and his sup-posedly unlimited gold find when the phone startled me. I picked it up with a little trepidation, thinking Dorothy might resort to tracking me down at home to quiz me.

"Hi, sweetheart," said Drake.

"Hey! How's the job going?"

"Not making much progress yet," he answered. His voice sounded tired.

"How big is the fire now?"

"Probably three or four thousand acres. The wind blew quite a bit today. But I guess it could have been worse. I dropped about a hundred buckets of water and foam, but it's like pissing on a house fire—not much effect."

"Do they know how it started?"

"Nothing definite yet. It started out in a clearing in the forest. That much is obvious from the air. We could see a definite pattern where it branched out from the starting point and went like crazy after that."

"I heard on the news it was man-made."

"That's the scuttlebutt here. Fire Manager said he'd bet some kids were out partying in the woods. They do that a lot around here. Go out somewhere on the reservation, light a big bonfire, drink a lot and do a few drugs. Next thing you know the fire's out of control and they've all dis-appeared and nobody's talking."

"Is it all on Indian land?"

"So far. There are a couple of ranches in the path, so that's a danger too, but they're hoping to get a line cut and get the thing contained in the next couple of days."

We chatted a bit more and I told him a little about my

day. "I may drive down to White Oaks tomorrow and see if I can get a line on whether the old man has been there recently. This woman—the daughter—is tenacious as a bulldog. Guess I better come up with something to appease her."

"White Oaks isn't too far from here. Too bad I'll be out flying all day."

"Well, it's too far for me to drive down there and back in a day. Maybe I'll just come on down there and bunk with you at your hotel."

Drake told me to drive carefully and we finished the call with a bunch of miss-you type gooey stuff. After he'd hung up I pulled the road atlas out of the hall closet. White Oaks was about fifty miles, mostly over winding mountain roads, from where he was staying. I'd have to see whether it was really practical to go there for the night.

Now that it looked like I was planning a trip, I decided I'd get to bed early. I cleaned up the remains of my dinner, locked up, and took one of McBride's books to bed with me.

I awoke about six the next morning, out of sync with my normal sleep pattern because Drake wasn't there beside me. Decided to pack a few things and get going. I grabbed enough for an overnight stay, including food for the dog, and phoned the office to leave a message on the machine for Sally to let her know my intentions.

By seven Rusty and I were in the Jeep, headed south on I-25. We pulled off at one of the exits on the edge of town where I topped off the gas tank, checked under the hood, verified the tire pressure, and bought a breakfast sandwich and large coffee. Modern travel has become such a one-stop affair.

I ate the sandwich in the car, giving the last bite to the

dog, before we pulled out of the service station's lot. Back on the interstate, I sipped my coffee and listened to a radio host taking calls on the topic of the road construction mess in Albuquerque. It felt good to be out of the city for a bit, zipping along ten miles over the speed limit.

The countryside became pure desert the farther south we traveled. Flat-topped mesas stood regally on our right, while the Rio Grande River showed as a strip of green vegetation cutting through the land between us and the pale purple shape of the Manzano Mountains to the east. I exited south of Socorro onto highway 380, wishing I'd planned it better. If I'd arrived here closer to noon, one of the world famous burgers at the Owl Bar would have been a real treat. Maybe I'd catch one on the way home.

By ten o'clock I'd passed through the little crossroads town of Carrizozo, turned north and found the sign for the turnoff to White Oaks. Nine miles of road winding through a land of pale earth dotted with scrub piñon and juniper led me into the old mining town. A cemetery, whose metal archway entrance stood on the right-hand side of the road, greeted the visitor first. I cruised past it, planning to come back later and browse the names of the inhabitants. Mine tailings dotted the hills on my left, small heaps of orange and yellow mineral residue showing brightly against the surrounding earth. I drove through the town once.

End to end it wasn't more than a mile or two. A few buildings remained along the main drag, with others, including a couple of sizeable Victorian homes, dotted around the surrounding hilly terrain. When I reached the northeastern edge I U-turned and retraced the route. On my right, I passed the shell of a once-massive sandstone building, most of its front façade chipped away but its two-story exterior walls intact. Across the road, adobe foundations and fragments of walls stood like silent soldiers in a field of scrub piñon and tumbleweeds.

I hadn't noticed a single car anywhere on my first trip through, but now I spotted a small pickup truck parked behind the town's one and only eating establishment. I pulled into the dirt flat spot in front of the tiny wooden building with the single word CAFÉ lettered in red paint on the front window. Rusty raised up from his spot on the back seat, suddenly interested now that we had stopped. I retrieved a bowl and canteen and poured water for him, which he lapped sloppily beside the open car door. When he was finished I ushered him back into the Jeep and rolled each of the windows down several inches.

"I'll be right back," I told him.

Grabbing my purse from the seat beside me, I walked up to the wooden porch and peeked in the window. A couple of lights burned overhead, the only evidence that the place might be open. I tried the door and it swung inward with a loud creak.

"Be right there, Jeb." A male voice came from the back somewhere.

I looked around. A polished wooden counter ran the length of the room on the left side, with red leather-topped chrome stools in front of it. Three sets of tables and chairs jutted out from the right wall at intervals, leaving only a narrow aisle between the end of each table and the stools at the counter. Behind the counter were an industrial sized coffee maker, a soda dispensing machine, and a shelf containing a long line of beer bottles. Through a window cut into the back wall, I could see a kitchen with a long grill, a variety of pots and utensils, and one of those chrome spinners that waitresses clip your order to. I took a seat at the counter.

"Little early today, ain't ya?" The man who stepped out of the back room was wiping his hands on the bottom edge of the large white bib apron he wore. His jaw went slack when he finally looked up and saw me. "Well, you ain't Jeb, are ya?"

"No. Sorry."

A wide grin spread across his round face, making his jowls overflow the top of the blue chambray shirt he wore. The top of his head was nearly perfectly round; his white hair had been clipped so short at first glance I thought he was bald. A pair of red suspenders emerging from behind the white apron disappeared over his broad shoulders, no doubt holding up the pair of dark blue work pants that the apron didn't quite manage to cover. He ambled slowly to the back of the counter.

"Well, you're a damn sight prettier than Jeb anyway."

I think I blushed.

"What can I get for ya?"

My very early breakfast had worn off. "Are you serving lunch yet?" I asked.

"I'll serve ya anything ya want, anytime ya want it. I don't hold with these places that serve one kinda food till exactly a certain time then cut ya off and only serve somethin' else. Food is food. I cook it all."

"Well, then maybe something like a tuna sandwich?" I ventured.

"Tell ya what the best thing on the menu is." He leaned heavily on the countertop and extended his index finger on the glossy surface. "The cheeseburger and fries. Ain't none of them pre-formed patties or none of them frozen little sticks they call fries in them fast food places. I use my own ground buffalo meat that a guy near here brings me. Make the patties myself. Cut the fries myself too, out of a whole potato."

I caught myself glancing at his hands. They were freshly scrubbed, the nails clean and well trimmed.

"Course, I make a pretty mean enchilada plate too. Get my corn tortillas made fresh from this little ol' Mexican lady over in Carrizozo. Use the ground buffalo meat for them too. And my sauce is my own recipe. Now anyone can make a green chile sauce—that's pretty simple. But a fine red sauce is a rare thing. Rare indeed."

I felt myself wavering. Both of his suggestions sounded far better than a tuna sandwich. I told him so. "So, which would you recommend?"

He pinched his lips together and looked at some unseen place in the distance. "Me, I think I'd go with the burger. Don't know why, exactly. That burger meat just looks real tempting today."

"Okay—sold."

"You got it." He slapped his hand down on the counter and pushed himself back to a standing position. "Want a Coke or somethin' while I'm cookin' it?" He'd already reached for a glass and filled it with ice.

"Sure, a Coke would be great."

"So, what brings you to White Oaks?" he asked, setting the Coke down in front of me. He started toward the kitchen at the back. "Go ahead, talk while I'm cookin'. I like somebody to visit with while I cook."

"I'm looking for an old man who told his family he was coming here to do some prospecting."

"Yeah? You an investigator or somethin'?" He peered through the window at me, ducking to avoid the chrome spinner. The burger meat sizzled in the background.

"Sorry, I should have introduced myself. Charlie Parker. I'm with RJP Investigations in Albuquerque."

"Pleased to meet ya. I'm Keith Randel." He turned away to flip the burger, then stuck his head back through the window. "So, who's this guy you're looking for? Maybe I know him."

"His name is William McBride. He's in his eighties." I started to fish in my purse for the photo Dorothy had given me.

"Willie? Well, hell yes, I know Willie," Randel chuckled. "He's been coming around for years."

"Really? Have you seen him recently?"

He raised an index finger and turned away. I could see him shuffling things back at the grill. He emerged a minute later with a platter; the surface was filled by the thick oversized burger snuggled into its onion roll and the fresh-cut fries glistening with oil. He set the platter in front of me and reached to the back counter to hand me a set of flatware tightly wrapped in a white paper napkin. The fabulous meaty smell wafting up at me nearly made my knees weak.

"Let's see," he said, shuffling around the end of the counter to plop onto a stool two places away from mine. "Guess I saw Willie, what, about maybe a month, two months, ago?"

I swallowed a generous bite. "His daughter says he left Albuquerque in February."

"Guess that'd be about right," he said. "It was pretty cold, as I recall. Willie'd come in here and get me to fill up his coffee thermos for him."

"Was that the only time you'd met him?" I dunked a fry into a puddle of ketchup I'd made on the platter. It was still practically sizzling and I bit gingerly into it with just the tips of my front teeth.

"Oh, hell no. Willie was a real regular. Guess he'd get fed up to about here," —Keith indicated a spot under his own quivery jowl—"with that family of his. Then he'd head for the hills and do a little prospecting. Didn't do too bad with it either. Found him a little gold every now and then."

I nodded, understanding perfectly well how someone could get fed up with Dorothy.

"Yep, he'd come down here two, three times a year. Used to bring him a sleeping bag and just camp out up there near the mines. Last few years, though, I think he stayed at one of them motels in Carrizozo. They got a couple there that're pretty cheap. Guess his old bones just got to where the cold ground hurt 'em."

I'd made my way through most of the huge burger, but just couldn't finish all of it. I wiped the grease off my lips with the remains of my crumpled napkin.

"That was wonderful," I told Keith. "Your recommendation was absolutely right."

He beamed as he carried my plate into the kitchen.

"Could I get you a piece of pie or a milkshake for dessert?" he offered. "I got a lady, bakes the pies at home. And I make a real milkshake, nothin' from one of them powdered mixes."

I groaned, holding my stomach. "They sound wonderful," I laughed, "but there's no way another bite is going to fit in here."

He refilled my Coke, though, clearly not ready to give up his only visitor.

"So, Keith, you have any idea where Willie might be now?"

He leaned over the counter again and gathered his lower lip up with his upper teeth. Eventually he said, "I think . . . if I had to guess . . . I'd think Willie would have come in here, showin' off anything he might have found. My guess is that he's gone somewheres else."

"I wondered whether he might have gone up there into the hills and gotten hurt. He could be lying there injured," I ventured. Even as I said it though, I knew if Willie had indeed been injured up in the hills he was likely dead. No way an eighty-four year old man, unable to move, would be able to survive for two months. "Did he always go up there alone?" I asked.

"I don't rightly know," Keith said. "I 'spect he usually did. But he was pretty good friends with ol' man Tucker up at the museum. They mighta gone out prospecting together."

"Maybe I should see if I can talk to Tucker."

"You could try. I ain't seen him around town in a few weeks." He chuckled. "Which is surprisin'. With only about twenty of us living here anymore, it ain't too hard to see everybody in town mite near ever' day."

"Think Tucker might have gone up in the hills with Willie and they're both missing?"

"Naw, I kind of figured it was more like Tucker went down to El Paso with that girlfriend of his for a wild weekend, and she snagged him into marryin' her. She got her a cute little place over to Ruidoso and she been buggin' him for years to get married and settle in with her. Hell, they're both in their eighties, so I guess it's high time they started doin' whatever they damn well please with their lives."

I had a hard time picturing the octogenarian lovers. My skepticism must have showed on my face.

"Course, Tucker coulda just caught a cold or somethin' and went on over to stay with his daughter awhile. She always babies him right along anytime he's sick or anything. Think I'da heard about that though. Ain't nobody got any secrets in a town this size."

I could certainly believe that. I also began to believe that I wasn't going to get much more out of Keith Randel at this point. I asked him how much the burger, fries and Coke came to and he started to give me change back from my five-dollar bill. I waved it away and added another dollar on the counter as a tip.

"Where's the museum Tucker works at?" I asked.

He ambled around the end of the counter and walked over to the front window. "See over there?" he asked, pointing across the road.

I joined him at the window.

"That rock building with the little bell thingy on top. That's the old schoolhouse. Now it's the museum. Ya get to it by taking the first road there to your left. You'll drive down this little wash and up the other side. If ya see a car in the lot, somebody's there. If not, they ain't."

I thanked him and climbed back into my Jeep. A dusty pickup truck was just pulling in beside me and the middle-aged woman at the wheel gave me a long, hard stare.

Guess any stranger was cause for speculation in a town this size. Rusty greeted me enthusiastically until he discovered that I hadn't remembered to bring the remains of my hamburger for him.

Backing out of the tiny parking area, I scanned the highway in both directions. The woman had slid out of her truck and was watching me from the front door of the café. I followed Randel's directions to the old schoolhouse and was pleased to see that there was a compact red car in the parking area. Maybe Tucker really was here. I pulled the Jeep into the shade of a piñon tree.

Before I reached the steps of the old rock building, a woman came out the door. She was probably in her sixties, with yellowed gray hair pulled tightly back from her weathered face into a ponytail. She wore a pair of brown denim jeans over her thin hips, a plaid flannel shirt, and a blue denim jacket that had been worn nearly white in places.

"Hi there," she greeted. "Want a tour of the museum?"

"Actually, I'm looking for a man named Tucker," I told her.

"Pop? Well, you and ever'one else."

"You're his daughter?"

"Yep."

"Keith Randel down at the café told me Tucker might be staying with you."

She looked puzzled. "No. He just up and went off with that friend of his, Willie McBride, awhile back and I ain't heard nothin' since."

I introduced myself. "I came to town looking for Willie," I explained, filling her in briefly on the fact that Willie's family were looking for him. "Where did they say they were going?"

"C'mon in," she invited. "I gotta get off my feet."

She led me into a wide hallway that stretched the full length of the building. To the right I caught a glimpse of an old-fashioned kitchen with a woodstove and metal topped counters. I followed her through a doorway on the opposite side of the hall; it led to a large classroom full of desks. A raised platform at the other end of the room held a teacher's desk, a piano, and two flagpoles—one with the American flag and one with the New Mexico state flag. A potbellied woodstove stood against the far wall. I noticed that the blackboards circling all four walls were actual sheets of plywood, painted black. Years worth of chalk writing and erasure dusted the surface.

"Have a seat," the woman offered. She was standing crookedly with her left hand pressing against her hip. "Sorry, my back ain't the greatest these days. Got pitched off a horse a couple weeks ago and it's been botherin' me ever since."

We moved toward two of the old-fashioned school desks.

"By the way, my name's Sophie," she said. "Sophie Tucker. *Don't* say it. I get razzed about it all the time."

"I know. I get razzed about being Charlie Parker all the time too. And I'm not the least bit musically inclined."

"Me neither," she laughed. "Now, you was asking about Pop and Willie?"

"Willie's family seem to think he came to White Oaks to do some prospecting. But they haven't heard from him in almost two months."

"Not surprising," she sighed. "Those two old guys've always been pretty independent."

"Did they tell you where they were going?" I repeated my earlier question.

"Not really. Pop never answered much to me. He lived on his own, you know, and pretty much came and went as he wished. Even had a lady friend over in Ruidoso, and he'd drive down there to see her pretty often."

"Would she know where they are?" I asked.

"Nah, she's been driving me crazy, callin' every few days to see if Pop's back yet. She can't tell you nothin'."

"So, Willie and your father—I don't even know his first name—they have a favorite place around here?"

"Bud. That's what everyone calls him. His real birth-certificate name was Delmar. But nobody never called him that. Just Bud." She shifted slightly in her seat to get more comfortable. "Yeah, I could point you in the direction of their favorite spots. I ain't had time to go poking around up there, what with this bad back of mine. But you're welcome to try. But I got this feeling you won't find 'em up there."

"Why's that?"

"Willie's truck is gone." At my puzzled look, she continued. "See, they left Pop's car at his house and they took Willie's pickup to this spot—well, I'll show it to you. Anyway, it's a place they park, then they start out hiking from there. I drove up there more'n a month ago. The truck's not there. *I* think they got in their heads to head for Arizona and start lookin' for that Lost Dutchman place. They both been talking about *that* for years."

"And they'd just go off like that without telling you?"

"Oh yeah." She shrugged. "Like I said, Pop's a real independent cuss."

"Do you have a map of this place up in the hills here where they started out?" I asked, glancing around.

"Well, the museum's got nothin' like that for sale or

anything, but I can sketch it out for you. And I'll take you up to the startin' point. Heck, I don't think we're getting any museum business today anyhow. Just let me lock up."

I stepped outside to the front porch while Sophie went around and switched out lights. She emerged a couple of minutes later.

"Okay, just let me get this key . . ." she puffed, struggling to yank a large key ring out of her tight jeans. She finally succeeded and pulled the door closed and inserted the key into the old-fashioned lock.

"School's been closed since the 1950s," she said. "Along with the post office and most everything else in this town. But I attended classes here and so did Pop."

We walked down the steps together.

"These two old wooden buildings?" she said, indicating one at either side of the school. "Those were the outhouses. One for the boys and one for the girls. Let me tell you, in the middle of winter, I could hold it all day. We had indoor plumbing at home. Just follow me in your car. I'm going straight home after this."

I did as Sophie instructed. The road she took bore to the northwest, leading generally in the direction of the mine tailings I'd noticed on the way into town. We'd gone 2.8 miles by my odometer when she tapped her brakes to let me know we were at the end of the road. She pulled to the left and I edged in beside her, rolling down my window.

"You can go up there about another twenty yards or so and park your car," she said, making some marks on a scrap of paper sack. "Then you'll see a path marked by an old wood sign. The sign's faded now, but the path's good and wide. It leads in about another mile, then you'll see some old buildings—probably fallen down by now, most of 'em—and a coupla mine shafts. Be real careful around those. They can cave in." She handed me her roughly drawn map.

I thanked her and waved as she backed her little red car around and made the turn back to town. I did as instructed and parked at the trailhead.

Rusty was thankful to get out of the Jeep at last. He relieved himself on a piñon tree and sniffed the area. I strapped the canteen over my left shoulder and stashed my purse under the back seat, taking only my keys and a tube of lip balm with me, in addition to Sophie's map. When the sound of her car's engine finally faded it was utterly quiet up here. I could see a few landmarks in town, including the school building and the entrance to the cemetery I'd passed coming into town.

"Come on, kid. You want to run a bit?"

The dog eagerly raced ahead of me, up the trail. I, too, was ready for some exercise but walked at a slow enough pace that I could watch for clues along the path. The early afternoon sun was warm and the hills sheltered me from the breeze that had funneled down the main highway through town. It didn't take long to come to the little collection of buildings Sophie had described. As she'd said, they were pretty dilapidated.

There were four buildings in all, made of rough wooden planks, weathered now to a smooth gray. A few bits of jagged glass remained in a couple of the window openings but most of them stood wide open to the elements. I saw evidence that curio seekers had made regular raids. Signs had evidently been mounted on two of the buildings, indicating that they had some commercial purpose originally, but they were long gone. Only a few nail holes and a background of slightly lighter wood showed their earlier presence. I peered through the window openings where I could, finding nothing but bare dirt floors inside.

Beyond the cluster of buildings I could see a small hole in the hillside, framed by some heavy timbers. A mine shaft.

I walked over to it and knelt to peer into the hole. Beyond the first ten feet or so it was utterly black. I hadn't thought to bring a flashlight, but even with one I doubted I'd venture inside. The bracing around the shaft's walls leaned at an angle and didn't look at all steady. I stood up and glanced around for Rusty.

The dog was sniffing around the old buildings. I left him alone and followed another path leading west. Against a small embankment I found another mineshaft opening. This one was quite a bit larger and looked sturdier but without a light I wasn't about to go in. I wandered back toward the buildings.

Rusty met me before I reached them, a prize dangling from his mouth.

"What do you have here?" I teased, stretching my hand out toward him.

He dropped a red kerchief into my hand.

The material was bunched up and felt stiff with the residue of dried mud caked on it. I opened it out as flat as I could get it but it retained most of its wrinkles.

"Where did you find this?" I asked Rusty.

He waved his long tail and back forth slowly, staring up at me with ears perked. Really, Charlie, did you expect an answer?

"Well, hey. Lassie would have turned right around and rushed back to the scene." His tail continued to wag. "And there'd probably be a big bag of gold nuggets right under the kerchief, too." I told him.

Actually, Lassie would have picked up the bag of nuggets and carried them to Timmy in the first place. I patted Rusty on the head and scratched his ears. He may not be ultra smart, but he's mine.

I looked at the kerchief again. The fabric, despite the beating it had taken, was relatively new. There were no holes or worn spots and the color hadn't yet faded, as it would have if it had spent years out in the New Mexico sun. I wondered if it might have belonged to Willie or Bud.

I held the kerchief out to Rusty and shrugged my shoulders, asking where he'd found it. He smiled at me and wagged. What a help.

I walked back toward the collection of old buildings, to the last spot I'd noticed Rusty nosing around. One of the structures sat apart from the others, slightly up a small rise, and I hadn't given it much attention on the way in. My canine fellow-sleuth bounded along beside me; now that there was action to follow, he was ready. He raced ahead to the little house. For the first time I noticed that this one had a wooden porch and a front door. The door stood open. I followed the dog to the opening.

The buzzing of flies was my first clue. For some odd reason, the thought went through my mind that I hadn't noticed a single fly since I'd been in town. Obviously, they were all here in this little cabin. Hovering around the man's body that lay sprawled on the wooden floor.

FIVE

Decomposition was pretty far advanced. Instinct told me this because I actually don't know much about it. I glimpsed a dingy pair of jeans, a plaid shirt, and short white hair before I buried my nose in the crook of my elbow and backed out the doorway. Rusty surged forward, wanting to get a good close-up whiff, but I grabbed his collar just in time and yanked him backward.

Outside, I blew out every bit of air in my lungs and drew in a fresh breath of untainted air. Blew all that out and took in some more clean air. My heart was racing at about ninety beats a second and my arms and legs had somehow become jelly-like. I stood there, staring at the cabin, for a full minute that seemed more like a full hour. I felt light-headed and realized I was hyperventilating.

Stop it! I commanded myself. It would be pretty stupid to stand here and pass out just because I couldn't control my jitters. I slowed my breathing and shook out my arms and legs. As soon as I let go of Rusty's collar, he tried again to head for the open doorway.

"Oh, no you don't," I said, grabbing him again. "I'm putting you in the car."

I had to drag him at first, but after we'd gotten out of sight of the cluster of buildings he found something else to attract his attention and he stayed with me. I kept up a pace that was just short of a jog and was feeling much more clear-headed by the time we'd covered the mile and could see the Jeep in its parking spot.

My mind raced as I tried to think what to do. Our gruesome find would have to be reported, obviously, but to whom? I only knew two people in White Oaks and neither was exactly an authority figure. I turned the Jeep around and headed toward the café.

The sun had dropped lower in the sky and shadows were lengthening as I hit the highway through town. The little café building sat alone in the middle of its plot of earth and I feared that no one was there. No lights showed through the windows and I didn't spot Randel's truck until I pulled into the parking area.

Turning the doorknob, I tried to make a hasty plan as to just how I was going to handle this.

"Keith?" I called out. "Are you here?"

"Well, hey there, Miss Charlie," he grinned, shuffling out of the back room. "Back for those enchiladas now?"

"Not just yet," I said. I found I was having to concentrate just to keep my breathing under control. "Who's the law enforcement agency in charge around here?"

"Well, we got no police department in White Oaks. County Sheriff is who you gotta call." His eyes narrowed. "You got a problem with somebody in town?"

"I may have just found the body of Willie McBride," I blurted out. Damn. Now why did I do that? I didn't know Keith Randel very well and for all I knew anybody in this town could have killed Willie—if the body really was Willie. I took a deep breath.

"Do you know the sheriff?" I asked as calmly as I could manage.

"Well, sure. Randy Buckman. Everybody 'round here knows Randy." He raised one thick index finger and started to add something else.

"Can you call him? Ask him to get out here now?" I said, interrupting.

"Now wait just a second here, young lady. You got yourself a mite upset now. Set yourself here and let me get you something." He brewed a cup of tea and shoved it toward me. "Now—I'll call the sheriff." He ambled slowly toward a phone on the back wall.

"Hurry!"

He stopped in his tracks. "Now, girl, didn't you say you found a body?" He waited for my nod. "Now that tells me that the guy's already dead, right?"

I gave in with another nod.

"Well then, no amount of rushin' around is gonna save him at this point, right?" He pointed at the counter with his finger. "Drink your tea."

I obeyed blindly, too wrung out at the moment to argue. He whirled the old rotary dial on the wall phone and visited amiably with the dispatcher for a good two minutes. Finally, he got down to business.

"Randy around?" he asked. "Uh-huh, uh-huh. Well, send him on out to the café here soon as you can." He ended the call with, "Say hey to Johnny and the kids."

I sipped slowly at my cup of tea through all this and found that it really did settle me a little.

"Buckman'll be here in about thirty, forty-five minutes," he said.

I looked at my watch. It would be pitch dark in another two hours.

"Just slow down, Charlie-girl. You ain't on city time anymore. Things might happen slower out here, but the sun comes up and the sun goes down and everything else still gets done somewheres in there. Now, I'm gonna fix you a plate of enchiladas. Red or green?"

I let the tension seep out of me. "Green, please."

"Comin' right up." He shuffled into the kitchen.

"While you're doing that, I'm going out to the car to feed my dog," I called out.

"You got yer dog with ya? Hell, bring him on in here. I can make him somethin' too. Would he like a burger?"

I chuckled. "I'm sure he would, but he really better have his own food. I'll get it." And here I'd thought Pedro's was the only restaurant in the world that would allow Rusty inside. My heart softened toward Randel.

Out at the Jeep I scooped some of Rusty's nuggets into his bowl and invited him to get out. He trotted along beside me into the café without a second thought. I set the bowl on the floor beside my stool and he went right to it. A couple of minutes later, Keith brought my steaming plate of food.

"Hope chicken's okay," he said. "Figured you had red meat at lunch."

"Chicken's my favorite," I said truthfully. "Thanks for keeping my diet somewhat balanced."

I'd just finished mopping up the last of the green chile sauce with a flour tortilla when we heard the clomping of boots on the wooden porch. The door swung inward and Sheriff Randy Buckman stepped inside. He was in his fifties, over six feet tall and slim. His uniform looked as crisp as if he'd just put it on. He removed his black felt Stetson and nodded to me. He gave Rusty a sharp glance but didn't say anything.

"What's the story, Keith?" he asked, taking a seat two stools away from me and reaching for the cup of coffee Randel had already poured.

"This here's Charlie Parker from Albuquerque," Keith said. "Says she's found herself a dead body."

Buckman turned to me. His brown eyes were kind, despite the furrow between the dark eyebrows that might have otherwise hardened his face.

I briefly explained what I'd been doing up at the old mining camp and expressed my suspicion that the body might be that of either William McBride or Bud Tucker.

"Did you touch anything up there?" he asked.

"I pushed the door open. Well, it was standing open about four or five inches. I just pushed it until I could see inside. I may have leaned against the doorjamb. I really don't remember."

"Didn't move the body, though?" he asked.

Remembering the feeling of liquid rising in my throat and the way my breath had come in gasps, I didn't want to admit that I'd nearly passed out. "No, I didn't even go into the room," was all I said.

"I met Tucker's daughter, Sophie, at the schoolhouse. She's the one who showed me the trail to the mines. Someone should probably tell her personally, before the news gets around town." My eyes flicked briefly toward

Keith as I talked to the sheriff.

"Let's find out what there is to tell first," said Buckman. He stood up and laid a dollar on the counter.

Randel picked it up and leaned over and stuffed it into Buckman's jacket pocket. "You know you don't pay for coffee in my place," he said kindly.

"I'll radio for the coroner," Buckman said. "Then I guess I better get up there. Gonna be night soon and I'd rather not be toting a body down the hill in the dark." He looked at me again. "You want to come up there? Don't need your help especially, but if you can keep your hands off things you're allowed."

My investigator side told me that this would be one of the few times I'd ever be allowed at a crime scene and I should probably go along to see what evidence I might find. My other side cringed away from going back into the cabin and viewing the body any more close up than I already had.

"Guess it's only my concern if the victim turns out to be Willie McBride." I told him. "If you don't mind sharing your findings with me, I think I'd just as soon stay here."

"Fine with me." He handed me a card. "You can call me later." He strode out to his squad car where I could see him speaking into a handheld microphone. A minute later he pulled out and drove up the highway without strobes or siren.

"He's a good man," Keith said. "Sensitive-like. A woman'd do good to catch a man like him."

I wagged my shiny new wedding band at him. "I've already got myself an excellent man, thank you," I said, smiling.

"Probably take 'em a couple hours to get back here," Randel offered. "You can hang out here and drink coffee if ya want. Ain't no hotel here in town."

"Thanks, but I think I'll head down the road. It's been a long day." I reached for my purse and left money on the counter for my dinner. Bidding Keith goodbye, I walked out to the car with Rusty following.

The sun was nearing the horizon as I drove away from White Oaks. My mind was a jumble. I wondered whether the body of the old man would turn out to be McBride or Tucker, or someone else. Was his death from natural causes, or not? How soon would the news spread through White Oaks? Would Sheriff Buckman really share his information with me?

I consulted my road map quickly and memorized the series of turns I'd need to make to take me to the south end of Ruidoso where Drake was staying during the fire. An hour later I was sitting across from my husband at a local restaurant where he wolfed down a huge plate of roast beef, mashed potatoes and gravy, green beans, and a salad. I sipped on a glass of wine. I'd phoned Drake on his cell as I approached the town and we'd agreed that it would be simpler to meet for dinner before settling down at the hotel. I didn't mention that I'd already consumed a rather large order of enchiladas.

We filled each other in on our respective adventures of the day, I making light of the dead body portion of my outing. Drake looked bone-tired and smelled of woodsmoke. Within thirty minutes after our arrival at the hotel, we'd shared a hot shower and had fallen into an exhausted sleep in each other's arms. I was not at all prepared for the alarm clock's insistent tweet at four-thirty in the morning.

"Snuggle down and sleep awhile," he murmured in my ear as he pulled himself out of bed.

I groaned and rolled over. My good intentions said I'd get up and have breakfast with him, but my baser nature sent me right back to sleep. I didn't become conscious again until I rolled over and looked at the clock to discover that it was eight-thirty. Drake had been so quiet I hadn't even realized when he left. But his flight suit and helmet were gone, along with his government-required boots. I pictured him now, hovering over leaping flames for the past two or three hours.

I got up and pulled on the same jeans I'd worn yesterday and a clean red T-shirt from my overnight bag. The early spring air was chilly, as I discovered when I walked Rusty outside, so I added a flannel shirt to my ensemble. I left Drake a note letting him know that I planned to head back to Albuquerque today.

In the middle of town, we again found a fast-food place with a drive-through where I got a combination of traditional breakfast foods all piled onto a bun. Rusty had already cleaned his own bowl back at the hotel, but that didn't stop him from wanting a share of my food too.

Sipping the last of my coffee, I pulled Sheriff Buckman's card from my purse and placed the call on my cell phone.

"Sheriff's office," said a female voice with a soft hint of Spanish in it.

I asked for Buckman and was told that he was out on a call. I left my number with her and requested that he call me as soon as possible. I hung up, hoping I'd hear from him before I left the area.

Feeling fidgety because of all the unresolved questions, I cruised north through the winding streets of Ruidoso and back onto the highway toward Carrizozo. I spotted two county sheriff department cars in the parking lot of the little drive-in restaurant at the town's main intersection and, on a whim, decided to see if Buckman was driving one of them. As luck would have it, I found him sipping coffee with another officer at a back booth.

"Sheriff? Charlie Parker—remember me?"

Buckman looked up. His gray-flecked hair had a molded reproduction of his hatband pressed into it. His eyes looked tired, like he'd been up late last night, but he smiled.

"Sure. I just got a call from my dispatcher saying you were looking for me."

I felt a little foolish, having left the message and then tracking him to his breakfast table. I guess it showed on my face.

"It's okay. Sit." He indicated the bench across the booth, next to the other officer, whom he introduced as Montoya.

"I have to head back to Albuquerque today," I told him. "Just wondered if there's any news I can give my clients."

"If you mean, should you tell them the dead guy was William McBride, we're not sure yet."

He signaled the waitress for more coffee and paused while she poured it. I waved off the extra cup she'd brought for me. He stirred heavy doses of sugar and creamer into his.

"But you think it could be him?" I asked, once she'd left.

"Could be. We knew that McBride was pretty well

acquainted with Keith there at the café and we asked Keith to take a look last night when we brought the body down. He identified the clothing as McBride's. Apparently he was wearing those items the last time Keith saw him."

"Sounds like it's probably him, then," I said. I should have been pleased to wrap up the case so quickly, but really didn't want to go back with sad news.

"Very likely. But we never jump to conclusions. The body itself was badly decomposed. Randel couldn't identify it. We'll have to go to dental records for a positive ID."

Which still meant contacting Dorothy and her family and letting them know of the possibility that this was her father.

Buckman read my mind. "We'll contact the family," he said. "You don't have to do that. In fact, based on the information you gave me yesterday, I already have one of my deputies making the call." He sipped from his mug and sent some kind of eye signal to Montoya, who had not said a word so far. The deputy nodded and excused himself. I stood to let him slide out of the booth.

"If the body turns out not to be McBride, then what?" I asked.

"Well, our job will be to ID this victim, then find his killer. If McBride fits in there somewhere, we'll deal with that when we get to it."

"Killer?" I whispered. "The man was murdered?"

SIX

Somehow, instinctively, I'd known there was foul play involved but the words popped out anyway.

"There'll be an autopsy, of course," Buckman said, taking another sip of coffee. "But I'd guess the .22-sized hole in the shirt and the pool of dried blood on the floor of that cabin will lead us in that direction."

Montoya returned and nodded to his boss. I stood again to let him back to his seat.

"Family dentist's been contacted," he said. "Martha says he's FedEx-ing the charts today."

"Okay," said Buckman. "We'll get on with the autopsy and should have an answer tomorrow. Meanwhile, maybe I can get you to do something for me?"

"Sure," I answered.

"It'd save me a trip to Albuquerque."

"What is it?"

He reached over and picked up a paper sack that sat on the bench beside him. "I want to try to ID this." He pulled a plaid flannel shirt from the sack. It was the one the dead man had been wearing. "You're acquainted with McBride's family. Could you show it to them and see if they recognize it as his?"

I took the shirt and turned it over. A neat square of material had been cut from the front. I raised my eyebrows in a question.

"Ballistics tests. Lab cut out the bullet hole," he explained.

"But you'll have the dental records tomorrow," I suggested.

"Just thought I'd get this as secondary proof. You never know what's going to come in handy."

"Okay. I'll probably see the daughter tomorrow," I said.

"Don't leave it with them," he cautioned. "Keep it in your possession until you can get it back to me."

"Chain of evidence?"

"Something like that," he said. "If our victim is William McBride, you know that any of his family members could be suspects."

That thought hadn't occurred to me, but it wouldn't be the first time family members reported a missing person when they knew perfectly well what had happened to him.

Buckman had me sign a receipt for the evidence then scooted to the edge of his seat, the signal that we were finished for now. I slid out too and we walked to the front door together.

I'd parked next to his patrol car and he noticed Rusty in the Jeep for the first time.

"Nice dog," he said.

The red-brown subject wagged furiously.

"He's kind of the hero of all this," I said. "He's the one who found the kerchief and led me to the body."

"Kerchief? You didn't say anything about a kerchief yesterday." Buckman's face had turned stern.

"I didn't?" I thought back to my first meeting with the sheriff at Randel's café. I couldn't remember exactly what I'd said. And where was the kerchief now? "Really, I wasn't hiding anything," I stammered. "Let me think . . . what did I do after I had it?"

I opened the door to the back seat in which Rusty sat, noticing that Deputy Montoya lightly rested his right hand on his pistol grip. The dog wanted to leap out and greet his new friends but I ordered him back. There on the floor of the back seat was the crumpled red kerchief. I picked it up by its very edge and handed it to Buckman.

"It was just like this," I told him, feeling like I had to justify myself. "All matted and dirty and muddy. Rusty had picked it up and he brought it to me. I thought Willie might have dropped it and I wanted to have the family identify it if they could. But that was before I found the body. Honest."

He turned the cloth over in his hand without a word.

"I guess I carried it down to the car after I left the cabin. Must have tossed it in here when I let Rusty into his seat."

"I'll take this to the lab," he said. "This crusty brown substance might not be mud. Could be blood. Typing it may help lead to the killer." He finally met my eyes and smiled, just a little one. "Thanks," he said.

Buckman and Montoya climbed into their cars and I was dismissed. I sat in the driver's seat for a couple of minutes, deciding what to do next. White Oaks was so nearby, I really had to make one more quick run out there.

Randel's café was open but he wasn't alone this time. I recognized Sophie Tucker's compact red car in the parking area and there was another vehicle I didn't know, a blue pickup truck.

All eyes turned toward me, the town stranger, when I opened the door. Keith was quick to give me one of those wide grins that sent his jowls jiggling and brought out the pinkness in his face. Sophie's face was reserved, not nearly as friendly as yesterday. I realized that my finding the body most likely meant one of two things to her: either she'd just lost her father, or there was the possibility that he would now be a suspect in a murder case. Neither choice would make her happy. The unknown truck belonged to a small, dark Spanish man wearing ranching work clothes, who was just on his way out. He nodded as he passed me.

"Set down here, Miss Charlie, and have yourself some coffee," ordered Keith. He'd already poured a cup and placed it in front of an empty stool near Sophie's. I sat there, wondering what to say to her.

"Ain't your fault," she said.

I looked over at her. Her weathered face was subdued but not angry. "Thanks," I said. I suppressed my natural tendency to over-explain and left it at that.

The three of us didn't exchange another word for a good two minutes. Randel had poured himself a cup of coffee into which, I noticed, he added a healthy dash of Bailey's from a bottle under the counter. He caught me watching him.

"Anyone else?" he asked, extending the bottle.

Sophie pushed her mug toward him and I did the same. We drank in silence for another minute or two.

"Guess I better get out to my place and get some chores done," Sophie eventually said.

"The sheriff told me he has some dental records coming from Albuquerque. One way or the other, you should have some news in the next day or two," I said.

She shook her head in resignation. "If that cussed old man of mine ever went to a dentist, he sure never told me about it. If he had've, I'd know today." She patted my shoulder as she stood up. "For now, I'll just keep busy."

I watched her back out and pull away from the building. Keith sloshed a little more Bailey's into his mug, but I declined a second shot for myself.

"What's your take on all this?" I asked him, sensing that his tongue might become slightly looser with the help of the liqueur, now that we were alone.

"Well," he began with a deep breath. He rested both hands on the front of his massive belly. "Want to know what I think? Or you want to know what I *know*?" The lazy grin spread across his face again.

I felt the corners of my mouth pinch impishly. "Okay, I'll bite. Tell me what you know."

He hit a button on the cash register and the drawer sprung outward. He wiped his fingertips on the front of his apron, reached inside and extracted the plastic section containing the coins. From beneath it he pulled out a weathered brown piece of paper. He turned and handed it to me.

"Open it," he said.

I glanced up at him as I took the paper. Unfolding it carefully, I saw that it contained a hand-drawn map, similar to the one I'd found at Willie's house.

"Willie's?" I asked, holding the map up.

"His *treasure* map," Keith grinned. "The old man told

me, many times mind you, that if he ever disappeared this was where he'd be."

"This isn't the Lost Dutchman Mine, is it?" I asked. "He'd told a lot of people about that dream."

"No . . . ma'am," he said, wagging his finger back and forth. "This's one he really found. And he said someday he'd go back there."

"So, how's he going to get there if you have the map?"

"Willie knew his mine backward and forward," Keith said. "He drew this map as a safety precaution. In case he got Alzheimer's someday, or got hit over the head or something."

I noticed that the drunker he got, the less "hillbilly" his speech became.

"And he trusted you with this map—why?"

He winked at me and took a slug of the Bailey's right from the bottle. "Because I know geological patterns and could find this place, based on this map. If he ever got lost, he knew someone could find him."

"And now? You think he's hiding out here?"

"Wouldn't surprise me a bit." He downed the remainder of his coffee and began wiping the counter where Sophie's place had been. "Course, I guess by this time tomorrow we'll have us a better idea about that."

"What are you suggesting?"

"You keep that map, Charlie-gal. Somethin's gonna come outta this. You just keep your eyes open."

I stared hard at him for a moment. Was he pulling my leg? Who was this guy who could talk about geology and map reading one minute and sound like he'd just come out of the Ozarks the next. I busied myself finishing the last of my coffee. When I looked up again the wide grin was back on his face.

I stashed the folded map in a flat side pocket of my purse and finished my coffee.

"Sure you don't want me to fix you some eggs?" Randel asked as I began making my moves to leave.

"No, thanks. I better be getting back to the city. Think I've done about all the harm I can do around here," I said.

"Gimme a hug," he said. He came around the end of the counter to fold me into a massive embrace. "You take care, Charlie-gal."

"I will." I walked out to the Jeep, with fond thoughts of this enigmatic man who was cook, geologist, and town confidant.

Rusty greeted me enthusiastically, hoping I'd brought some kind of treat for him—a slab of ham, perhaps. He settled again into the back seat after he was convinced there were no goodies forthcoming. I decided to make one more run up to the mining camp before heading back to the city.

I parked in the same spot I had yesterday, noticing that the surrounding scrubby bushes had been trampled and there were several new sets of tire tracks, no doubt from the sheriff's department vehicles and the coroner. Once again, Rusty led the way down the trail. I followed at a brisk pace, wired by all the coffee I'd consumed.

The little cabin at the far end of the camp was less frightening today without the body lying on the floor. All the flies had vacated. The only sign of the violence that had occurred here was the dark brown stain on the wooden plank flooring. Without the body covering most of it, I was surprised at how large it was and that I hadn't noticed it on my first visit.

I looked carefully at the flooring in the rest of the small room. No other blood drops, spatters, or smears that I could see. It appeared that the victim had been shot and had fallen right where I'd found him. Sheriff Buckman had mentioned a .22 caliber hole in the shirt. That meant a pretty direct hit to a vital organ, I thought. A .22 doesn't have much stopping power unless it hits just right. Of course, the victim had been old; I'd gotten that much from the patch of snowy white hair I'd seen. It wouldn't take much deadly force to kill off a man in his eighties.

For the first time, I took a close look at the cabin itself. It consisted of one room; wooden walls that had become warped enough over time to show daylight through cracks. A single window on the back wall, the glass long since broken out. A woodstove of some kind must have stood against the west wall at some point—a round hole partway up the wall with a metal flange around it indicated where the chimney pipe would have exited. Stove and stovepipe were gone now, probably at home somewhere else in the valley. A niche in the east wall still contained bits of some framing, which might mean there were built-in bunks at one time. Only a few boards remained nailed to the sides of the small enclosure. Anyone using the cabin in modern times would have had to spread out sleeping bags on the floor. I couldn't imagine two old men being comfortable here in February.

More likely, they would have slept in one of the old mines. Better protection from the wind and elements. They could build a fire at the entrance for warmth and to keep stray coyotes away. I stood on the porch of the cabin and stared out toward the largest mineshaft opening, the second one I'd noticed yesterday. It might be worth a look.

Stepping carefully, I scanned the ground at the opening. Outside, there were several sets of footprints. One was definitely mine from yesterday. The others were probably caused by the sheriff's men, if they came up this far, or by recent casual onlookers. I doubted any footprints from a month or two ago would have survived. Just inside the shaft opening, there was evidence of a campfire, as I'd speculated. A layer of sand covered the charred sticks and blackened rocks. I walked about ten feet into the shaft, bending over to avoid bumping my head on the overhead timbers. No sign of human occupation, no vital clue, no personal possession of William McBride's waited for me there. Detecting is never as easy as it looks on TV.

I walked back to the Jeep and whistled for Rusty. He trotted up empty-mouthed. Even he didn't have a clue for me today. Ten minutes later we were on the road to Carrizozo.

SEVEN

I couldn't work up much enthusiasm for visiting Dorothy Schwartzman upon my return to Albuquerque, but knew I wouldn't be any more thrilled about it in the morning. There was the matter of having her identify the plaid shirt. I might as well get it over with.

From my purse I pulled the address she'd given me. It was in a section of town that had been developed in the late '50s and early '60s, middle class three bedroom brick homes for the most part. I got off I-25 at Carlisle and took Constitution east. I found her street without any trouble. Large, deciduous trees were beginning to leaf out with fragile bright green tips and the fruit trees were in full glory, covered with pink and white blossoms.

The Schwartzman home was a spread-out red brick with white painted trim. Twin blue spruces flanked the sidewalk that split the grassy yard in two. Neat flowerbeds, filled with flourishing pansies in purple and yellow, bordered the front porch. Two cars sat in the driveway and two more were parked in the street out front. If they had company, I was even less thrilled about showing up with my evidence bag. But I took it with me anyway and bravely rang the doorbell.

A woman about my age answered. She had chin-length, fluffy brown hair and wore jeans and a snug-fitting white T-shirt on her slim, model-like frame. She held a streamer of white computer paper that trailed to the floor behind her.

"Oh! I thought you'd be Bobby," she said, gathering up the long stream of paper.

"I'm Charlie Parker. I need to talk for a minute with Dorothy if she's here."

"Sure, come on in." She pushed the screen door outward to admit me. "Mother!" she shouted, toward the back of the house. She turned back to me. "Charlie, you said?"

"Yes. Your mother hired me to investigate the disappearance of your grandfather."

She rolled her eyes and glanced back in the direction she'd directed her shout. "It's this stupid reunion," she whispered. "Mom's got it in her head that *everybody* has to be here. She just doesn't get it that Grandpa doesn't care about it."

"Oh, Charlie! I wasn't expecting you today," Dorothy said, bustling into the room wiping her hands on a towel. "I'm just making up some of the desserts for the reunion."

"Could I talk to you privately for just a minute, Dorothy?" I asked.

"Melanie, excuse us, please." Dorothy issued it more as an order than a request.

Melanie gave me a weak smile and ducked out of the room. Dorothy ushered me to a white brocade sofa. She made a production of folding the hand towel while I sat down. She took a seat on a pale aqua chair next to the sofa and placed the folded towel in her lap.

"Now, what's this about?" she asked.

"Did someone from the Lincoln County Sheriff's Department contact you yesterday?" I asked.

"A woman asked if I knew the name of my father's dentist. I gave it to her and she thanked me." Her face registered mild puzzlement. "Why?"

This wasn't going to be easy. "A body was found at a small mining camp near White Oaks," I said. "It was an elderly man, but they haven't identified him yet."

"Oh, my." Dorothy's face registered a look of disbelief.

"There's no easy way to do this, I guess. The sheriff asked me to see if you could identify this shirt." I pulled the plaid shirt from the bag and handed it to her.

She turned it over in her hands and looked at the tag inside the collar. "It looks familiar," she said slowly. "He has several plaid shirts and I don't remember this one specifically. Melanie and Bob gave him one for Christmas a couple of years ago and he wore it quite a lot. It could be this one."

"Could we ask Melanie if she recognizes it?"

"It will upset her. She's very close to her grandfather."

"The police really need to know."

"Let me get her," Dorothy said, rising.

She returned a couple of minutes later, trailing behind her daughter. Whatever Dorothy had told Melanie had left her visibly upset.

"What's this about Grandpa's shirt?" she asked in a quivery voice.

I stood up and carried the shirt to her. "Do you know if this is your grandfather's?" I asked.

She looked at it and nodded. "It's the one we gave him for Christmas. Why do you need to know this?"

"We don't know for sure," I told her. Her petite face crumpled when I told her about finding the old man's body.

I put an arm around her shoulders and led her to the sofa. Dorothy took a spot primly on the side chair again. Melanie leaned forward, elbows on knees, and held her face in her hands, staring out at a point somewhere in the middle of the beige carpet.

"Will we know something definite by the end of the week?" Dorothy finally asked. "This is certainly going to put a damper on our reunion." Her fuzzy gray curls dipped with the emphasis she put on her words.

Melanie clenched her fists and turned to Dorothy. "Mother! You and your damned reunion! Just shut up about it!"

"Well!" Dorothy's curls were bobbing like nervous corks on water now. She stood up and stomped back to the kitchen.

"I'm sorry," Melanie said to me. "I never . . . I mean . . . I just never have the courage to speak to Mother like that. I mean . . ."

"It's okay, I know what you mean."

"She just, I don't know, just never seemed to care that much about Grandpa. Now she's got this burr under her saddle about this reunion. I just wish the whole damn thing would go away."

"I can't promise much. Finding answers in the next couple of days may be impossible." I watched her mood sink again. "Hey, you want to get out of here for awhile?"

I asked. "Maybe go have a cup of coffee or a drink?"

She brightened a little. "I could use a break. I've been here all day. It's getting a little overwhelming. Let me take my own car and I'll meet you somewhere."

She showed me out after we'd agreed on a little neighborhood bar on Lomas, just a few blocks away. I pulled away from the curb, wondering if Dorothy were watching me from her kitchen window. The woman had always set me on edge. She seemed obsessed with finding Willie, but only because of the reunion. I hoped Melanie would open up over a drink and shed some more light on her mother's attitude.

I'd parked behind the bar and secured a corner table by the time Melanie arrived. She'd donned a short leather jacket over her T-shirt and I noticed several male heads turned as she walked through the room. We both ordered wine and reached for the basket of crunchy nibbles at the same moment.

"I'm trying to get a picture of your grandfather's habits," I told her after our drinks had arrived and we'd skimmed over a little idle chitchat. "Did he often go out prospecting by himself?"

"Oh, all the time," she said. "When I was a little kid, sometimes he'd take me with him. It was fun for me, but I got the idea—later, of course—that he was perfectly happy to be out there by himself where he could get some serious work done."

"So he thought of his prospecting as a job? Did he actually find much?"

"Oh, yes. Well, every time I went out with him, he'd find a few little nuggets. I thought they were just pretty little sparkles. I had no idea what gold was worth. I guess, in retrospect, he probably netted a couple hundred dollars worth a day."

"I wonder where he kept it. Dorothy gave me a key to his house and I looked around there for some idea about where he'd gone. Didn't see any sign of any gold nuggets lying around."

She crunched a minute on a pretzel. "I imagine he cashed in some of it whenever he needed money. You probably saw that his needs are simple." I nodded agreement. "Maybe that's all there ever was, just a few nuggets. Could be, he carried it with him. I don't know."

Or had a secret hiding place. I remembered the map Keith Randel had given me, but didn't mention it to Melanie.

"So what's this big deal your mother has about this family reunion? It looks like she's making it quite a production."

She rolled her eyes again. "I don't know. I swear, Mother has *never* pushed family togetherness like this before." She stared into her wine glass for a long minute. "Something you have to understand about her, Charlie. Mother was one of those women who wanted a career many years before the feminist movement made it the thing to do. In the '50s, when every other woman in America was having babies and being a housewife, Mother applied to law school."

I guess my face registered my surprise.

"Oh yeah. She got turned down three times. This is family lore that was drilled into us from the time we were little. Well, she finally got accepted but it was still a battle against the all-male powers-that-be to finish school, pass the bar, and get hired to a very secondary position in a small local firm. It was the only job she could get and it grated against her constantly when she realized that she'd never rise much above that starting position.

"She'd married my father when they were both in law school, when her dreams were still vivid and exciting. By the time she was thirty she'd become an embittered woman who felt stuck where she was in life. If she stayed home to raise the two kids they'd produced, she'd be admitting defeat, admitting that she was just one of the masses of women who were 'doing nothing' with their lives—her words, not mine." She paused to take another deep sip of her wine. "As it turned out, the decision was made by fate, and that probably served to make her even more bitter."

"What happened?" I asked.

"My father, whose position was with a bigger firm and better prospects, had a stroke. I think his firm helped the family out a bit financially—I never really knew—but eventually they had to cut him loose because he was unable to work. Mother had no choice. Her salary couldn't support the family and his medical bills and keep two kids in day care. Her firm was already lukewarm about having a woman lawyer on staff and they probably put even more pressure on her. She eventually caved and gave up her dream. Quit the firm to stay home with the family and care for Dad. We had to go on welfare for awhile. It was humiliating for her, I'm sure.

"I don't remember many of the details. I was about seven at the time. I just knew that, for once, she was there when I got home from school. We always had food and clothes. Beyond that, I wasn't privy to anything behind the scenes. When I was ten my father had another stroke and that one killed him."

I made a sympathetic motion.

"I didn't really miss him. He hadn't been there mentally for a long time. I did miss her. We were now into the 1980s and feminism and discrimination were big buzz-words. Even though we had Dad's life insurance money, Mother wanted her career. She had no trouble getting into a prestigious firm then, and she made the most of it. Suddenly, Roger and I were latchkey kids and the home cooked dinners came to a screeching halt. There were a series of cleaning ladies who would sometimes be there when we got home. Some of them were even nice to us. But I guess Mother thought we were old enough to fend for ourselves after school. It never even occurred to her that we were lonely."

"Sounds like she must have been happy though. Did it improve her disposition?"

"Hah. Not really. I don't think she ever became finan-cially successful. And, believe me, Mother definitely equates money with success. If you don't make lots of money, you're nobody. Well, she continued to rail against her bosses and the system and everything else she could remotely attribute to discrimination. Well, you've seen the result. She's never been happy."

"Sounds like she just never allowed herself to be happy," I commented.

"That's about it. Whatever she had was never good enough."

"And so this reunion is all about . . ." I shrugged.

"About pretending that we're just one great big, wonderfully happy family. She's invited all her siblings and their families. They're spread out all over the country now. I think the guest list at last count was somewhere around fifty people, and I don't know if that even includes the littlest ones. She wants to do this big meal at her house, for which she'll do most of the cooking. Heaven knows why." She sipped again. "I guess so everyone will look at her and think what a wonderful homemaker and mother she turned out to be. Now that's a laugh—her wanting to show what a great homemaker she is, when it's the last thing she ever wanted in real life.

"And of course, part of this image of the big, perfect family is, in her mind, having Grandpa . . ." her voice broke off. "Do you think there's any hope of that?" she asked, giving me a long, hard stare.

"I don't know, Melanie. I just don't know."

EIGHT

We parted outside in the parking lot, with my promise to find out what I could. She'd also asked me to come to the reunion dinner on Sunday. I agreed without really wanting to, but figured I might pick up some clues by meeting the other family members. I didn't hold much hope for a happy outcome to this one. I drove home, heated myself a bowl of soup, and fell into bed for the night

I spent the weekend puttering around the house. I was still enjoying our new addition and found I liked straightening and tinkering with the little bit of decorating I still had to do. On Saturday, Dorothy called to restate Melanie's invitation to the reunion dinner and I found myself trapped into going. Sunday evening I drove up to the northeast heights once again and hunted for a parking spot among the dozens of cars that lined her street.

Dorothy opened the door herself, wearing a silk broomstick skirt in shades of coral and brown, with a rust-colored tunic top and a string of silver and coral heishi around her neck. Her gray curls were upswept in back with a spiral curl dipping low over her forehead.

"I hope you have some good news for us tonight," she whispered through her teeth.

"It's only been a couple of days, Dorothy. I don't have any news yet," I told her.

She dropped my elbow and ushered me through the living room to a large den at the back of the house, where six large round tables had been set up for dinner. Across the crowded room I spotted Melanie as she finished setting butter dishes on a couple of the tables.

"Hi, Charlie," she greeted. "So glad you came. I've put your place right here next to mine. Bob, my husband, will be with us."

Dorothy stood at the doorway into the kitchen and rang a small crystal dinner bell. Talk among the guests gradually faded away. "Dinner is ready," she announced.

"We're doing this buffet style," Melanie whispered in my ear. "Let's go fix our plates and we can visit while we eat."

By process of deductive reasoning, aided by hints from Melanie, I began to figure out who the family members were. Seated at our table were—besides Melanie, Bob, and myself—one of Dorothy's sisters, Beatrice, her husband Ralph, and a sullen teenager named Heather. Dorothy presided over a table with another sister and spouse and a few people about Melanie's age, presumably children of Dorothy's other siblings. Another table hosted Dorothy's brother Felix, rugged and outdoorsy with a craggy face and deep tan, and a svelte woman in her sixties whom Melanie said was Felix's date. Altogether, I came up with four in Dorothy's generation, about ten of their respective children (and children's spouses or dates), and an assortment of teens and kids who belonged in there somewhere. If Willie had been here, he would have been the patriarch over the four generations.

"Well, Dorothy's really outdone herself," Beatrice sniffed after we'd finished our dinner and were well into the desserts.

"She worked hard to put it together," Melanie acknowledged. Her eyes became red around the edges. "I just wish Grandpa could have been here."

Beatrice stiffened. She busied herself with her chocolate mousse but had a hard time eating any with her lips clamped shut so she ended up just stirring it to death in its crystal glass.

"Aunt Beatrice, what's the matter?" Melanie asked.

Ralph tried to dissuade the question with a subtle headshake but no one noticed it. Heather didn't say a word but a spark of interest had appeared in her eyes. I attempted to tune my senses to every little nuance while appearing as though I hadn't the slightest interest in the conversation. I doubt I succeeded.

Beatrice fired a poison-dart look toward Dorothy at the other table. The other woman was in an animated conversation and didn't notice. Ralph nudged his wife. "Bea, settle down," he whispered. She turned on him.

"I'm not settling down," she hissed. "It eats at me every time I see my sister. The thought of how she's controlling Daddy and making him do things he wouldn't normally do." She scraped furiously at the sides of her dessert dish. She looked at Melanie. "She's got all his important papers hidden somewhere and won't tell any of the rest of us what's going on. I know for a fact that she got him to take the rest of us off that insurance policy of his and make her the only beneficiary. Lord only knows what he's done with his will by now."

Melanie looked like she'd cry any minute. I glanced around the room to see who else was listening in. All the other tables were absorbed in their own conversations.

"I'm sorry, dear," said Beatrice, patting the middle of the table as if she were touching Melanie's hand. "I don't mean to upset *you*. I know it's none of your doing."

Bob put his arm around Melanie's shoulders. "It's okay, honey," he said in a low voice. To the table at large he launched into a story about how legend in his family had it that his great-grandpa Joey had changed his will twenty-seven times in the last year of his life. It got to be such a game of musical chairs in the family, trying to guess who would be in and who would be out, that everyone finally gave up and told the old man they didn't care. After that, he wrote them all back in equally. "Willie will probably do exactly the same thing," he tried to assure them.

I got the sense that no one was buying it.

"I just hope he's really alive somewhere," Melanie said, sniffing into her napkin.

I squeezed her hand and told her I hoped so too. People were getting up and milling around now and I felt myself drooping. It had been a long day. I said goodbye to Melanie and Bob, looked around for Dorothy but didn't see her, so I ducked out the front door without any fanfare. By the time I got home I didn't have the energy for much of anything. I watched television for a few minutes and caught myself dozing off so I went to bed. It was only nine o'clock.

Rusty woke me the next morning at daybreak by resting his large head on the edge of the bed and staring at me until his presence became undeniable.

"All right, all right," I groaned. I slipped on a robe and let him out the back door. The thought crossed my mind that I'd just tippy-toe back to bed for another couple of hours, but the phone rang as I was crossing the living room.

"Randy Buckman here." His voice seemed softer and less officious over the phone line. "I hope I didn't wake you."

I swallowed to clear the fuzziness from my voice. "No, it's fine. I was already up."

"I'm getting an early start today on that White Oaks case," he said. "The dental charts aren't here yet but, being as I have to go to court this afternoon, I thought I'd clear away a few other things. You have any luck with an ID on that shirt?"

I told him that Melanie had definitely recognized it. "The family is pretty upset about this," I fudged. "They've got a big reunion going on now and I'm afraid any outcome except Mr. McBride turning up alive and well is going to put a real damper on all of them."

"Well, let's see what the dental charts turn up. I'll notify them as soon as possible. If the body is his, it's better that they know as soon as possible, I'd say."

"I'm sure you're right." Privately, I was just glad he would do the notifying. I hung up the phone, feeling down because the case was ending so quickly and so badly.

Rusty scratched at the door just then and I let him back inside. Fed him a scoop of nuggets and myself a piece of toast. By then I was feeling decidedly grubby sitting around in my robe, so I opted for a very long, hot shower where I shaved my legs, shampooed and conditioned my hair, and gave myself a mini-facial. I followed all this by polishing my toenails and sitting back on the new chaise lounge in our bedroom while they dried. Having done all the girl-stuff I could think of, I slipped into jeans and a cotton sweater and put on sandals so I wouldn't ruin the new polish job.

Today was Monday, I realized, so I needed to get to the office at some point and catch up on my incoming mail. Other than that, the day was promising to be long and uneventful. I had hoped Drake would be able to get home for the weekend, but he hadn't and I wasn't sure when he'd get any time off. Fires don't quit burning because the fire-fighters are tired, unfortunately.

I drove to the office about nine, missing most of the rush-hour traffic. By noon I'd finished most of my work and left instructions with Sally for a few projects Tammy should work on during the afternoon. If she finished early, I told Sally to have her switch on the answering machine and lock up. I considered calling a friend and making lunch plans but it was short notice and I ended up just doing a few errands on the way home. The answering machine in the kitchen was blinking when I carried the groceries in.

"Charlie, it's Randy Buckman again. Give me a call and I'll fill you in." *Beep*. "Charlie, it's Melanie Ritz. The sheriff just called to tell us that the, uh, man you found wasn't Grandpa. Can you call me?" *Beep*. No more messages.

I called Randy Buckman first.

"So the body wasn't William McBride?" I blurted the instant I had him on the line.

"Did I say that in my message?"

"No," I admitted, "I had a second call on my machine, from McBride's granddaughter." I sat down at the kitchen table. "So where does the investigation go from here?"

"Well," he said, "our other logical supposition is that

this could be Bud Tucker. I'm still trying to find out whether we can get some dental records on him. Coroner didn't have much luck getting fingerprints."

"And if this isn't Willie McBride, I guess my case is still open and now I'm looking for a missing person."

"Wait a second. If the victim turns out to be Tucker, then McBride becomes a suspect. He was the last guy seen with Tucker. Finding him now becomes a police matter."

"Sophie told me the two men took McBride's truck and now it's missing. Locating it might be a good start. And the other day when I went through some things at his house, with his daughter's permission, I learned that he banked at First Albuquerque Bank. I don't know if he had an ATM card, but you might want to see if he's drawn out any money."

"Well, thank you so much for that little lesson in procedure," he drawled.

"I'm sorry." I felt myself blushing. "I didn't mean to tell you how to do your job. Just thought I'd share a little information."

"It's okay. You did save me some time. I'll see how much I can accomplish before the banks close this afternoon."

"Would you let me know if you find out anything? I know you don't have to, but I think it's in everyone's best interests to find McBride quickly and maybe I can help."

He didn't exactly guarantee anything, but he didn't refuse either. I hung up after promising to return the plaid shirt. I hadn't mentioned Keith Randel's theory about McBride and his gold mine.

I finished putting away my groceries and found myself pacing the kitchen floor, at loose ends. The rest of the week loomed ahead with my office duties caught up, Drake out of town, and my case at a standstill; I wasn't sure what to do with myself. It was only two o'clock. I could drive down to White Oaks and return the shirt to the sheriff and maybe do a little more exploring on my own. And I might be able to spend a little time with Drake.

Once more I gathered a few provisions for a couple of days out of town. I was just stuffing undies into a duffle bag when the phone rang.

"Charlie, it's Randy Buckman again."

"Wow, that was quick."

"Sometimes the wheels of justice actually move with some precision," he said. "What you said made sense, about us wanting to find McBride as quickly as possible. So, I'll share with you if you'll do the same."

"Certainly."

"No sooner had I put an APB out on McBride's pickup truck than I got a strike. A towing company in Las Cruces has it. It sat in the bus station parking lot for a couple of weeks before somebody decided to have it towed away. They've had it over a month now and want their money. We're having it brought here to Ruidoso for processing."

"So Willie probably drove to Las Cruces and took the bus somewhere else."

"Or someone did. It's more likely some unknown perp found the two old men while they were up at the mining camp. Killed 'em both and took Willie's vehicle. McBride could be lying in one of those mine shafts or somewhere out in the desert between here and Cruces. If that's the case, we may never find him. But we'll work on it as long as we've got the manpower."

That was a possibility I hadn't considered.

"Right now we're treating it as a search and rescue mission, getting some folks over here to help us look. At least we can scour the mines and surrounding area. Normally State SAR won't handle a body retrieval but the local coordinator is a buddy of mine. He's agreed to pretend that there's some hope of finding McBride alive."

"I'm coming down there," I told him. "I'll bring back the shirt and maybe I can help with the search."

He argued a little about my participating in a search since I wasn't officially on the search team, but didn't forbid me from coming. I finished my packing. Deciding that having Rusty along with me would be more hassle than help, I called my neighbor, Elsa Higgins, and asked whether she'd mind dogsitting for a couple of days or so. As always, she was incredibly accommodating and I walked the dog over to her house. Thirty minutes later, I'd topped off with gas and was on the road.

I arrived in White Oaks to find the town in a flurry of activity, relatively speaking. The parking area at the café contained five vehicles, including the sheriff's. I joined them and went inside. Buckman sat at one of the tables along the right wall, along with two other men and a woman. All were dressed in black and wore belts bristling with radios. Randy waved me over.

"Charlie, this is Ron Pitt, the search and rescue coordinator. Charlie is a private investigator hired by McBride's family."

Pitt rose slightly and shook my hand. I let the error in my job description slide on by.

"Any news yet?" I asked.

Pitt's radio squawked and he raised it to his ear. Buckman stood up and steered me toward the counter.

"Nothing around here," he told me. "But I got a line on McBride's bank account. He did have an ATM card, which is kind of unusual for a man his age. They don't usually go for modern technology. We discovered that his card has been used twice—once in Las Cruces and once in Phoenix. I'm waiting for the banks to see if they can get a usable photo of the person using the card and fax it to me."

"That should tell us a lot, I would think," I ventured.

"We'll see. Look, I gotta get up to the mining camp. You stay around here; there're already too many people milling around up there." He went outside and got into his patrol car.

The SAR group were busy with their heads together over maps and sketches, their radios constantly buzzing with static and blurry voices. They paid no attention to me. I wandered back to the lunch counter and caught Keith's eye.

"Hey there, Charlie," he greeted. "Fix ya somethin' to eat?"

"Maybe just a Coke for now," I said.

He filled a red plastic cup from the fizzing dispenser and set it on the counter. I glanced around. There were three other people at the counter, all dressed in hiking gear and boots.

"They been out here all day," Keith volunteered. "Little groups of 'em come in to get some food, and out they go."

"Remember that little item you gave me the other day?" I asked, tilting my head toward the cash register.

"Uh-huh," he nodded.

"You said you knew how to translate it?"

"Sure." He lowered his normally booming voice. "Get yourself a topo map of the Superstition Mountains and I'll pinpoint 'er for ya." He winked.

"One more thing," I asked. "Tell me how to get to Sophie Tucker's?"

"I can tell ya, but I'll also tell ya that she ain't there right now. She's over to the schoolhouse."

"Thanks." I sipped my Coke in silence and he turned to wait on his other customers. I finished the drink and left a few minutes later.

A sheriff's department car blocked most of the road leading to the schoolhouse. As I signaled to make the turn, the deputy climbed out of the vehicle. I recognized Montoya.

"Can't go up to the mining camp," he said.

"I know. I only want to go as far as the schoolhouse. Is Sophie Tucker still up there?"

He turned and gazed out toward the old building. "Yeah, I think her car is there."

"I just wanted to see how she's doing."

He waved me on through and I noticed in my rearview mirror that he watched until I made the right hand turn at the school. I parked next to Sophie's little red car and went inside. She answered my shout and I tracked her voice to a classroom at the far end of the long hall. She was busy with a feather duster, attacking stray motes on the desks and books that decorated the room.

"You doing okay?" I asked, taking a seat at one of the student-sized desks.

"Pretty good," she said, dusting even more furiously. "There's no official word yet. They won't let me see the body. Sheriff says I couldn't tell nothin' by looking anyway."

She picked up a few books from the teacher's desk and formed them into a stack. "Finally rounded up a dentist Pop went to once, but it was twenty or more years back. Guy's retired now and they aren't sure if they can dig out any records, but they're trying. Everybody's been real nice.

I mean, they all know this is pretty hard for me." A tear slipped down her weathered cheek. "Alls I can do now is keep busy." An unhappy chuckle escaped her. "My house ain't never been so clean, I'll tell you. And I'm about to get this place whipped into shape too."

I made some sympathetic noises. "Need any help?" I asked.

"Nah. I don't want to finish it too soon. Wouldn't have anything to do then but sit around."

Sensing that she really wanted to be alone, I gave her my cell number and told her to call if I could do anything. I patted her shoulder and left. I'm not very good at hugs and comfort, I guess.

Montoya watched me drive toward him and gave me a small wave as I pulled out onto the highway. Without much of a plan, I headed toward Ruidoso.

The desk clerk at Drake's hotel didn't seem too inclined to give me a key to his room and it was only after I'd produced identification that he quit eyeing me as if I were a hooker. I parked near the door to the room and carried my one duffle inside. I washed my hands, switched on the television set, and dialed the number to Drake's cell phone that rings directly to his headset when he's flying.

"Hello!" he shouted, the whine of the turbine engine strong in the background.

"Hi, hon, it's me." I shouted back.

"I can hear you fine," he said, lowering his voice. "Everything okay?"

"Yeah, I won't keep you. I'm here in your hotel room in Ruidoso. Can you meet me in town for dinner when you're finished?"

"Sure. I'll call you when we shut down for the day. It'll be around dark."

I hung up and paced the room a couple of times. The TV wasn't holding my interest, but I remembered an errand I could do in town. Picking up the phone book, I located what I needed and wrote down the address.

The woman in the map store looked like she wasn't thrilled to have a customer come in at ten minutes to closing, but I assured her I would be quick. I told her which topo map I was looking for and she pulled it from a cabinet of wide, flat drawers. I paid for it and left her to close up and go home, still pretty much on time. With an hour or more to wait for Drake's call, I leisurely browsed a small gift shop next to the map store before I headed back to the hotel. By the time his call came, I was ravenous.

"They're calling the fire ninety percent contained," he told me after we'd loaded our plates at the all-you-can-eat buffet where I'd met him for dinner.

"So, how much longer will you be here?"

"Hard to say. Another couple of days, for sure. Maybe longer. They'll keep their contract ship on the job because they're already paying him anyway. The rest of us, call-when-needed ships like mine, they'll release as soon as they've got things under control."

I filled him in on my progress.

"Guess it's good news that the body wasn't your client's father," he said, taking a forkful of mashed potatoes.

"The granddaughter was certainly happy about it when she found out," I said. "The sheriff reminded me, however, that just because we didn't find Willie it doesn't mean that he isn't also out there somewhere. His truck was abandoned in Las Cruces and his ATM card was used twice. They think his body might have been dumped in one of the mine shafts around White Oaks."

"But you don't think so," he said, giving me a long, pointed stare.

"Well . . . remember Keith Randel, the guy who runs the café there? He's a pretty canny old guy. He said something that makes me think Willie might have wanted to disappear."

"Leaving his friend dead in a mining shack?"

"Maybe Willie didn't know Bud was dead. Maybe he left while Bud was still alive. Someone else could have killed Bud."

"And stolen Willie's truck?"

"Maybe. Or maybe the killing and the truck are totally unrelated."

I speared a chunk of lettuce, chewing it fully while my mind whirred around the possibilities. "It's probably more like the police are saying, that someone else killed both the old men and took the truck to get away."

But something about that theory nagged at me while Drake went back to the buffet to get dessert. I couldn't quite put my finger on it.

"Want some?" He offered his dessert plate, which contained two cookies and a blob of chocolate pudding. I took one of the cookies. My brain felt weary.

"Meanwhile," he said, "I can't wait to get back to the room, take a nice hot shower, and jump your bones."

Twenty minutes later, we were back in the room where he proceeded to do just that.

NINE

Drake was out of the room before daybreak the next morning. I gave him a lingering kiss at the door then scurried back to nestle into the covers again. My body was still languid from last night's bedtime joys and it was after nine o'clock when I finally gave up the luxury of the warm bed to shower and dress.

I'd switched on the television set, thinking I might catch a newscast, but when I emerged from the shower the station was airing an old rerun of *Unsolved Mysteries*. I rummaged through my duffle for clean underwear and shirt but came upright when I heard the commentator mention the Lost Dutchman Mine. Backing to the end of the bed, I plopped down in front of the set. A colorful character with a craggy face and white beard, wearing a plaid shirt and suspenders, was being interviewed.

It wasn't a new story. Legends of the mine have floated around for years. But the man telling his story seemed particularly knowledgeable about the area and the thought jumped into my mind that he might know Willie McBride. I jotted down his name—Rocky Rhodes. It had to be a nickname. Surely no one would really stick a baby with that.

The segment ended and a few minutes later the show

was over. I had no idea how long ago it had been filmed. Many of the rerun episodes were at least six or seven years old. It could be that this old man would be long gone by now. But I figured it was worth a shot. I called Information for the Phoenix area and got a listing for R.W. Rhodes in Apache Junction. When I dialed the number it rang at least twelve times with no answer. I gave up and finished dressing.

"Can a person still get some breakfast here?" I asked Keith Randel an hour later as I walked into his café. The place was clear of searchers and deputies for a change.

"Well, hey there, Charlie girl. You sure can. I'll fix you anything you want, any hour you want it." He gave me his wide grin and proceeded to pour coffee into a mug for me.

"Some scrambled eggs, ham, and wheat toast?"

"You bet." He headed for the kitchen while I took a stool at the counter, setting my purse and the map I'd purchased yesterday afternoon on the seat beside me.

"I got that map you mentioned," I called toward the kitchen. "Maybe you can show me the spot you were telling me about?"

"Sure thing."

I glanced around the room again. "So, have the searchers left town?" I asked.

"Naw. They was all here this mornin' early for breakfast. Ate mite near everythin' in the place. You just happened to catch a slow time." His arms worked the grill, stirring the eggs, flipping the ham. He reached for a plate on a shelf above the window and scooped the cooked food onto it.

My mouth was nearly watering by the time he set the plate down in front of me. I unwound a set of flatware from inside its paper napkin and cut the first bite of ham from the thick slice he'd given me. Keith refilled my mug and puttered at the other end of the counter while I sated my initial hunger pangs.

"Let me take a look at that map," he suggested.

I pulled it off the stool and put it on the counter.

"You got that other little one too?"

I reached into my purse and pulled out the small sketch he'd given me from his cash register.

He spread the large topo map carefully on the counter, unrolling it from the bottom and weighting the corners with salt and pepper shakers and a sugar jar. His jaw worked back and forth as he studied the layout. I spread strawberry jam on my toast as I watched him peruse the map.

"Okay, here we go," he said at last.

I pushed my plate aside to my left and wiped the crumbs off my fingers.

"Here's your highway coming in from the south," he said. "Now—*here's* your little map. See this spot here?" He pointed to a place where a small creek bisected a trail. "That there's this same place." He indicated a T on Willie's sketch.

"So if I get to this spot," I said, pointing to the topo map, "I just take it from there on the little map?"

"Right. Now Willie told me this map of his, it don't follow no set trail. Guess he climbs over all kinds of boulders and stuff to get to his spot."

"Okay." I was beginning to envision myself completely lost among the saguaros and rattlesnakes.

Keith seemed to sense my growing uncertainty. "You can do it," he assured me with a wink. "Jus' take this map an' follow Willie's marks. Like these three little circles, one on top of the other? That'd be a rock cairn. Wiggly line's a stream. Like that."

Uh huh. Sure. I rolled the two maps together and stuck them down in my purse. I was stirring sugar into my fresh cup of coffee when the door creaked. Randy Buckman walked in. He nodded a greeting my way.

"Thought that was your car out there," he said, taking the stool to my left. Keith poured him a mug of coffee and he busied himself with the ritual of sugar and cream. Took a tentative sip before he addressed me again. "Got the dental records back," he said quietly. "It was Bud Tucker. I just went up and told Sophie. And we found something else."

"What? Out at the mines?" I asked. I noticed Keith at the back counter, wiping at non-existent spills, eavesdropping for the gossip mill.

"Yeah. Well, actually, just above shaft number eight. Hidden in a clump of sage."

I raised an eyebrow, wanting to grab his shoulders and shake the information out of him.

"Packet of mining tools wrapped in an old blanket," he said. "Don't know exactly what that means."

"No clues about who they belong to?"

"Not really. It's old stuff. I mean, not something you'd be able to go out and buy today. But not antique, either. Could easily belong to either McBride or Tucker."

I pondered that while I took another sip of my coffee. "You said they were hidden in the sage? Like someone purposely wanted them out of sight?"

"That's my guess. Everything was neatly wrapped, stuck between two good-sized bushes. Doesn't seem like they would have just fallen there."

"Why would Willie hide his tools, then leave without them," I mused.

"Maybe they're Tucker's tools," he countered. "Or maybe we have some unknown third party—or parties."

"Any other evidence?"

Something in his face clicked shut. "Some. But with close to fifty searchers prowling around out there, anything as subtle as a footprint is long gone." He chugged down the rest of his coffee and met my gaze straight on. "I've got as many law enforcement men out there as I can, but unless we find Willie's body, I don't hold much hope for ever knowing what happened out there."

He rose stiffly, his leather belt full of police gear creaking, and slapped a dollar bill on the counter. "Thanks, Keith," he said, raising a hand to both of us as he walked out.

"So, does that shoot down our theory that Willie took off to go mining in Arizona?" I asked Randel as he turned back toward me.

"It might," he said, rubbing one pudgy hand along the side of his face. "But I don't count nothin' settled until the cows come home."

I flashed him a look. Did people really say that? "Well, guess I better get going," I told him. "Lots to do."

I gathered my purse and maps and left money for my breakfast.

"You take care, Charlie." He came around to my side of the counter, started to shake my hand, then converted it to a massive bear hug instead. "Take care."

"I will." For some reason my voice was a little husky.

Outside, the April wind had picked up, changing the sky

from gorgeous and clear to a blustery near-Arctic temp that made me want to scurry for my winter coat again. Across the road, a tumbleweed rolled by, lodging itself against the porch railing of an abandoned retail building. Another car pulled into the café's parking area, kicking up a flurry of dust. I quickly turned my back to avoid getting my eyes full.

"Deserved it, you ask me." Two men clad in Levi's and western shirts emerged from the dust-covered dark blue Pontiac. Their conversation came in snatches between gusts of wind.

". . . Bud Tucker . . . since that bank deal."

". . . tempted to do it yourself?"

The man on the far side of the car noticed me and closed his mouth abruptly. He tilted his head toward me in greeting then turned toward the café. The other man turned to give me a quick stare from under thick, dark brows. I offered a stupid half-smile and opened my car door, sliding behind the wheel as the two men stomped their boots on the wooden porch and went inside.

Knowing they were probably watching through the windows, I backed out and cruised slowly up the highway into town.

Why hadn't I looked at this angle before? I'd been so focused on Willie McBride, placing him at the center of the picture, that I'd failed to consider that Bud Tucker might have been the real target here. He obviously had enemies— that much was apparent—and I hadn't even bothered to ask some routine questions. I pulled over at a Historical Marker sign, one of those the State of New Mexico is fond of putting out with little tidbits of information about wherever you happen to be standing at the moment.

Staring at the sign, but not really seeing it, I pondered Bud Tucker. I really didn't know anything about him except that he was Willie McBride's buddy. Maybe I needed to ask Sophie some more questions about her father. I glanced around. I didn't know where Sophie lived, but the whole town wasn't much more than a mile-long stretch of highway and her little red car wouldn't be that hard to spot. I pulled out onto the road again and cruised along slowly, not seeing another vehicle.

A few cross streets bisected the main highway, attesting to the fact that the town had once been fairly good-sized. One of these dirt lanes meandered over the hilly terrain and appeared to lead to a large brick Victorian house near a streambed. A flash of red caught my eye and I made a quick right hand turn and headed toward it.

Sophie's car sat outside, its paint oxidized out to nearly the same shade as the faded red brick of the house. The wraparound porch badly needed a paint job and the plastic hanging baskets around its roofline needed new plants. A gray cat perched on the chipped wooden railing, eyeing me suspiciously. A second cat, a calico, trotted up to me as I got out of my car, sniffed my shoe tentatively, then began to rub against the leg of my jeans. I reached down and scratched her ears, which brought a rumble of purring.

"Charlie? Hi." Sophie stepped out onto the porch, drying her hands against the legs of her jeans. Her eyes were red-rimmed but dry. Her hair was pulled back into its customary braid and her plaid shirt was tucked in neatly, emphasizing the slimness of her waist. "I'm just taking some bread out of the oven. Want a slice, with a hunk of butter melted over it?"

Well, who could resist? I followed her through the front door.

We walked down a wide entry hall, passing a parlor on the right, dining room on the left. The furniture consisted of simple, ranch-style pieces in pine with blue and green plaid upholstery. Victorian touches still showed in the woodwork and light fixtures. We passed a flight of stairs leading up to the second story—turned mahogany spindles topped by a thick handrail—and emerged into a sunny kitchen filled with the heady scent of baking bread. The walls were pale yellow and the uncurtained windows with their southern exposure held narrow shelves laden with pots of houseplants.

"Have a seat," Sophie invited, pulling a chair away from the heavy pine-topped table.

Two loaves of bread sat, still in their baking pans, on wire racks on the linoleum counter top. On the opposite side of the sink, a drainer held clean mixing bowls and utensils.

"I was just about to cut myself a slice, and I've got hot water for tea." She held up the kettle as a question to me.

"Yes, please."

She pulled two mugs from pegs on the wall and started the tea ritual of dunking a teabag into the steaming water she poured into each mug.

"This bread won't slice real neatly while it's hot," she said, her back to me, "but I just can't resist it when it's right out of the oven." She dumped each loaf onto a wooden board, turned them upright, and pulled a long bread knife from a drawer. "You heard about Pop, I guess?"

"Yes, I'm sorry it turned out this way. Willie's family still wants me to find him," I said. "I'm just trying to make some sense of it all—your father's death and how that ties in."

Sophie stopped slicing and rested the heels of her hands on the countertop. "I know," she said, heavily. "I can't imagine who'd want to hurt a couple of harmless old men."

She carried the two cups of tea to the table and turned back to the counter to pick up the blue willow plate with four thick slices of bread, which she set in the middle of the table between us.

I set to work buttering a slice and tried to ask the question casually. "Did your father have any enemies?"

"No!" The answer came too quickly and she realized it. "Well, at least I don't think so."

I chewed slowly. The bread was heavenly. Sophie swirled the knife around and around, working the butter on her slice. "I don't know," she finally said. "Maybe."

"This is purely hearsay," I began, deciding to get right to the point, "but was there something about a bank?"

She looked at me sharply, like she wanted to ask how I knew that. "That goes back a long ways, Charlie."

I remembered the angry look on the man's face at the café. Long time back or not, some people were still mad. "Want to tell me about it?" I asked.

She sighed. "You really think it matters?" Without waiting for an answer, she continued. "Well, maybe so. Pop used to be on the board of directors for the local bank. Didn't really work there or nothin'. He just went to meetings now and then. Guess it kinda sounded important, and it got him out of the house, a little time away from bein' both mom and dad to a snotty little girl. Mom died when I was only about three or four. I don't really even remember her. The bank position gave Pop a chance to have some buddies, you know."

"You were really young at the time?"

"Oh, ten or twelve years old. I guess I was a pistol. Anyway, I was plenty old enough to take care of myself once or twice a month when Pop went out to his meetings."

I swallowed the last bite of my first slice and reached for another. "He ever tell you what was going on at the meetings?"

"Nah. I didn't care. During the day we worked the ranch together. I rode right along with the cowhands. Finished up to eighth grade in school, then didn't see much point in it. Cows don't much care if you can diagram a sentence or read Shakespeare." She chuckled.

"So your dad went to meetings . . . ?" I prompted.

"Well, yeah, he'd told me once, back when they invited him to be on this board of directors, he said 'Guess I'm a prominent businessman in this town now, Sophie.' He sounded kinda proud of that. Like somebody needed to tell him he was worth somethin'. Which is just a lot of horseshit, far as I'm concerned.

"Anyway, I was just a kid so I didn't ask much about it. But I do remember that was about the time we moved to this house. There was only about four or five fancy houses in town and here we were, living in one of 'em. It was somethin', all right. Before that, we just lived out at the ranch—four or five miles out, it is—in a three-room wooden house. Not much more than a cabin. It's still there. Pop moved back out there when I got married."

At my startled look she held up one hand. "Marriage didn't last much longer than the ceremony," she said dismissively. "It was more than twenty years ago."

"So, was the ranching business going that well, or did the big house have something to do with the banking?" I asked, getting back to the subject.

"Don't really know." She picked up her second slice of bread and started buttering it. "Guess it might have."

"And the trouble? What was that about?"

"I still don't know that, to this day, I don't. I just know that I was about fourteen, fifteen maybe. Workin' the ranch every day, ridin', brandin' . . . you know. Sometime in there, the bank closed down, sudden-like. Bank president—can't even remember his name now—he got run outta town, maybe went to jail, can't really remember. Pop just went back to bein' a rancher, 'cept we did get to keep the big house." She stared at the ceiling for a long minute. "One time, lotta years later, after I was grown, Pop showed me the deed to the house once. Said 'Don't you worry, Sophie. This place is yours after I'm gone. No mortgage. It's free and clear.' "

I decided to share what I knew. I told her about the tiny snatch of conversation I'd caught at the café. "I don't know who the men were. It just struck me that at least one of them was still very angry with your father and it had something to do with the bank."

Her eyebrows pulled together in the middle. "Can't think who that'd be. Guess it might be just about anybody. I never did let myself get too wrapped up with the people in this town. Ain't healthy. I like the ranch better."

"I wonder where I might get more information about the bank," I said. "Is there a newspaper office here in town?"

Sophie let go with a belly laugh. "Now that's rich," she cackled. "You never lived in a small town, I guess. Newspaper'd be a joke here. Ever'body in town'd know the news before they could print the damn thing up."

I gave an appropriately chastened grin.

"Course, the town used to be a lot bigger," she continued. "Used to have a post office, even. That closed down in the '50s. May have been a paper somewhere back there too. Just don't remember anything about it myself."

I drained my teacup and thanked her for the information as I left, my mind fast-forwarding to other possible sources of information. The calico cat rubbed against my legs again as I left and I shooed her away before getting into my Jeep. The obvious prime gossip-mill in town was Randel's café, but I'd already been there once today. Besides, I wanted a little more background first so I'd have some intelligent questions to ask. The nearest town of any size was Carrizozo, so I headed there.

An inquiry at the gas station was all it took to get the location of the newspaper office, where I was led into a surprisingly modern room complete with microfiche reader. The woman, who introduced herself as co-owner of the paper, assured me that all their issues dating back to the turn of the century had been stored on film. I asked whether she remembered something about a banking scandal in the '40s but she didn't. I loaded a box with film rolls dating from 1941 to '45, deciding to start there.

By five o'clock I'd scanned enough film to make a trapeze artist dizzy and still hadn't come across the story. When the woman came in to tell me she was getting ready to close up for the day, I asked whether there was anyone else in town who might remember the story.

"Well, sure," she responded with a smile. "My father owned the paper until Joe and I took it over five years ago."

I smiled through clenched teeth. Why hadn't I thought of this thirty rolls ago? "Could we give him a call?" I asked. "I'd like to come back tomorrow and look some more, but it would help if I had a starting place."

"Sure thing." She punched the digits on the phone quickly. After a couple of minutes of "How's Mom?" and "Umm, your bursitis again?" she got to the point. "There's a lady here who wants to ask about some back issues," she told him, handing the phone over to me.

I sympathized about his bursitis too and finally got him to settle on the topic at hand.

"Yeah, sure," he said, finally. "Christmas of '46. That was it. I remember it well, 'cause Molly—that's my daughter there you're talking to—she was born in November. There she was, just a baby, getting us up at all hours, and I had this big story to cover. Had to drive to Ruidoso to the courthouse to sit in on the trial of that banker fella. Just look on them film rolls. Molly's husband, Joe, he put all that stuff on film for us awhile back. Works great, and you can print copies of anything you want to keep."

I thanked him for the information and told Molly I'd come back the next day to go through them.

"Well, I have to be somewhere in the morning," she said. "Tell you what—you could just stay here now and finish if you'd like."

"Really?"

"No problem. Just shut off the machine and the lights

when you go. You can just twist this little thing on the doorknob to lock up."

"That's very trusting of you," I said.

"You have an honest face," she said, smiling. "Besides, I'm just going to be shopping at the market next door."

"I shouldn't be too long," I assured her. "Now that I have the date, it should go pretty quickly."

She looped a purse strap over her shoulder and left me at the microfiche reader. I went back to the cabinet where she'd gotten the original film rolls and browsed them until I found the last few months of 1946 and early 1947. Starting with Christmas week, I followed the trial, then scanned backward to the first mention of the story on October 15th.

BANK CLOSES IN WHITE OAKES, the headline read.

Local residents of the town of White Oaks were shocked to learn that the town bank has closed its doors. "The first inkling we had was this morning when I went to make a deposit," said local businesswoman, Betty Brierling. "At first I thought somebody had just forgotten to unlock the door. I knew it wasn't a holiday. So I knocked at the door, then I peeked in the windows." Brierling stated that she was shocked to see the manager's desk was gone and the vault door was standing open.

In a phone call to federal banking authorities, the News Express *has learned that the bank was closed on their orders, after an audit on Friday uncovered severe shortages of cash and irregularities in accounting procedures. At this time, no other details are known.*

I printed those pages, then scrolled to subsequent dates.

*According to William "Bill" Walker, a local business-
man, he and many of the townspeople were approached by
one Phillip Stanton with a plan to further develop the
town. "I guess we were ripe for his kind of deal," said
Walker. "White Oaks hadn't seen prosperous times for at
least fifty years and the town was on its way downhill.
Stanton had the whole thing planned out. Housing developments for a retirement community, stores, a community center, the whole thing. Lots of us went for it. We'd each
invest what we could toward the amenities, then we'd get
our money back tenfold as the housing started to sell. He
even showed us contracts from homeowners who'd already
bought in. People were going to be moving here from all
over the country."*

*Testimony at the trial of bank president Sam Curry
revealed that the bank's officers and directors had fully
backed the project. Stanton, who had skipped to an
unknown location, had convinced the officers of the
validity of the project and they had, in fact, put deposi-
tors' money at risk in the development.*

*In a bizarre set of coincidences, the sum of three mil-
lion dollars had been wire transferred from the White
Oaks bank to the account of River Oaks Development late
Thursday afternoon, October 12th. On that same day,
River Oaks Development wired the money to Sagebrush
Properties, who then wired it to Stonebridge Land and
Cattle. A convoluted set of documents showed that Phillip
Stanton had a hand in each of these entities but no actu-
al transfer of funds to him directly can be traced. Despite
a warrant for his arrest, Stanton has not been located.*

"In short, the investors and the bank are out every-

thing they invested," testified Warren Collins of the Federal Banking Commission.

The *News Gazette* went on with follow up stories about Sam Curry, the bank president being sentenced to ninety days in jail and two years probation. After serving his brief jail time, Curry quickly disappeared. Several businesses immediately folded, and all but two of the former directors left town quickly and quietly. Bud Tucker was one of the two who stayed.

I looked at the stack of pages I'd printed and rubbed my itchy eyes. It was nearly eight o'clock. Following Molly's directions, I turned off the equipment and locked the door. Drake would probably be back at the hotel by now. I dialed the number on my cell phone as I started the car.

"Hey there, have you had dinner yet?" I asked when he answered.

"Just finished. I didn't know if you'd be back tonight."

I told him where I was and that I'd fill him in when I got there. "I'll grab a fast food something on the way," I said.

By nine o'clock Drake was in the shower and I had just finished a semi-soggy burger. My head was so full of the complexities of the banking scandal that I knew I wouldn't fall asleep right away. I stretched out on the bed and turned on the television. I had just begun to doze when Drake shook my shoulder gently.

"Isn't that your client, hon?" he asked.

Preoccupied and half groggy, I hadn't been paying attention to the news report. "What are they saying?"

He nodded his head toward the TV.

". . . at least two dead." An on-scene reporter with her collar pulled up against the blustery wind was speaking into her microphone.

"So, just to recap, Chris," said the female studio anchor gravely, "there's been a six-car pileup on Interstate 40 near the Carlisle exit. Fifty-nine year old Dorothy Swartzman of Albuquerque, apparently the driver of the lead car that started it all, has been taken to the hospital. The extent of her injuries is unknown at this time. But we do know that two other people died at the scene."

"A real tragedy," agreed her male counterpart. He turned to the other camera. "It was a big day at the zoo today for a group of kindergarten . . ."

"Did I catch that correctly?" I asked Drake. "Did they say Dorothy caused the crash?"

"Sounded that way to me."

"I wonder if I can reach Melanie." I went to the room's desk and rummaged through my purse for the number. It rang four times and a machine picked up. I left a message, giving her the number at the hotel and my cell phone. Told her to call me when she got in, no matter how late.

"So." I said, plopping back down on the bed. "I wonder what this means. . . ."

TEN

The phone rang at six-thirty. Drake had left for the fire scene more than an hour earlier and I'd wired myself with two cups of room-brewed coffee. I planned to head for the hotel's coffee shop for some real food, then I'd make the decision whether I'd go back to Albuquerque or see what else I could dig up in White Oaks.

"Did I wake you?" Melanie asked. "I just got in and got your message."

"How's your mother?"

"She'll be fine, physically. She's got a broken leg and a mild concussion. They're keeping her in the hospital a day or two for observation."

"Did she tell you how the accident happened?"

Melanie sighed. "She claims she saw a hitchhiker who looked just like Grandpa and she was going to pull over and pick him up."

"On the Interstate?" For one thing hitching was illegal there and, for another, how would she recognize someone while driving sixty miles an hour?

"She swerved across two lanes of traffic. I don't think she understands yet that she caused two people to die." Melanie sounded bone-tired.

"Is there anything I can do?" I offered, unsure what it would be.

"No, I don't think so. Needless to say, this has put a real damper on the reunion. Everyone was there at the hospital last night, but when it became obvious that Mom would be all right, they all started talking about going home. Couple of them have kids whose spring break is almost over anyway. Guess they'll all be heading out today or tomorrow. I'm just going to get some sleep, then start shuttling them to the airport."

I ended the call by telling Melanie that I wasn't much closer to locating her grandfather but that there had been some new developments in the case. I'd fill her in when I got back to town. I didn't mention Randy Buckman's theory that someone had murdered both the old men and that searchers would find Willie's body soon.

After polishing off a plate of pancakes at the coffee shop I went back to the room and left Drake a note saying that I planned to go back to Albuquerque later. I'd call him this evening. I loaded my duffle into the Jeep and headed toward White Oaks one more time. The news accounts of the town's banking scandal and the possibility that Bud Tucker had been the killer's real target had bothered me all night.

The road leading into town was beginning to feel shorter with each trip. At the outskirts I'd passed the town cemetery every time but had never stopped. Now I noticed a gathering of cars there, including Randy Buckman's cruiser. Tucker's funeral. I'd forgotten all about it. I pulled into the dirt parking area and stopped behind Sophie's little red car. A small knot of people was gathered around an open grave to the right of the entrance.

If you ever want to meet the entire population of a small town at once, just hold a funeral. Keith Randel, Sophie, Buckman, and an assortment of others were all there, their typical ranching attire dressed up by the addition of a clean felt Stetson here, a bolo tie there. A petite woman with fluffy white hair was sobbing into a sodden ball of handkerchief. Bud Tucker's lady friend from Ruidoso was about to watch her hopes of marriage get lowered into the ground. The man I'd seen yesterday at the café, the one whose words sounded so angry, stood at the edge of the group. I approached quietly and stood next to him.

A minister, differentiated only by the fact that he wore a small cross pinned to the lapel of his wool jacket, read the twenty-third Psalm. Sophie stood on the opposite side of the grave from me. Her face was composed, her eyes dry. She stared at a point somewhere in mid-air over the silver coffin. She didn't acknowledge me.

Keith stood with his hands clasped in front of his large belly, expression respectful if a tad impatient. I could tell he'd rather be behind his grill, although he knew all his potential customers were standing out here in the open air. He gave me a quick smile and wink. I edged closer to him, mainly because I couldn't openly study the angry man next to me unless I put a little distance between us.

The minister said something, the intonation indicating he was finished. Four pall bearers stepped forward to lower the casket into the ground, and Sophie reached down to gather a ceremonial handful of dirt. The white-haired woman looked near collapse as she gripped the arm of a young man next to her. I noticed that Randy Buckman's eyes continually scanned the crowd. He'd obviously come to the same conclusion I had, that Bud Tucker might have been the target of a local resident.

I tapped Keith on the arm and he bent his ear close to me.

"Who's the man in the buckskin vest?" I asked.

"Rory?"

I shrugged.

"Rory Daniels," he said. "Family's lived in these parts forever, I guess."

I opened my mouth to whisper another question but Keith was on the move. "Gotta go get the café open," he said. "C'mon over. I'll buy you a cup of coffee."

He gave my arm a quick squeeze and headed toward his small pickup truck as quickly as his massive size permitted. I caught up with Sophie as she rounded the grave. She wore a pair of crisp new jeans and a burgundy western shirt trimmed with a single row of fabric ruffles at the yokes. Her hair was braided down the back of her head and a small silver cross hung from a delicate chain around her neck.

"You doing okay?" I asked.

"Sure. I'll get used to it eventually." Her weathered face was solemn but her eyes were clear.

"I have to head back to Albuquerque today," I told her, mentioning briefly Dorothy and the car accident. "Here's my number. Just call me if you need anything. Or if you think of anything that might help locate Willie."

She nodded and brushed on by. The little crowd had thinned, heading for their cars to get out of the breeze that was picking up steadily from the west. I spotted Rory Daniels getting into the same dusty blue Pontiac he'd been driving yesterday. The other man, whom I'd not noticed in the group, was with him. The two looked . . . satisfied.

I walked slowly back to my Jeep, leaving only a dark-suited man, presumably from the funeral home, standing beside the open grave. Keith's café was hopping when I pulled into the parking area. He'd been right in his assumption that everyone in town would want lunch right after the funeral. Conspicuously missing was Sophie Tucker's little red car. Had she gone home alone? Was this the town's way of shunning her for her father's past transgressions? I hesitated a minute, debating whether to go out to her house or stay here and try to catch the local gossip.

Gossip won out. I parked and went inside.

Only one stool at the counter remained empty so I took it, followed by the eyes of everyone else in the room. Keith spotted me and held up the coffee carafe.

"Could I get iced tea this time? I've had enough coffee this morning to wire a small city."

He brought me a tall glass of tea with a lemon wedge affixed to the rim. Conversation drifted back to normal in the room as I squeezed the lemon and gave the liquid a stir. A woman I'd not met before came up to the customer seated next to me and asked for his order. Keith was back in the kitchen, his arms working busily at the grill.

"Ma'am?" The waitress was looking at me. She was in her forties, attractive, with short dark hair styled puffy on top and a generous mouth coated in bright pink lipstick. She wore a flowered shirtwaist dress, and I thought I'd seen her at the funeral.

"Nothing just now. I had a late breakfast."

She moved on to the tables behind me. I kept one ear cocked toward the table where Rory Daniels and his friend sat, to my right. At one point, Daniels's voice became tense but his friend shushed him and they began talking about the calving season. Soon plates of food began to appear on the stainless steel window ledge and the waitress began to dispense them to the various tables. People didn't linger. Needing to get back to the work of ranching, they ate, paid, and left in quick succession. When only myself and one other customer remained, Keith's waitress pulled a purse from behind the counter and turned to go.

"Thanks, Mona, always 'preciate it," he said.

"Anytime. You know that." She stood on tiptoe and planted a solid kiss on his jowly cheek, leaving a pink lipstick mark. Laughing, she rubbed it off with her thumb and left.

"Didn't realize you had a waitress," I told him when he came over to refill my tea after the other customer had gone.

"Oh, Mona. She's kinda like a lady-friend. Helps out when things get busy. We catch a movie over to Ruidoso now and then."

"You don't have to explain her to me," I told him, smiling at the slow flush that reddened his cheeks. I took a long sip of tea. "Maybe I'll have some of those world-famous enchiladas now. Smelling all that food made me hungry."

"Chicken, with green?"

"You bet." Doesn't take long for a good cook to differentiate the green chile eaters from the red.

"That Rory Daniels, the guy you pointed out to me at the cemetery?"

"Yeah?" He peered at me through the kitchen window while he assembled the enchilada plate.

"What's his story? I saw him yesterday. Caught just a few words, but enough to give me the idea that he sure hated Bud Tucker. Then he's at the funeral today?"

"Hell, ever'body was at the funeral today. That was mite near the whole town."

"But if he hated Tucker . . ."

"Could be he wanted to be sure Bud got buried. Never know about that stuff." He brought the steaming plate out and set it before me.

I cut a vent through the tortilla to let steam escape. "What's behind it? Do you know what he had against Bud?"

He leaned heavily against the counter. "Goes a long way back. Way 'fore my time here. Guess the whole town nearly went broke back in the '40s. Some Eastern fella showed up with a scheme and lots of 'em went for it. Rory's pa was one, I know that much. Poor ol' guy never was the same. They say it turned his hair white overnight—and he was only in his twenties. Rory was a new baby then. But his pa never did recover. Died when the kid was 'bout ten or so."

"What about Rory's mother?" I asked, savoring another forkful of chicken, cheese and chile.

"Never met her myself. Never met the pa neither." He straightened a set of salt and pepper shakers and began to wipe the counter with a rag. "Guess she died 'bout the time Rory growed up. That was about in the '60s, '70s, I guess."

"And Rory blamed Bud Tucker for that?"

"Guess so. I hear Bud was one of them bankers back then. Let all the people lose their money. Rory's family was poorer than dirt after that."

"The newspaper reported that the bank president went to jail, but the other directors weren't held responsible."

He looked up and grinned. "Been doin' a little research, have ya?"

"Well, some. Just trying to figure out some motive for all this. I can't see that some random stranger would come along and kill a couple of old men, just to steal Willie's pickup truck."

"Been killin's for less," he commented. "Plus, we don't know but what those two old men had 'em a big stash of gold somewheres."

"True." I puzzled over it as I scraped the last of the chile off my plate. "Just seems like they'd both have chosen a bit better lifestyle if they'd been rich."

"Sometimes havin' riches ain't the same thing as havin' *things*." His eyes met mine firmly as he said it.

I had to agree with that.

"But, gee, Keith, that was all so long ago," I said. "How could Rory Daniels still be this angry with Bud so many years later?"

He shrugged. "Can't say for sure." He began to wipe vigorously at the countertop. "Some things you get taught as a kid, they don't never go away."

I watched his rag rub the same spot repeatedly.

"My own pa grew up in Arkansas," he continued. "Hated Andrew Jackson worse than anything. Taught me to hate him too." He rubbed harder at the countertop.

"Now you *know* neither me or my pa was around in Jackson's time, but I still can't *stand* that man. Don't even want his name spoken."

I almost laughed but toned it down to a rueful grin. "Guess some things run pretty deep, huh."

He met my eyes firmly. "They do. Always remember that."

I paid my check and decided I'd drop in to see how Sophie was doing, one last time before heading back to the city.

Her car sat in front of the brick Victorian so I pulled in beside it. Sophie was on the porch, lifting the previous season's hanging flower baskets down from their hooks. She'd changed from her good jeans and shirt into a faded pair and a worn flannel shirt with the tails hanging free.

"Figured I'd better get these things cleared away. Can't decide whether I want to plant them again this summer or just toss them away." She set the two baskets down.

"I'm heading back now. Better see what else I can do for my client."

She nodded without comment.

"Sophie, could we talk for a minute?" I felt awkward standing down in the yard, while she watched me from the porch.

"Sure." She leaned a hip against the railing and crossed her arms over her chest.

I climbed the steps so I'd be at her level. "What's happened here?" I asked. "A couple of days ago you were open and friendly with me, now . . . something's different."

Her gaze dropped to the wooden porch, then slowly climbed from my shoes to my hair. Her mouth stayed pinched. "My Pop was not responsible for the people in this town losing their money."

My mouth opened.

"I know you been snooping around and digging at past history. I know there's a few, like that ass Rory Daniels, who want to believe it. But it ain't true. Pop didn't—" her face crumpled and she took a deep breath—"he *didn't* take their money."

She sniffed, a moist sounding deep one. "Don't you think I'd of known it? All these years, fightin' to make a few bucks off this ranch, worryin' about the price of beef, the weather, the bills." She paced the length of the porch twice. "If that old fart had a stash of money around some-wheres, I sure never saw it. Him and Willie going off all the time *prospecting*. Shit-fire! If he ever found anything, it wasn't much. And he sure didn't bring it home to help out around here.

"These last few years, with Pop gettin' too old to be much help at the ranch, that's when we really coulda used the money." She leaned against the railing with both hands, facing out into the dusty yard. "There wasn't any money, Charlie. Believe it."

"I do, Sophie," I said quietly. I patted her on the shoulder and walked down the steps to my car. She was still standing at the railing when I drove away.

ELEVEN

All the way home I thought about Sophie. The newspaper accounts hadn't said anything about Bud Tucker being accused of keeping any of the missing money. Everything I'd read seemed to clear the bank's directors and place the blame squarely on Phillip Stanton, the easterner who'd masterminded the whole development scheme. Sophie was such a young child at the time, odds were she didn't know first-hand what her father's role was. But from the rancor I'd just witnessed, she'd fallen heir to a lot of the town's bitterness. Couple that with constant financial worries and the fact that her father was aging—could she have decided he was better off dead?

Then there was Rory Daniels. He, too, was a young child when the whole scandal broke. But he'd watched both his parents die far too young and no doubt he'd had his own share of financial pressures over the years. His anger was still very near the surface. Could he have happened along while Bud and Willie were at the mines, lost his temper with Bud, and shot him? Maybe the two old men *had* found gold—that could be a motive for Rory. Willie might have gotten away and was now hiding, in fear for his life—or not. Maybe the search party would still find him. And if Willie was also dead, how did his truck get to Las Cruces and his bankcard get used as far away as Phoenix? Rory hadn't skipped out, but had he left for a while and come back? I'd have to ask a few more questions.

My head was spinning by the time I reached the outskirts of Albuquerque, but I had to admit the drive had gone quickly. I longed to go home and hug my dog, but the hospital was on the way and I should stop in and see Dorothy.

Her room was on the third floor at the end of a long hall that smelled of antiseptic and old food trays. I barged in without knocking and found Dorothy and her brother Felix in a tense-looking conversation. Felix started when he realized they had company. He touched Dorothy's arm and backed away from the bed.

Dorothy looked smaller and less intimidating with her leg elevated in a thick cast and a white square of gauze taped to her forehead. Her gray curls had been brushed down low in front to partially hide the bandage, but she'd lost a lot of her fearsomeness. Felix, on the other hand, was taller and more muscular than I'd remembered. Dressed in khaki slacks and a navy short-sleeved polo shirt, he was in remarkably good shape for a man in his sixties. His impossibly black hair and thin mustache didn't show a thread of gray against his tan face

"Hi, Dorothy, how are you doing?" I said, standing back from the bed.

"I'm sick of this place," she whined in her nasal tone. "The food is simply awful and I haven't had a decent night's sleep."

"Well, they're letting you out tomorrow," Felix told her, patting her arm gently.

"Can you take care of yourself at home?" I asked.

"I'll be going to Melanie and Bob's house. Probably have to stay there until I get this cast off. Can't see how I'd do much for myself on crutches. I just hope they have a decent mattress in their guestroom."

Lucky Melanie.

I filled them in briefly on the search and rescue operation to find Willie, although there really wasn't much to report.

"Sorry to hear that Bud Tucker got killed," Felix offered. "Dad was sure fond of him."

"Melanie said you were trying to pull over to pick up someone who looked like your father," I said to Dorothy. "Did you have any reason to believe he was back in Albuquerque?"

"Well, I . . ." She fumbled for a reasonable explanation.

"I mean, had he contacted you? I need to know if any family members hear from him," I said.

"No, he hadn't contacted me. I just . . . well . . . I guess I just hoped." She dabbed at one eye with the corner of her sheet, although I didn't see any moisture there.

"Melanie said the rest of the family were going home today," I said.

"The younger ones have already left," Felix said. "Of course, I just live in Socorro, so that's an easy drive. I'll stay on while Dorothy needs me."

"Felix is a professor at the college."

"Geology 101," he added with a chuckle.

"Bea's children all left earlier today," Dorothy said. "I

think she was going to stay over one more night at my house and get a flight out tomorrow afternoon."

"Well, I'm sorry the reunion didn't quite end up as planned," I said. "At least everyone got to see each other for awhile."

"Everyone except Dad," Dorothy added bitterly.

"Well, I just wanted to see how you were doing," I said, shifting from one foot to the other. "And to be sure you still want me on the case to locate your father."

Felix shot a glance over to Dorothy but she didn't catch it.

"Certainly. Now, more than ever, we need to know what's happened to him," Dorothy said. "I'm sure if he's up there by those mines, that sheriff will let us know what they find."

"I'll be in touch with the sheriff too," I assured her.

Felix gave me a tight grin.

Out in the hall, I paused outside Dorothy's door, pretending to fumble in my purse for my keys.

"I told you to be patient!" Felix's voice sounded like sandpaper.

"I just—" she hissed.

"Shh!"

The squeak of his shoes told me he was crossing the room. I did a couple of giant steps before slowing to a leisurely saunter toward the elevators. I could swear I felt his eyes boring into my back. What were those two up to?

Thirty minutes later, across town, I'd dropped my duffle inside my front door and was walking through the break in the hedge between my house and my neighbor's, Elsa Higgins. Rusty bounded out to greet me the second she opened her back door.

"Hi, Gram, how did he do?" I asked.

My eighty-seven year old surrogate grandmother beamed. "Good as gold," she said. "You know, it's a nice feeling of security to have a big dog like him around."

Rusty leaned against my legs, pushing hard, while I scratched his ears and roughed up his fur.

"Want to stay for dinner?" Elsa asked. "I made stew."

"Sure. Let me go check my messages and throw a few dirty clothes in the washer."

"I'll bake up some cornbread and have it all ready about six," she said.

I trudged back through the hedge with the dog at my heels. The answering machine had only one message, from Melanie. Just a quick "call me" with no further explanation. I dialed her number and got her machine, so I told her to try me again after eight o'clock.

Rusty watched avidly as I unpacked my duffle bag. He sniffed each item I pulled out, waiting in anticipation for some stray dog biscuit to slip out. When none came, he led me back to the kitchen.

"Been a little spoiled, have you?" I teased. No doubt Elsa had given him treats every time he begged.

I started a load of laundry and checked my e-mail—all junk—then left a message for Drake that I'd made it home okay and would be in later. Called the office, where the only news was that Ron's fishing trip was going great and he'd decided to stay two more days.

Although I knew Elsa would welcome me anytime before six, the past few days were beginning to catch up with me and I felt the need to unwind. I stretched out on the living room sofa and forced my mind to go blank. I awoke an hour later to insistent knocking on my back door.

"Everything okay?" Elsa asked. She held her light jacket together in front against the evening chill. "It's six-thirty and I thought you might have run into trouble."

"Oh, god, I'm sorry," I said. "I really meant to only close my eyes for five minutes."

"You work too hard. Well, everything's ready so just come on over any time."

I switched on a couple of lamps and checked to be sure the front door was locked before grabbing a denim jacket and heading out the back door.

Elsa's kitchen smelled wonderful and I was glad I'd agreed to come. She ladled out bowls of hearty beef stew and I ran a knife through the pan of cornbread, making neat squares of it. We ate in silence for a few minutes.

"How is your case going?" she asked, wiping crumbs off her mouth with a napkin.

"I don't know," I moaned. "I feel stuck. There's a contingent of search and rescue people out there now, combing the hills for Willie's body, thinking that whoever killed his friend might have also killed him.

"For some reason, I think there's more to it than a simple robbery gone wrong. But I've discovered that people in White Oaks have old grudges against Bud Tucker, so he may have been the real victim. His own daughter is very protective of him. Then there's Willie's family—what a bunch! Dorothy's sister, Bea, told me that Dorothy got her father to change the beneficiary on his insurance policy so Dorothy is the only inheritor. But I overhead Dorothy and Felix, their brother, whispering about something that made them both pretty tense."

I drained my glass of iced tea. "I just don't know. The whole thing is getting more complicated by the day."

Elsa carried our bowls to the sink. "Well, I have to say—from more than a few years' experience—that families and the way they treat each other can get pretty mind-boggling."

"No kidding," I laughed. "And this group just got together for a reunion. I can't imagine why they'd want to. None of them seem to like each other."

I glanced at the wall clock above the stove. Eight-fifteen. "I better get going soon," I said. I'm expecting some calls. I squirted dish liquid into the sink and aimed the hot water to form a puff of suds.

"I can do those later," she protested.

"I know, but I don't mind helping. These few things won't take long." I dunked the two bowls, two plates, and few pieces of silver into the hot water.

"Guess one of your calls will be from Drake." Her eyes crinkled at the corners. Ever since Elsa had met Drake, she'd been infatuated. If she'd been forty years younger I think I'd have had a serious rival.

"Yeah, he said they've almost got the fire under control. They'll probably release him to come back home after that. If something else around the state doesn't start burning, I may actually get some time with him."

With dishes stacked in the drainer and hands dried on a nearby towel, I asked Elsa if there was anything she needed before I headed home. A couple of minutes later Rusty and I started back to our place. The phone was ringing when I walked in.

"Did I catch you at a bad time?" Melanie asked.

"No, this is fine," I assured her. "What's up?"

"Just thought I'd check to see how things are going. I talked to Mother awhile ago and she said you'd stopped in at the hospital."

I told her I had, leaving out the part about Felix and Dorothy's strange whisperings. I filled her in on the little bit of White Oaks news that pertained to Willie. Figured Bud Tucker's problems with the townsfolk were not part of the McBride family's business.

"Your mother told me she's coming to stay at your house after she's released?"

"Oh, yeah." Her voice sounded weary already. "Bob isn't exactly thrilled, but I don't see much other choice. There isn't money to cover home care for her at her house, so I guess this is it. We'll see how long it takes for me to start pulling my hair out."

I could certainly sympathize, but didn't say so. First thing that'll pull bickering families together is for an outsider to butt in.

"So, what's next?" she asked.

"Your mother said your aunt Beatrice wasn't leaving until tomorrow afternoon. I'd like to touch base with her one more time if I could."

"Sure, I don't see why not. She's staying at Mother's. You could call first, just to be sure she'll be there."

I wasn't sure what information I'd get from Bea, I thought as I hung up the phone, but it was worth a try. I was short on viable evidence and I figured just about any of the players might be able to throw a crumb my way.

When I called Bea to suggest a meeting, I found her positively excited.

"I was hoping I'd get a chance to talk to you," she said. "Just wasn't sure how to find you. Anyway, I've got something exciting to share." We decided to meet for breakfast.

Drake called while I was transferring the clean laundry into the dryer. We didn't talk long. He said the fire was contained and he'd call and let me know as soon as he was released. I was in bed by nine, ready to wilt after the long day.

I spent a restless night, despite the fact that I'd felt bone tired when I first hit the bed. Apparently I'd gotten my deep sleep during the hour-long nap before dinner. Wakefulness stirred me several times during the night and I finally gave up at six o'clock, opting to get up and start the day early rather than toss around uselessly. I let Rusty out, and took a quick, hot shower to rinse the cobwebs from my brain.

Beatrice and I had agreed to meet for breakfast at a Denny's at nine o'clock. I was a few minutes early so I ordered coffee and started to browse the novel-length menu.

I spotted Bea standing near the entrance scanning the room, so I waved her over. More than before, I noticed how opposite she was from her sister. Slightly over five feet, looking slim in jeans and a cotton sweater, she lacked both Dorothy's imposing size and pushy manner.

"Hi, Charlie," she greeted. "I'm so glad you caught me before we had to leave."

We browsed the menu and placed our orders.

"Well, I've certainly found some interesting evidence since we talked the last time," she said, reaching into her oversized purse and pulling out a sheaf of papers.

"Remember, I told you I thought Dorothy'd gotten Dad to change his will? Ralph shushed me, but I knew I was right."

She pushed a document across the table at me.

"This is a copy," she said. "You'll notice it isn't signed yet. And this—" she produced a similar sheaf, "—is the old one."

The waitress brought our food and I held the papers out of her way.

I scanned the pages quickly. "Wills? Two of them?"

"Exactly. The old one was drawn up years ago. Dad left equal shares of his property to each of us children. Now the new one—" She fluttered her hand toward the papers in my right hand. "—that was drawn up in January. By Dorothy's lawyer, not the one Dad always used. The wording is tricky, but basically it gives her the right to handle his estate, deducting any fees she may reasonably incur—" She paused for emphasis. "Meaning that, as I see it, she could completely drain the estate before any of the rest of us see a dime."

"Will it be a large estate?" I asked, picturing Willie's ramshackle house in the valley. "I mean, is it really worth her time to go to all this trouble?"

"On the face of it, probably not," she admitted. "But looks may be deceptive. I understand that the part of town where he lives is becoming pretty hot property. His house may not be much, but the land is surely worth something."

She was right about that. Many of Albuquerque's newly successful business people were opting for the semi-rural atmosphere of the north valley and had driven land values sky high. A thought struck me.

"Could Felix somehow be involved in this?" I asked, holding up the papers.

Her brows pulled together as she cut a wedge from her omelet and chewed on it. "I don't know. He and Dorothy are cut from the same greedy cloth, I can tell you that."

I spread strawberry jam on a toast triangle while she pondered the question further.

"You know, as kids it was always Dorothy and Felix bossing Ella and me around. We just kind of took it, I guess. Now, Dorothy's kids didn't turn out that way. Melanie and Roger are both good kids who've gotten on with their own lives since they got out from under her thumb. Makes Dorothy mad, I'll tell you, not to run those kids' lives anymore."

"But Felix's name isn't on the new will? More than yours, for instance?"

"Not really. But maybe I should reread it to be sure. It would be just like him to wiggle his way in there somehow."

"Or like Dorothy to try to cut him out?" I thought of the tension in the room at the hospital.

"That too," she agreed. "Anyway, I've made copies of both wills. I'm going to stop at the bank and sign a notarized statement that the new one was unsigned as of this date. That way, whatever happens, if Dad turns up, uh, well, not alive, at least she can't try to push this thing through as the valid will."

"Good idea," I agreed. "You know, this might be another reason Willie decided to disappear when he did. Maybe she was pressuring him to sign and he didn't want to." I didn't dwell on the fact that Willie might not be missing of his own accord. At least it seemed to take away any motive Dorothy or Felix might have had for wanting him dead yet. They needed that signature first. And it certainly provided a better explanation for Dorothy's pushiness about finding her father quickly. I'd never fully bought the family reunion story.

I wrote down Bea's home address and phone number before we parted, promising to keep her up to date on my progress, even though Dorothy was technically the client.

There didn't seem to be much I could do on the case at the moment. I placed a call to Randy Buckman but he wasn't in, so I left a message. The day had turned beautiful, the sun bright and warm, and the wind silent at last. I spent the rest of the morning puttering in the yard, trimming the shrubs and setting out a few bedding plants I'd bought more than a week ago. I realized I'd forgotten to carry the portable phone outside with me when I went back inside and found the answering machine blinking.

"Charlie, Randy Buckman here," it began. "Just to give you an update, we've decided to terminate the search for Mr. McBride. There's been no trace at all and the odds are his body is somewhere between here and Las Cruces, out in the desert. At this time, my department doesn't have reason to believe he's in our jurisdiction. We'll be pursuing the murderer of Bud Tucker but, frankly, I think he's long gone."

He didn't suggest that I call him back but I did anyway, after scrubbing the garden soil from under my fingernails. I caught him on his way out the door, according to the dispatcher.

"Just wanted to let you know that McBride's family still wants me to try to locate him," I told Randy after our initial hellos. "Can we still share information on this?"

"Depends," he said. "You know there are certain things I can't divulge."

"But you think someone killed Tucker on the spot, abducted Willie and his pickup truck, killed Willie along the road somewhere, and abandoned the truck in Las Cruces."

"That's about it."

"When you processed the truck, did you find prints? Or blood?"

"Lots of prints, several sets. We're getting Bernalillo County to take some sample prints from McBride's house so we can eliminate those. We've run everything through the national system and haven't come up with any known felons. Doesn't mean much, though. Killer could be somebody small-time or it could have been a crime of passion, somebody who shot Tucker without thinking, then had to get out of there quick. McBride and his truck might have just been handy. No blood on the truck, but that might not mean much either."

I told him I'd let him know of anything I learned about his case, reasoning that Dorothy and Felix's possible shenanigans with Willie's will didn't seem to have much bearing on Bud Tucker's death. And I still wasn't convinced that Bud's death and Willie's disappearance were connected. It seemed to me that Bud had one set of enemies and Willie another.

A few minutes later under a steamy hot shower I had a brainstorm. There's something about the lulling effects of hot water pounding the body that stimulates a person to think. Mulling over the few clues I had so far in the case, I knew what I had to do. But first I wanted to check out one of Beatrice's assertions.

I toweled off and slipped into a pair of clean jeans and white T-shirt. Planting one hip on our new king-size bed, I pulled the phone book from the nightstand drawer and looked up the number of a real estate agent friend. I fluffed my wet hair while the phone rang.

"Shirley Mason." The officious sounding voice didn't jibe with the petite blond I knew, who was likely sitting in her home office right now wearing shorts and a halter top.

"Don't you just love a friend who only calls a couple of times a year, and then just when she wants a favor?" I joked.

"Charlie?"

"The same. How are you?"

"Thriving. Hey, I heard you got married! Wow, what a change for you." Her bubbly voice always cheered me up, reminding me that I really should be a better friend and call more often.

"I hate to admit this, but once again I'm calling for a favor. I'll buy you a lunch for this one though," I promised.

"Hey, it doesn't matter. What's up? Another big case?"

"I don't know how big. But here's the question. I'm curious about the value of a certain piece of property in the north valley."

"Do we have a listing on it?"

"No, it's not for sale. A client may soon inherit this place and is wondering what it's worth." The story wasn't too far off the mark.

"Give me some details," she prompted.

I gave her the address and a brief but accurate description of the house. "I would imagine that the land is worth more than the structure," I added.

"The land, or the mineral rights," she said.

"Mineral rights?"

"Probably nothing, but we did have a property in that area that brought a hefty price a year or so ago because of something to do with the minerals."

Shirley went on with a few more gossipy personal tidbits, we set a lunch date for the following week, and I thanked her for the information.

Interesting, I thought, hanging up the phone. Who would have thought about mineral rights on a piece of city property? Who would have known to ask? Someone with some inside knowledge about exploration.

Someone like a geology professor at a university.

TWELVE

This was beginning to make more sense than ever. Felix, with his knowledge of geology and access to inside scuttlebutt at the university, would know of any new finds well before it became common knowledge. He could have easily pushed Dorothy to get Willie to change the will, then planned to get rid of the old man before anyone else could figure out what they were up to. But if another property owner had already sold for a whopping big price, the news would soon get around. They had to act quickly.

So, had Felix jumped the gun, getting rid of Willie before the new will was actually signed? Such a screwup would definitely explain why Felix and Dorothy were having words at the hospital. Maybe Felix wanted Dorothy to forge a signature on the will. He knew Willie would never turn up again and he wanted the paperwork to all be in order. Dorothy didn't know Willie wasn't alive—if her story was true about swerving across the traffic because she thought she saw him—and she'd rather have his actual signature to assure there wouldn't be a legal battle later. Plus, there was the fact that she'd hired me to look for him. She wouldn't have wanted anyone poking around if she knew he was dead. Unless . . . I was simply being used to add legitimacy to their story.

I sat on the edge of bed, staring at a space somewhere in the middle of the room. Just what was going on here? The endless possibilities were making my head hurt.

The phone rang, startling me out of my endless-loop reverie.

"Hi, hon, it's me." Drake's voice came through louder than usual, with the sound of turbine engine whine in the background.

"Hi, sweetheart, where are you?"

"On my way home. They just released me from the job and I'm spooling her up now. There's still daylight to make it back. Couldn't wait one more day to be home with you again. My ETA is about five o'clock. Want to meet for dinner about six?"

"Pedro's?"

"Sure. I'll call you when I land." His cell phone clicked off with a chirp.

With something better to do now than mull endlessly over the McBride family problems, I stepped back into the master bath to finish drying my hair. As promised, Drake called at five to close his flight plan and again forty-five minutes later to let me know he was on the way to Pedro's.

Our favorite eatery is a tiny place near Old Town, run by a cute Mexican couple who have always treated me like one of their kids. Pedro and Concha, the proverbial Jack Sprat and his wife, make the best chicken enchiladas and margaritas anywhere (sorry, Keith). Rusty and I arrived a few minutes before Drake, and we took our customary table in the corner. Pedro held up one finger and raised his shoulders in question.

"No, two," I said, shaking my head. "Drake will be here in a minute."

By the time my honey had walked through the door Pedro was setting the perfectly blended drinks on our table.

"Umm, missed you," Drake said, giving me a long kiss.

"I just stayed with you night before last," I teased.

"Yeah, but I was too tired to do much about it." Something told me that would change tonight.

"I just had a thought," I told him, taking a tortilla chip and dunking it deep into the salsa bowl.

He gave me a look that said, "Uh-oh."

"Okay, it is for the case I'm working on, but we could mix business and pleasure. I need to go to Arizona." While drying my hair this afternoon I'd decided that, twisted complications aside, my job was still to locate Willie McBride. And his ATM card had last been used in the Phoenix area.

"We could visit Paul and his family," I continued. "And, if there's time, we could even buzz up to Flagstaff to see your mother."

"I can't commit to that much time away," he protested. "Not during the fire season."

He had a point. But I had a point too, and I didn't want this to become the source of our first big argument.

"Okay, what about this? We take the helicopter and you forward calls from your business line to your cell phone. If you get a call, you're off the hook for any more family visits. You can just leave from there for the job. I'll get back home however I can."

The corner of his mouth scrunched up skeptically. "Let me think about it."

Our enchiladas arrived just then, giving us a break from the conversation.

"I suppose we could rent a car once we get there," Drake said, wiping the last of the sauce from his mouth.

"Sure. And Rusty can go with us so there's no particular time-frame for getting home."

He pulled his cell phone out and called the mechanic at the airport. They went back and forth about an upcoming three hundred hour inspection and Drake seemed satisfied when he hung up.

"Day after tomorrow," he announced. "Chuck says they'll need two days to complete the inspection, then we're good to go."

I held my breath over the next two days, waiting for the inevitable call to come that would drag him away from our plan, but by Saturday the coast was still clear. We packed two light bags and all the gear Drake would need if another fire call came in. He suggested I do the piloting to help build my hours, so at seven A.M. we took our seats, Rusty in back, Drake riding along as passenger, and me in the right seat. I'd done my preflight and cleared our departure to the west. After we'd cleared the Albuquerque International Airport's airspace, we'd swing south-south-west. I was still getting used to the aircraft's Global Positioning System and Drake had coached me through its programming so our course would take us directly into the Mesa Airport. I'd told him I really didn't feel ready to deal with the air traffic at Sky Harbor, Phoenix's massive international airport. Besides, Mesa was closer to our destination anyway.

Luckily, the beautiful spring weather held and I was

able to maintain a track about two thousand feet above ground level without hitting any noticeable drafts. Little more than two hours later we were seeing the metro area on the horizon and I followed my GPS heading straight toward Mesa. The tower cleared me for landing among a group of general aviation craft and I set the JetRanger down gently.

"Great job," Drake grinned. "You'll be ready to take over some of my flights soon."

"That was a piece of cake. No way am I ready for any fires or rescues."

I noticed that he didn't argue with me.

Rusty was eager to get all four feet on the ground again. I unbuckled my harness and went around to his door. Clipping a leash on his collar I headed him toward a dirt patch near one of the hangars that served as the doggie facilities. He took his time, sniffing every strange scent he could find. By the time we returned to the aircraft Drake had our personal things unloaded and was locking his fire gear into the rear cargo compartment.

"I brought along another portable GPS," he told me. "Just in case we get out hiking around. It's in your bag."

"Good idea." We headed for the car rental desk, where I'd reserved a mid-size that turned out to be generic silver in color.

Thirty minutes later we were cruising the streets of Mesa with Drake at the wheel and me acting as navigator, map on my lap, trying to remember the turns to Paul's house. My middle brother and I weren't as close as Ron and I, and I'd only been to his house two other times. The city had changed dramatically in the five years Paul and

Lorraine had lived here; none of the landmarks looked familiar at all to me and I was relying heavily on the map.

"Did you plan for us to stay at their house?" Drake asked.

"Oh, I don't think so. The last time I remember, it was total chaos. They don't have much space and those two kids of theirs would drive me nuts after a day or so." I remembered the last time they'd dropped in on a moment's notice to spend a few days with me. "No, I think I'll get a lot more investigating done if we stay in a motel. I'm thinking something down near Highway 60 will be convenient for us.

"We'll just drop by now and invite them to lunch or dinner. Spend enough time to be sociable."

The house looked virtually the same as the last time I'd seen it, right down to the bicycles lying on the front lawn, except last time they'd been bright plastic Big Wheels. Getting no response to several pushes at the doorbell, I scribbled a note telling them we were in town and would like to take the family to dinner. Knowing my brother, the offer of a free dinner would certainly bring them out. I wrote that we'd call them once we settled into our motel.

"Okay, let's find a room," I said, rejoining Drake in the car.

We located a place on Power Road that accepted dogs as guests and had inexpensive phone rates. I dug around in my purse while Drake brought our bags inside. Rocky Rhodes, the man I'd seen interviewed on *Unsolved Mysteries* was listed in the directory and answered on the second ring. I gave the condensed explanation of who I was and asked whether we might meet with him.

"Sure, sure, come on out," he agreed. He gave directions to his place in Apache Junction, just east of us.

"Ready to learn something about the Lost Dutchman Mine?" I asked Drake after hanging up.

"Whatever milady wishes," he said gallantly. I can never tell when he's making fun of me and when he truly wants to be included in my sometimes-outlandish plans.

Rhodes lived in a walled community of doublewide trailers, one that nearly matched at least a dozen other such neighborhoods near his. He responded to my tap almost immediately. I introduced Drake and myself.

"You don't want to leave your dog out there in the car, you can bring him inside," he said, noticing Rusty's head jutting out one of the fully open windows. "He won't hurt nothin' in here."

Drake released the prisoner and whistled for the dog to join us. He spent the first five minutes sniffing all corners of the living room, then settled beside me at the edge of an orange and brown plaid sofa.

"I think I mentioned that I'd seen your interview on television," I began.

"Yep. Course that was a few years ago," Rhodes answered. "Guess I look a little older now."

He did, but not by much. He'd done away with the beard. I'd guessed him to be in his seventies by his white hair and liver-spotted hands, but his posture was still erect and he moved with the agility of a man accustomed to regular outdoor activity.

"I'm afraid I didn't explain my own mission very well," I told him. "I've been hired by an Albuquerque family to locate an eighty-four year old man whose habit is to go off prospecting by himself."

"And you're here because of the Lost Dutchman. 'Cause it's the prize of all prizes, the thing any decent prospector would go after."

"Well, something like that," I laughed. "Mr. McBride had frequently mentioned it to his family."

"McBride? Willie McBride?"

"You know him?" Surely it couldn't be this easy.

"Well, sure I do. Known him many years."

"Have you seen him recently?"

"Well, gosh, let me think." He rubbed his grizzled chin with the knobby fingers of one hand. "Guess he was by here a year or so ago."

"Not more recently than that?" Drake piped in.

"Well . . . I'm thinkin'. I'd say it's been a year or so, but then my memory's not what it used to be. Hold on. I got a book I can check." He rose a little stiffly from his orange recliner and crossed to a desk on the far side of the room.

I watched him pull a cloth-covered diary from a drawer. He paged through it slowly while I fidgeted in my seat. If we were really this close, I wanted answers now.

"Yep, see here. June, it was. Last June. Guess that's a little less than a year. I wrote that he stopped by the house here, wanted to go up into the Superstitions." He rubbed a hand through his hair.

"Now, June woulda been way too hot to going out roaming those hills. I remember telling him that. It gets a hundred-fifteen out there, easy, in the summer. Told him he oughta wait till it cooled off."

"So, maybe he did come back later," I suggested.

"Well, let's see." Again, slow paging through the diary. "I'm skippin' the hot months now," he said. "Going right to October, November . . . Hmm, looks like I wrote about him again in the early part of December. Guess he was here then too. Funny, it seems longer than that."

He continued to page through the book.

"Nothing as recent as this year, February or later?" I asked. "That's when his family lost track of him, February."

He flipped forward another chunk of pages, then slowed to a page at a time. "Nope," he said finally. "Don't see anything else about Willie."

And I'd thought we were getting so close. Another thought came to me. I pulled the topo map and Willie's little sketch from my purse.

"Did Willie ever talk about his own mine?" I asked. "Something he had his own claim on, here in the Superstitions?"

Rhodes looked steadily at me. "Maybe."

I held out the hand-sketched map Keith Randel had given me. He gave it one quick glance.

"Where'd you get this?" he demanded.

"Is it Willie's mine?" I countered, pulling my hand back so he couldn't snatch the small piece of paper.

"Where'd you get it?"

"Let's just say, a mutual friend. Willie left it with him and told him this is where he'd be."

"That sounds about right," he conceded. "Musta been somebody he really trusted. He took me up there once but never would give me anything in writing. I kept telling him he better register the claim. He said he did, but I wasn't ever sure about that. Willie was the kind who wanted the riches but didn't want to handle any paperwork."

"So the mine really does exist," I said.

"Oh, yes. Like I say, he took me there once, showed me that little map once, too. Guess that's why it startled me that you had it. I know Willie drew it."

"If he wanted to hide out, do you think that's where he'd go?"

"Makes sense to me—*if* he could get up there. It's pretty rugged. We didn't have an easy time of it fifteen years ago, when we was both a bit younger. Last time I saw Willie he was slowin' down. Don't know as he could make that hike anymore.

"You ever been up in the Superstitions?" he asked, giving me a sharp look. "No? Well, that land is rough. And that map—here, let me show you somethin'."

I held out the map again. He pointed a gnarled finger, tracing a dotted line Willie had drawn.

"This here's Willie's trail. Now, it ain't any real trail, mind you. Best as I remember you gotta aim yourself from one landmark to the next. Like this—this'd be a giant saguaro. This here—this'd be a rock cairn. Stuff like that. Follow 'em into the hills till you hit a pretty deep wash. That's the wiggly line he's got here. 'Long the side of that wash is where the mine entrance is. Now don't expect to just see it—it's gonna be hidden real good. But if Willie did make it up there, you oughta see signs of him, footprints and all. Willie's a decent prospector but he ain't no Indian. Ain't worth shit at hidin' his own tracks."

"Mr. Rhodes, you've really been a big help," I told him as we stood to leave. "Would you let me know if you hear anything from Willie? Here's my card. His family is really worried."

"Family, huh. Would that be that daughter in Albuquerque, what's her name?"

"Dorothy?"

"Yeah, that's the one. Don't know as Willie would really want to be found by that one."

He caught my expression.

"You're not too surprised, either, are you? I never met her myself, but Willie tells me she's tryin' to start running his life, bossing him around. He didn't want no part of it. I don't know as I oughta turn him over to her."

"Look, I know exactly what you mean about Dorothy—the pushy part, I mean. She hired me to locate him for a family reunion. The reunion is over now, but there are still family members who are worried about him. His granddaughter, Melanie, for one." I rolled up the two maps. "I may not be able to convince him to go back, and I certainly can't *make* him see Dorothy. But I'd like to be able to assure the family that he's alive and well. Think you could help me with that?"

He scuffed a weathered boot against the carpet. "Long as you don't make him go back. I'll let you know if I hear from him."

Drake, Rusty and I headed back to the car. "I notice you didn't exactly promise not to take Willie back to Albuquerque."

"But I did say I wouldn't turn him over to Dorothy. I know that's probably some kind of a breach, since she's paying me, but I can't be party to the dirty tricks she's playing with his will. On the other hand," I said as we pulled out onto the street, "Willie is still wanted for questioning by the sheriff in White Oaks. I can't exactly ignore that."

We returned to our motel and stretched out for a short rest. When I dialed Paul's number again he was home so we made plans to meet for dinner at seven.

The restaurant was one of those 'family dining' places where kids eat free. Paul would have probably chosen something more upscale, since it was our treat, but the kids insisted and I'd learned long ago that Paul's kids usually got their way.

We met them out front and I registered quick impressions of the group I hadn't seen in almost a year. The two kids had each added an inch or two of growth, Lorraine had added another ten pounds to her post-childbirth middle, and Paul had added a few gray hairs.

I introduced Drake all around—Paul's family hadn't made it to our quick wedding in October. Lorraine lowered her eyes coquettishly and eight-year-old Annie latched onto his hand, developing an instant crush. Paul gave Drake a smile that didn't quite extend to his eyes, and it struck me that he was jealous. Paul's desk job high in the Bank of America building didn't hold much glamour compared to Drake's days at the controls of his helicopter. Drake immediately put him at ease, though, with a compliment on the beefy new SUV Paul drove. My brother launched into the story of the great deal he'd gotten on it.

Inside, we settled around a large table and browsed the menu. We were just receiving our salads when Drake's cell phone rang.

"Uh-oh, this can't be good," he said, pulling it off his belt. "Drake Langston."

I shushed Paul's two kids when it became apparent that neither of their parents would do it.

"Yes, Mike," Drake continued, "how are you? Yes, I'm available. Uh-huh. Okay, let me get some details." He pulled a small notepad from his shirt pocket and began writing rapidly.

So much for our having a few days off together, I thought. Okay, to be fair, I was the one who talked him into coming along on my job rather than taking some pure vacation time. I stabbed a chunk of lettuce and swirled it in honey-mustard dressing.

"Sorry," Drake apologized to the group. "I don't like to take calls at the table."

"Another job?" I asked.

"A fire near Heber. At least that's in Arizona, not too far away." He clipped the phone back to his belt and stuffed the notes into his pocket. "Got to head down there first thing in the morning."

Both kids perked up at the mention of fire, something I might have worried about if they'd been mine, so Drake entertained everyone with a few stories of forest fires he'd worked. By nine o'clock we'd returned to our hotel where we snuggled together tightly, knowing we were facing a lot more nights apart now.

THIRTEEN

I blew Drake a kiss in the gray early morning light as the JetRanger lifted off from its spot on the tarmac at the Mesa airport. The little details were now mine to deal with, getting Rusty and myself back to Albuquerque, turning in the rented car, handling Drake's business in his absence. But what I really wanted to do was to follow my leads on Willie McBride.

Drake had issued all kinds of cautions to me about not heading off alone into the mountains, about heat stroke, snakebites, and cactus. Knowing he couldn't actually forbid me to go, he'd just tried his best to make it sound too nasty to deal with. I knew immediately that I'd go anyway.

Rusty trotted along beside me and I opened the back door of the rented sedan for him.

"Okay, kid. What's next?" I pulled my maps of the Superstitions from under the seat. Drake was right in everything he'd said—it wouldn't do to get myself lost out there unprepared. I drove back to the hotel to work out my strategy.

I'd brought a small backpack from home, thinking it was just the right size for a picnic lunch for three. Now it would serve as a day trip kit for two. Into it went the maps, a compass, flashlight, sunscreen, snakebite kit (yes, we did own one), lip balm, three Power Bars, a large plastic zipper bag of dog food, and two bottles of water. On top of it all, I added the portable GPS, which Drake had forgotten to take with him. I hoped he wouldn't need it on his job, but I needed it for mine. From my purse I took some money and my cell phone, and added my driver's license, just in case someone had to identify me later.

I dressed in cotton slacks and shirt and tied a light jacket around my waist. Another canteen of water would go over my shoulder. I made sure Rusty drank all the water he wanted in the room before we headed out to the car. On the way out we would stop somewhere and stoke up on a high protein breakfast.

All this preparation might make an observer think I'm a real outdoors person but let me assure you that isn't the case. Although I was pretty rough and tumble as a kid, my adult life experience as an accountant hasn't exactly required it and, in general, I'd rather visit the dentist than the sun, the bugs, and the snakes. It's only a result of my marriage to Mr. Preparedness that I've learned that it pays to face the great outdoors in a ready state.

The sun was still fairly low in the east, the air temperature a pleasant seventy-something, when we parked the car at the trailhead. Rusty bounded from the car, excited to be doing something he considered fun for a change. I looped the canteen over my shoulder and took the maps, compass, and GPS from the backpack before slipping my arms through the straps. I booted up the GPS and waited until it fixed on our position. I programmed our current spot as a waypoint, then clipped the instrument to my waistband. Now, in theory, no matter where I might end up on the face of the earth, I could find my way back to this car. That is, if the batteries held out.

The trail was wide and smooth and Rusty roamed ahead, exploring rabbit smells, veering back to check on my progress from time to time. According to the scale on the map it looked like I'd go about a mile on marked trail before reaching the point where I'd need to start following Willie's sketch. The morning air smelled of sage and something very herbal. I took deep breaths of it, taking the time to notice a couple of landmarks once I was out of sight of the car.

Weaver's Needle rose in the distance ahead of me, a craggy upward-jutting rock that must have acted as a beacon for explorers of the area from the earliest times. On either side of us, canyon walls rose gradually, the hillsides dotted with cactus, from the fluffy-looking chainfruit cholla to majestic saguaros with their arms reaching toward the sky. Soon, the trail began a steady climb, narrowing at a series of switchbacks. My legs were speaking to me about the unaccustomed stretching. Rusty began to stick a bit closer.

I stopped at a small rise and consulted the map again. The marker I was looking for on Willie's map consisted of a dead saguaro skeleton with five rocks at its base. I scanned ahead but didn't see it. I drank some water from the canteen and offered Rusty some in a plastic cup. He took a couple of deep slurps and turned away.

"Hey, can't waste water out here," I scolded. "Finish this."

He looked at the cup again but clearly wasn't interested.

"Okay, but I'm only carrying this for you a little way." He kept trotting up the trail. "Hey, I'm not your slave, you know." My shout didn't carry much weight with him. I glanced again at the water in the cup, then tossed it with a splash on the ground. So there.

I stashed the cup in my pack and hiked on, hoping I'd see the marker before I went too far out of my way. Three sharp turns and another hundred feet in elevation and I found it. There on my right stood what appeared to be half a saguaro cactus. The top had fallen completely away and the base was pretty rotten. The once-majestic arms were now reedy-looking appendages, some pointing skyward, others fallen at haphazard angles. Sure enough, at the base were five reddish rocks, close enough in color and size, and placed at even intervals around the large cactus, that they couldn't have just been there by chance.

"Okay!" I shouted to Rusty. He stopped at his spot higher up the trail and turned to me. I nodded toward the turnoff and he bounded back.

A barely-visible track traced its way through the desert terrain. I checked my map to see what kind of marker we would be looking for next. It looked like it would be a wooden sign, something probably "borrowed" from a Forest Service trail, battered and lying on the ground. Unfortunately, Willie's map scale wasn't nearly as precise as that on the topo map so I'd need to keep my eyes peeled and do a lot of guesswork.

I pulled out the compass and checked my heading. If Willie's perspective was right I'd need to go due east for at least a half-mile then make a turn to the north. I glanced again at the pitiful track before me. There was nothing so defined as a path, not a footprint in sight. It was more like a wide space between plants. With eyes on the ground I started to follow it, thankful that I'd worn slacks instead of shorts as the woody branches of sage scraped against my legs.

About two hundred yards off the main trail I thought

I'd lost it. A rock outcropping crossed my path and I couldn't see whether I was supposed to go around it or over the rocks. I decided to climb up and see if I could pick up the trail by seeing it from above. Rusty looked at me curiously as I began the climb, being careful not to reach over any ledge without checking it visually first. Rattlesnakes aren't normally aggressive but a person can certainly startle them out of a nice sunny nap and get a fatal bite in return. My feet fumbled a couple of times on the round rocks but soon I had a vantage point twenty or thirty feet higher than the path I'd been on. I scanned the surrounding area and spotted the trail easily, winding through the desert beyond the outcropping.

Rather than attempt to descend over the round boulders below me I backtracked to the path and rounded the outcropping, catching Willie's path again on the east side. The sun was now directly overhead and I stopped to smooth sunscreen on my face and bare arms. Rusty trotted along as we headed east once more.

I nearly missed the downed-sign marker. Expecting it to be right along the path, I only caught it because of a fleck of white paint that still clung to it. It caught the sun at just the right angle to flash like a tiny mirror at me. The sign lay ten or twelve feet away from the path, on my right. I needed to turn left to the north. I paused to double check the map. It was drawn the opposite way and would have been an easy assumption to make a wrong turn. But my destination was clearly shown to the north.

An airplane droned overhead, a single engine thing that sounded like a bumblebee on steroids. I watched it head toward the city, disappearing behind the hills in just a few minutes. The silence that followed reminded me just how alone I was out here. Other than Rusty and a few jackrabbits, I hadn't seen another living creature all morning. It warned me that, although I felt confident that I could find my way back, no one else knew where I was. A tiny breeze raised goosebumps on my arms and I rubbed to make them go away.

"Okay," I said to Rusty, mainly to hear the sound of a human voice. "Let's get going."

He chuffed in agreement and followed my lead. Heading north again, I realized that the sun was now well past center. A glance at my watch told me it was already two o'clock. We obviously weren't going to make it to the mine and back in one day, as I'd hoped. And getting back to the car was something I didn't relish attempting in the dark.

Desert temperatures drop dramatically after sunset. It isn't at all uncommon to lose thirty degrees or more overnight, and I didn't think my light cotton clothing was going to work if it hit forty. I stopped and looked again at the map.

"Hold up a second, bud," I called to Rusty.

Even allowing for differences in scale, I'd guess we still had at least two hours to go before we'd come to the mine. *If* we could find it easily, which Rocky Rhodes had told me we wouldn't, and *if* Willie was there and agreeable to giving us a warm place to spend the night. Those were some pretty big ifs. I may be foolhardy at times, but common sense told me we better use our remaining daylight to get back to shelter.

"You know, I think this is about enough hiking for one day," I told the dog, trying to sound like I was happy about it. "We better head back now."

One nice thing about being a dog is that you aren't too goal oriented in matters other than food. Rusty gleefully turned around when I did and trotted back the way we'd come. He clearly didn't feel any of the disappointment I did at abandoning our mission. We reached the car at six, just as the glowing orange ball of sun hit the western horizon. I slipped the small backpack and my other equipment into the back seat and jammed my arms into the sleeves of my jacket.

"Told you it would be getting cool pretty soon," I said to the dog. "Besides, I'm starving. Ready for some dinner?"

Dinner is one of Rusty's magic words. His ears perked and his front legs bounced off the ground, spinning him in circles of joy.

"Let's get back to the hotel," I suggested.

All the way down the trail I'd wrestled with the problem of how I'd make it to the mine without running into the same problem, lack of time. I'd either have to find a quicker mode of travel, such as a horse, or prepare to stay out overnight. Neither idea had loads of appeal so I filed them away until I could relieve my dusty, hungry condition.

I knew once I reached the comfort of my hotel room I wouldn't want to go out again so I pulled into the drive-thru at a Kentucky Fried Chicken and got myself a boxed chicken dinner to go. Rigor mortis was starting to set in on my dead-tired muscles and it was somewhat stiffly that I pulled myself out of the car and headed toward my room. This physical effort stuff is excruciating.

In the room I set out a bowl of tasty doggie nuggets for Rusty but he was having none of it as long as there was fried chicken in the room. Unable to decide whether I'd feel better if I ate first or showered first, I decided to get him off my trail by getting the food out of the way. I switched on the TV set and pulled my dinner from the box. Peeling a few select strips of meat off the bones, I set them aside for Rusty and proceeded to devour my portion.

Afterward, I tore up the chicken meat and added it to his bowl, sticking the remains of the meal in the wastebasket and deciding that container would be safer out of the dog's reach. I put the basket on the high closet shelf and started peeling off clothes. When I came out of the shower Rusty was sitting in front of the closet door, staring at it wistfully.

"You're impossible," I told him.

I put on my robe, gathered the tempting chicken bones, and wrapped them tightly in the wastebasket's plastic-bag liner. I set it out in the hall with everyone else's room service detritus.

"There. No more." I showed the dog my empty hands and he finally settled down to sleep on the carpet.

The ibuprofin I'd swallowed before stepping into the steaming shower were finally beginning to take hold and I drifted off, reaching for the TV remote as I slipped off the edge of wakefulness.

Getting out of bed the next morning was no easy feat. Every muscle in my lower body was screaming at me. I did more painkillers and another hot shower while letting the little in-room coffee maker do its thing. I stepped from the shower in far less pain and with an idea.

Pulling the telephone directory for the metro area's East Valley, I looked up Rocky Rhodes.

"Mornin' there, Charlie," he greeted. "Did you make it out to Willie's mine?"

"How did you know?"

He chuckled easily. "Just sorta guessed it. By the way you were askin' questions, I knew you'd want to find it."

"Well, I didn't have any trouble finding the markers.

They were right in place. Just ran out of time," I told him. "I'm trying to figure out how I'm going to do it next time. Any suggestions? You said you'd been out there yourself?"

"Oh gosh, years ago," he said. "We always took some horses or mules. Course we were staying awhile and had some gear with us."

"Would you like to come with me?" I asked.

"I ain't really in shape for it now," he said. "Or I'm just gettin' too blame lazy."

"I guess you're right about the horses," I said, hiding my disappointment. "Where would I go about getting one?"

"I suppose most places that rent them wouldn't let you keep one out overnight unless they sent a guide with you," he said. "Don't know. Guess you could ask 'em."

I flipped to the yellow pages while we talked. There were a couple of stables in the area.

"Used to know a guy who took horses up in the hills all the time. Don't know if he still does, though. Suppose I could give you his number," he offered.

"Thanks, I appreciate it." I wrote down the number of his friend, along with the places in the phone book.

Before I could dial one of them, the phone rang.

"So, are you two enjoying a nice lazy vacation?" Sally's usual cheerful voice came through.

"Well, not exactly." I told her about Drake being called away and my dilemma about going back into the mountains a second time.

"You may want to check with this guy first," she said. "A Randy Buckman from White Oaks. He sounded a little excited when he called here. Said something about an explosion."

FOURTEEN

"An explosion? Literally?" I asked as soon as I got Buckman on the line.

"In one of the mine shafts on the west end of town. Cause is still under investigation, as is the identity of the two bodies."

"Oh, god. Two?" My mind spun forward to the possibility that one might be Willie McBride. "Any ideas about who they are?" I asked.

"I know what you're thinking," he said. "I can't say either way. Got some crime lab people coming down from Albuquerque. They're the only department in the state with sophisticated enough equipment to read this scene. It's a mess."

"We may have some ideas in a few hours. The bodies are charred beyond recognition, but we may be able to take a head count here in town to find out who's missing. It's a starting place anyway. Mainly, I was trying to get in touch with you to see if you'd found McBride elsewhere. Would at least help us eliminate him."

"No, I haven't. Not really any proof that he'd been here since he went missing from home either."

"You can check back with me later in the day," he

offered. "I may have some answers by then."

I hung up feeling very unsettled. The sheet of paper with the riding stables' phone numbers sat by the phone. There wasn't much point in my going back up into the Superstitions if Willie's body was lying charred in a mine shaft in New Mexico. I'd just be wasting time and resources and putting myself at risk in the unfamiliar environment. I made a snap decision.

The rental agency agreed to let me return the car in Albuquerque, so I hastily jammed our stuff into the bags and packed it all into the trunk. Rusty watched me bustle about, cocking his head, staying near enough to the door to be sure he wouldn't be left behind. Consulting my road map, I figured the quickest way to White Oaks would be to take Interstate 10 to Las Cruces, then up through Alamogordo. By ten o'clock we were on the road.

White Oaks was curiously quiet when I pulled into town, just as the sun dipped below the hills. My aching joints screamed at me as I slid from behind the wheel after spending hours in one position. I'd hoped to find Randel's café open but it was dark.

I let Rusty take a much needed run in the empty lot beside the café while I tried to decide what my next step would be. Finally decided to see if I could reach Randy Buckman. He answered with a weary voice after the third ring.

"I'm in White Oaks again," I told him, "but it's really deserted-looking here."

"It's been a long day," he said. "Everybody's probably getting tucked in for the night. I was just about to grab some dinner in Carrizozo, the place at the main intersection. If you want to join me I'll fill you in."

Food sounded good. I told him I'd be there in fifteen minutes.

"Well, we've got an ID on one of our victims," he said after we'd ordered—meatloaf for him, open-faced roast beef sandwich for me. "Rory Daniels."

My face must have registered the appropriate surprise.

"Looks like it's drug related." He watched for my reaction to that little bombshell.

"What! In White Oaks?"

"Know what you mean," he said, shaking his head side to side. "Took me by surprise too. And in a small community, that's not easy to do."

Our food arrived just then. I buttered my roll and took a forkful of mashed potatoes with brown gravy.

"Looks like Rory was part of a big export operation We don't think he was actually making the stuff out there in the mine. Probably just storing the chemicals. Usually with these meth labs, it's the lab that blows up, when they're cooking up a batch. But I guess some of those chemicals are pretty unstable and if two things get mixed together, bam!"

"So, the Albuquerque lab people figured this out?" I asked.

"Yeah. It's not really my forte, as they say. We got the DEA in on it now. They'll eventually find out who Rory was working with and where they were actually cooking up the stuff."

"So, if Rory Daniels was one of the bodies, who was the second?" I asked.

"Still don't know. Now that we know about the drug

stuff, my guess is it'll be somebody involved in that."

"But you called my office this morning," I pointed out. "Is there still any reason to think it might be Willie?"

"Ordinarily, I'd say not. And I wouldn't have called you at all, except for one bit of evidence." He paused to take a bite of his meatloaf and to drag out the suspense for me. "McBride's wallet was lying not twenty feet outside the mineshaft opening."

My brain went into a spin.

"But, the whole area was searched earlier this week. Why didn't anyone find it then? Was it burned? Do you think it means Willie was in the mine with Rory when the explosion went off?" I was having a hard time picturing the old prospector involved with a drug ring. Nothing was coming together.

"Wasn't burned," he answered. "But it wasn't there earlier in the week either. I'm real certain about that. Those searchers combed every inch of that ground."

"Then why didn't they find the chemicals in the mine?"

"We're calling a couple of them in for questioning to find out. Could be Rory had the stuff hidden down a small shaft, or maybe he'd disguised it somehow and they just missed it. I don't know the answer to that one."

"So how did McBride's wallet get there," I mused, drawing tine-marks in my remaining potatoes.

His radio squawked just then and he pulled it off his belt. A voice that sounded as if it were being spoken through a sieve said something I couldn't understand and Randy gave it a 10-4 in return.

"Gotta go," he said to me. "Here's my share."

He dropped a ten-dollar bill on the table and picked up

his hat from the seat beside him. I watched his trim form saunter to the door, with a small salute to the waitress as he left.

I fiddled with my food but found I wasn't hungry anymore.

Although the idea of being back home in my own bed tonight had enormous appeal, I couldn't face nearly another four hours of driving. I got a room at the motel connected to the diner and, after placing a call to Drake's cell phone to let him know about the recent turn of events, fed Rusty some of his food and crawled between the sheets. Sleep came almost immediately.

My eyes came open suddenly and my heart pounded as my brain registered only the conscious thought: where am I? Relaxing my rigid muscles, I turned my head to one side. A yellow square of light framed the window at the far side of the room. Red numerals glowed 3:15 on the night-stand clock. Another motel room. This one in Carrizozo. I finally remembered. Shit, I just wanted to go home.

I stretched out my limbs, my muscles crying out about the abuse I'd given them over the past two days, and rolled to my other side. After fifteen minutes I rolled back the other way. My eyes wouldn't close and my brain wouldn't stop.

Was Willie McBride still somewhere around White Oaks? Was his the second body in the explosion? If he had indeed gone to Arizona, why was his wallet here? If Willie'd become separated from his wallet weeks ago, why did it turn up now and who'd had it all that time? Had Willie used his ATM card or had someone else?

At 4:45 I gave up. There was no way I was getting back

to sleep. My eyes squinted shut against the sudden light as I switched on the lamp at my bedside. Rusty raised his head questioningly. One side of his face was squashed upward and his tongue peeked out, a tiny sliver of pink against his distorted reddish muzzle. His eyes weren't any more open than mine.

I swung my legs over the edge of the bed and stumbled toward the bathroom. He got up, shook himself, and looked ready to go for the day. It would take a little more than that with me. I always hate it when some early riser in a motel starts flushing and thumping about before daybreak but this time I had to be the one. Sorry, I couldn't help it.

Twenty minutes later I emerged from the shower feeling almost human. Slipped into the same clothes I'd taken off and tried to be fairly quiet about getting myself and my dog out the door. I left the key on the dresser and thunked the door shut as quietly as I could. The motel office was dark but I'd given them my credit card the night before. They could figure it out.

The early morning air was chilly, stars clear in the black sky, a tiny sliver of moon low in the west. Even with my light jacket on I shivered as I scanned the parking lot. No one moved in the little town and the only lighted establishment was a twenty-four hour convenience store across the road that catered to truckers. I started the car and headed for it.

Coffee. It was my only coherent thought as I parked in front of the store. An eighteen-wheeler with diesel engine rumbling was parked in an open dirt lot to the west, its driver nowhere in sight. A set of jingle bells tinkled as I entered the store, bringing a dozing clerk to his feet behind the counter. I followed my nose to the rear corner where I poured black, sludgy coffee into a large Styrofoam cup. I added an overdose of creamer and sugar to it, hoping for the best. At the counter I topped off my nutritious breakfast with a package of Twinkies

"Guy'll be here about six with fresh donuts," the clerk offered helpfully.

"That's okay, I'm in kind of a hurry." At this moment I couldn't imagine what would make me want to hang around another forty-five minutes for a donut. I handed over a couple of dollars and pushed the door open with my hip.

The coffee tasted every bit as bad as it looked, but I sipped at it gratefully anyway. I let the car idle while I opened the Twinkies, with Rusty hanging over my shoulder watching my every move. I handed him one, which went down with hardly a smacking of the lips, and put the gearshift into reverse as I took a nibble from mine.

"Back off!" I told him. "Not my fault you ate all yours. This one's mine."

He sat back on the seat but didn't relax until he saw the last bite of Twinkie disappear into my mouth.

I was beginning to get a nice little high from the infusion of sugar and triple-strength caffeine. The road was deserted, the sky beginning to lighten behind me, and all was well with the world. By the time we reached Socorro, I was jittery from my previous excesses and decided I better balance it out with something nutritious. A fast food drive-thru yielded a ham-egg-biscuit combination and a large orange juice, all of which I ate one-handed as I hit the Interstate again. By ten-thirty I'd argued with a clerk at the car rental agency, called Sally to come pick me up, and was sitting on the curb at the Albuquerque airport, my dog and bags beside me like a homeless person. It felt great.

On the way back to the office Sally briefed me on everything I'd missed.

"Tammy's given notice," she said. "Decided it just isn't her *thing*."

"Guess she expected something more glamorous working in a private investigator's office."

"Anyway, tomorrow will be her last day, she says. I'd take up some of the slack," Sally offered, "but with the baby . . ."

"That's okay. You only signed on to work part time anyway. We'll get someone else." Or I'll end up back full time, I thought grudgingly.

"When you get back, you should probably call Rick at Hastings and Ellison," she continued. "He's all hot right now because Ron hasn't returned his calls for a week. Even though Tammy and I have both told him Ron was out of town. At first he said that was okay, no hurry. Now, suddenly it's a big hurry."

"Have we heard anything from Ron?" I asked.

"Back on Wednesday. He swears he'll come into the office in the evenings and catch up on paperwork so he can start right in on some client work."

I muttered once again, but tried to keep it from Sally. It really wasn't her problem that I'd had only half a night's sleep. I asked her to take me home so I could drop off my bags and get my own car. I had a feeling it would end up being a long day.

FIFTEEN

By three o'clock I was actually feeling a lot more upbeat. Maybe it was a second wind, maybe I was just operating on overdrive, I don't know. After dropping my bags off at home and making sure everything looked undisturbed there, Rusty and I had piled into my Jeep and headed for the office.

I'd decided to take Tammy's resignation as a good thing. If a person's unhappy with their job, you really don't want them around anyway, I decided. She looked a little surprised that I didn't seem to care about her leaving, but oh well. I called Rick and soothed the client. It was one of the bigger law firms we worked for and I knew we'd miss them a lot more than we'd miss Tammy, so it was worth some butt-kissing to pacify them. I told them I'd be happy to start work on the case (although I wasn't sure how I'd work it in) or Ron would start on it first thing Wednesday. Wednesday was good enough.

After all that, I opened a huge stack of mail that had accumulated, sorting it into piles of Bills to Pay, Letters to Write, Computer Entries to Make, and Circular File—I'm not very patient with junk mail. By five, I'd paid all the bills and drawn up Tammy's final check, which I'd give her tomorrow.

My energy was lagging again when the phone rang.

"It's Dorothy Schwartzman," Tammy announced over the intercom.

I took a deep breath and tried to bring back my earlier perky feeling. "Hi, Dorothy."

"I haven't heard anything from you in a few days," she said, her nasal whine making my teeth grind.

"That's because I've been out of town, Dorothy. Remember I told you I was following up some new leads about your father?"

"Did you find him? What new leads?"

I hated admitting that I didn't have Willie in hand yet, but I briefed her on the little bit I did know, leaving out the part about the mine in Arizona. For some reason I felt protective of that information. I hadn't shared it with Randy Buckman either.

"You may have heard something on the news about a mine explosion at White Oaks," I told her, not knowing whether the news had covered it or not. "I should let you know that there is a possibility that one of the people killed there was your father."

"Oh dear," she said neutrally.

"The only thing that ties him to the spot was his wallet, found outside the mine. It may not mean anything. The crime lab people have determined that the cause of the explosion was chemicals used in manufacturing methamphetamines."

"I'm not following you here, Charlie. Surely you're not saying my eighty-four year old father was doing drugs." Her voice had become sharp.

"Not at all. He may have simply chosen the mine as a

hiding place and was unlucky enough to be there when the explosion happened." I had a half-dozen reasons why that was probably unlikely, but I didn't tell her that. "I just wanted to prepare you for the possibility that you could get a call from the authorities."

"Well, I appreciate that, Charlie, but I don't appreciate the insinuations about his character. I hope you haven't been spreading this to the news media or anything. Believe me, I'll have your license if this family's name is dragged through the mud," she snarled.

"Dorothy, I'm going to hang up now before I say something I shouldn't." I clicked off before I could blow.

My hands were balled into tight fists, I realized. I had to make a conscious effort to unclench my jaw. Have my license! This from the woman who insisted I work for her, even after I'd told her I wasn't a private investigator. The woman who'd invited me to her home for dinner, who called me whenever there was a problem. Who wanted immediate results on an impossible case. I took a deep breath and blew it out forcefully.

In times of stress my penchant for neatness tends to surface like oil on water. I slowly gathered the stack of receipts beside my calculator, tamping them into a tidy pile. I filed them in their proper folder. The few pieces of correspondence went into a nice, neat sheaf beside the computer, ready for me to write the letters tomorrow. I began arranging my desktop items, telephone precisely aligned with the edge of the glass top, stapler and tape dispenser close by. I came to the small plastic cube filled with paper clips, and then I lost it. I picked up the little box and squeezed it until the corners dug into my palm, then I flung it across the room. It hit the open door just as Tammy walked in.

She let out a small shriek.

I let out a ferocious growl.

Rusty jumped up from his prone position on the rug, ready to do battle on my behalf.

Tammy's wide eyes watched the dog nervously.

I took another deep breath. "It's all right," I assured her calmly. "Everything's fine now."

Rusty took his cue from my tone and lay down again on the rug.

"I just came to say goodnight," Tammy told me, a twitchy smile trying to form on her lips. She looked at the splatter of loose paperclips that had showered the floor when their container burst open. "Shall I . . . ?" She glanced down.

"It's fine." I handed her the final paycheck I'd drawn up. "Goodnight, and have a nice life." I sat with my hands clasped primly on my desk until I heard the back door close. Then my head went forward and I grabbed it with both hands, running my fingers down each side and squeezing two fistfuls of long hair. I'm just tired, I told myself. Not enough sleep, that's it.

"Charlie?"

The male voice, coming from right in front of me, sent my heart pounding.

"Ron! What—" I reached for my stapler, came up with a pen instead, and threw it at him. "You scared the shit out of me! What are you doing here?"

"C'mere," he coaxed, rounding the desk to stand beside me. "What's wrong, Sis?"

He took the hand that had just thrown the pen and pulled me into an embrace. His clothes smelled like woodsmoke. He patted my back and I let my forehead burrow against his shoulder. He made soft little there-there noises.

"A client just threatened me," I sniffed.

"What?"

"Well, not physically. She just said she'd have my license." I started to giggle between sobs. "Stupid old cow, she knows I don't even have a license. She's been a gigantic pain since day one, and I don't know where her father is, and Tammy just quit, and Rick Hastings was mad at you so I had to fix that." I took a jagged breath. "And Drake is out there, god knows where out in the sticks, risking his life to fight a fire that some jerk probably set because he didn't think the fire restrictions applied to *him*. . . ."

"Haven't had much sleep, have you?" he said, backing away to look at my face.

"No, I guess not." I felt a grin tugging at the corners of my mouth.

"C'mon, you're gonna drink a cup of tea while I pick up these paperclips."

Rusty rubbed against my legs, adding his own brand of comfort. Ron led me downstairs to the kitchen where he nuked a mug of water and peeled open a tea bag wrapper. I dunked the bag a few times then sipped at the tea gratefully.

"What are you doing here, anyway? You weren't supposed to get home until Wednesday." We settled into two chairs at the kitchen table.

He shrugged. "Just had a feeling, I guess." My eldest brother may be a little on the chunky side with hair that's getting sparse on top, but he's there for me.

"You look like a wreck," I told him. "Your pants have a big soot mark on them and that fishing hat looks like a car ran over it. And you smell like a campfire."

"I cleaned fish right before I drove home. Want a whiff of my hands?" He stretched them toward my face.

"Uh, no! Get 'em away!"

"At least you're smiling again," he teased. "When was the last time you ate?"

"Oh, gosh, maybe eight o'clock this morning."

"Well, Miss Always-Preaching-Nutrition, don't you think it's time?"

"Pedro's? A margarita might really hit the spot right now."

"Think he'll let me in, smelling like I do?"

"He lets Rusty in, doesn't he?" I pretended to give it some consideration. "Well, you better at least wash those hands."

We stood up and I rinsed my mug at the kitchen sink.

"You scrub on those hands awhile, I'll go clean up the mess I made in my office."

I was down on my hands and knees, stuffing silver clips into their container when the phone rang. Without thinking, I reached for it.

"Charlie, is that you?" Dorothy's whiny voice continued without pause. "Of course it is. Charlie, I'm still very upset about your insinuation that anyone in my family might be involved with drugs. I'm just not sure I still want you on this case. You just don't seem to be doing anything for me."

"Dorothy," I began, fighting to keep my voice steady, "did anyone ever tell you that it's not always about *you*?

Frankly, I don't give a shit about how this affects *you*, anymore. I'm not doing it for *you*. There are members of your family who genuinely care about Willie, like Melanie, like Bea. And I'm doing it for Willie. Did you ever stop to think what he might be going through? That he might be lost, or cold, or afraid? No, Dorothy, this isn't about you and people . . . like you." I'd nearly blurted out what I knew about Felix and the changed will. I clamped my mouth shut.

"Well!" she huffed.

"Dorothy, I apologize for the rant. It's been a very long day. You think about it. If you want us to continue on the case, we will. Ron is back in town now and we'll do our best. Just keep in mind that you may not like the outcome. Sometimes the truth isn't what we'd like it to be."

There was a long silence on the line.

"We all care about my father," she finally said tightly, "And we want him found. Please keep looking for him."

Ron walked in just as I hung up.

"Did I hear a teeny little note of anger?" His eyebrows went up as he looked sideways at me.

"I hope I did the right thing," I said. "It probably isn't smart to yell at a client."

"But she still wants us on the case, right? You know, bullies will usually back down when you stand up to them."

"Well, she didn't back down by much."

"Tell me about it over some enchiladas," he said, steering me toward the back door.

Back at home, later, I felt curiously light. I was glad I'd taken a stance with Dorothy, and it felt good to have Ron back, if only to listen and ratify what I'd done so far. My brief rant had released the right endorphins, apparently. The two margaritas probably hadn't hurt my mood a bit either.

I was actually humming as I undressed. The phone rang just as I was getting ready to step into the shower.

"Hi, hon, how was your day?" Drake asked.

I recapped it quickly, glossing over how much Dorothy had upset me. "How about yours?" I asked.

He described a fire out of control, with flames leaping a hundred feet or more into the air. His small helicopter was being used for recon by the fire management officers, while large tankers dropped load after load of fire retardant. As they began to get the fire under control they would use his smaller water bucket to catch spot fires and flare-ups before they could take hold.

"Take care, sweetheart. I miss you like crazy," I told him before we said goodnight.

Ten minutes later, after a quick shower, I slipped between cool, clean sheets. Rusty settled onto his rug beside the bed.

The dream felt very real, although I was aware that I was dreaming even as it unfolded. We were in a courtroom. I sat behind a table, alone. Dorothy Schwartzman stood behind the other table, tall and imposing in a severe pinstriped suit, much as I imagined she would have during her high-power law career.

"Your Honor," she was saying, "I submit that the defendant was hired to locate my father and to bring him back to me alive and well."

I tried to object that "alive and well" had not been mentioned at the time, but my voice wouldn't come out.

Dorothy kept talking. "You see, Your Honor, I have important papers for him to sign. I need him here."

"She wants him to sign a new will, cutting out all her siblings," I tried to shout. Again, my mouth moved but nothing came out.

"I further submit that the defendant acted as a private investigator, without a license and without the skills to properly complete the job."

"You hired me for the job! I told you to wait for Ron! I told you!"

She sent a smirking look toward me.

I looked at the judge but he didn't appear to realize I was in the room.

"I therefore, Your Honor, ask that the defendant be sentenced to life in prison for her crimes." She set her notepad down and took her seat.

"So ordered!" The judge rapped his gavel twice.

"Wait! You can't do that! I get to say something," I rounded my table, ready to get in the judge's face, but a bailiff grabbed me by the arm.

"Sorry, miss," he said, pulling my other arm forward, ready to put handcuffs on me.

"No! Wait!"

Wait . . . I struggled to consciousness gradually, thrashing against my restraints. Wait . . . I woke to find my arms tangled in the sheets. My legs were kicking ineffectually against my nonexistent opponent. My breath came in gasps.

Exhaling loudly, I flopped back against the mattress. I slowly turned my right arm until it became free of the fabric. The left came away easily once I stopped resisting. My heart was beating double-time and sweat coated me. It took a conscious effort to slow my rapid breathing. I lie there for a minute, getting my bearings, my first thought being *Thank God it was a dream.*

After a couple of minutes I sat up, then decided to get a glass of water from the bathroom. The cooling sweat made me shiver and I slipped on my terry robe. I sat on the edge of the bed, hoping the unsettling feeling would go away and I'd be able to fall asleep again. But my thoughts wouldn't slow down.

"Why did I agree to stay on this stupid case?" I said aloud.

Rusty stirred, stretching his legs straight out, but didn't awaken.

I switched on the bedside lamp, bringing a peachy glow to the far corners of the room and dispelling the ominous shadows. The dog raised his head partway, eyes slitted against the sudden brightness. When he saw I was still on the bed, he dropped his head back to the floor.

Dorothy, clearly, was an enemy. The elementary symbolism of the dream was telling me not to trust her; that she'd turn on me in a moment. Well, *yeah*, I thought. She already did that this afternoon on the phone. Her threat to "have my license" wasn't an idle one, I realized.

I got up and went to the kitchen. Without consciously deciding to do it, I poured some milk into a mug and stuck it into the microwave. While it heated, I paced.

We should go carefully from now on, I decided. I'd fill Ron in on every detail I'd learned so far and we'd create a case file with him authorizing me as his assistant to interview witnesses and perform certain duties. I'd talk seriously to him tomorrow about taking over from this point, conducting the rest of the investigation himself.

I took the warm milk from the oven and added a packet of

hot chocolate mix. The clink of the spoon in the mug brought Rusty from the bedroom. Ears perked and tongue lapping tentatively out, he displayed frank interest in the mug.

"Not for you, pal," I said, reaching out to scratch his ears.

He ducked, not wanting to be distracted by mere affection. I pulled a crunchy dog biscuit from the cupboard and offered it. He snatched it eagerly.

What else could I do to protect myself against Dorothy? I should have known, from day one, I chided myself. Anybody as pushy as she'd been, and a lawyer to boot, was bound to get nasty when things didn't go her way. I carried my hot chocolate to the living room where I turned on a soft light and burrowed into a corner of the sofa, my feet tucked under me. Rusty followed me, laying his chin on the sofa, doing his best to look adorable while not taking his eyes off me.

For some reason, Melanie's face came to me. She'd been so worried over her grandfather. And Bea, so unlike her sister. Actually, aside from Dorothy and Felix, they weren't such a bad group. And of course there was Willie himself. I still didn't have any idea whether he'd turn up dead or alive, but he deserved to have someone out there looking.

The warm drink gradually calmed me. I'd talk it over with Ron tomorrow. He'd probably have some ideas. I couldn't let Dorothy scare me off now. Especially knowing what her motives were. I couldn't let her attitude put me on the defensive—she was the one in the wrong. I drained the dregs of the cup and took it to the kitchen sink.

I could probably sleep now.

SIXTEEN

"She can't have *my* license pulled," Ron said matter-of-factly. "You're acting as my assistant, gathering information is all."

"Even though I've been in contact with a law enforcement agency down south?"

"Buckman actually enlisted your help a couple of times, didn't he?"

"Well, yeah, identifying the shirt, especially."

"Okay. Let's just let Dorothy cool off and we'll keep doing the job. She didn't actually say we were fired, did she?"

"No, she said she wanted her father found."

"Then that's what we'll do. What do you suggest we try next?" he asked.

"I think we ought to stay in touch with Buckman's office and see if they get an ID on that second body in the mine. Maybe you could do that," I suggested. "I'm going to call the other sister, Bea, and find out if she got her statement notarized about that unsigned will. I don't know how much weight it would hold in court, but at least she's making the effort to be sure Dorothy and Felix can't magically produce a signed one if Willie is dead."

"Good idea."

"Another area where you might get more answers than I could is in checking out Felix's credentials." I explained my theory that with his knowledge of geology Felix might know something important about the mineral rights on Willie's land. "Think you could find out whether he's been checking around, making any specific inquiries about that piece of land?"

"Will do—Chief." He gave a little salute.

"I guess I better handle a few domestic matters," I told him. "Talk to Sally this morning about how we're going to redistribute Tammy's workload now that she's gone. Or did you want to try getting another part-timer to replace her?"

"Whatever you think. I certainly defer to your expertise there," he said. "You ladies are the ones who'll feel her absence."

"Or not. You know, in some ways it was actually more comfortable with just you, me and Sally here."

He nodded a "whatever," and I left his office to head downstairs. Ron and I had come in early this morning, wanting to get caught up before the phones started ringing and the day officially started. I went into the kitchen for a second cup of coffee and was just pouring it when Sally came through the back door.

I broached the subject of Tammy right away and we decided that the two of us could manage without another helper.

"I can certainly take some work home with me," she offered. "I can do letters or case files on my own computer, if you don't mind. Main reason I can't put in more time at the office is because of Ross's schedule. We'd agreed that one of us would always be home with the baby."

I agreed with Sally's assessment and decided I, too, could reorganize my work.

That bit of business off my mind, I placed a call to Bea in Seattle. She sounded sleepy when she answered.

"Oh, gosh, I'm sorry. I'd completely forgotten about the time difference," I apologized. I asked her about the notarization and she assured me she'd done it.

"Bea, I don't know how all this is going to turn out," I began. "Dorothy was pretty upset with me yesterday. Stopped just short of firing us from the case."

"Well, don't worry about that," Bea said. "Dorothy rarely has anyone stand up to her, but when somebody does she'll usually back down. And if she does fire you, I'll simply hire you myself. I'm not going to sit by and let those two play any games with Dad's will and his property. I hope you find him alive so he can boot them out face to face." She laughed. "Now that was a really strange mixture of old clichés, wasn't it? Guess it's still too early for me."

"I'll let you get back to sleep then," I said. "And, Bea? Thanks for believing in me."

I hung up, feeling better, finding a new determination to find Willie McBride. I really wanted to see the good guys win this one.

I could hear Ron's voice on the telephone in his office, so I settled in to answer some of the correspondence that was waiting for me.

"Charlie?" Sally's voice came over the intercom. "Randy Buckman's on the line, says he's returning Ron's call, but I thought you might want to take it."

"Hi, Randy, what's up?" I greeted.

"Who's Ron Parker?" he asked. "I wasn't sure what he was calling about."

I explained that Ron was my partner and we were just catching up on shared duties since he'd returned to town.

"What we were calling about was to find out whether you'd had any more luck in getting an ID on the other body in the mine," I said.

"No ID at this point," he said. "But a strange bit of evidence has turned up. Found a little bundle of personal items—a change of clothing, Buck knife, some matches and a blanket, all rolled up together like a person might put into a backpack or take with 'em for camping out."

"Do they tie in to Willie McBride?" I asked.

"Well, yeah, they do. I took 'em over to the café and had Keith take a look. He said he remembered Willie carrying that bundle in with him a few months back. Now why he carried the stuff into the café, rather than just leaving it in his truck, I don't know. Could be he'd loaned the truck to Bud Tucker, something like that, I don't know. But the bundle was with him shortly before he disappeared."

"So, that might mean the body is his?" I felt a strong stab of disappointment.

"Can you hold on a second, Charlie? My other line's ringing."

A firm click stuck me on hold.

"Well, this is interesting," he said when he came back on the line a couple of minutes later. "That was the coroner's office. From the skeletal remains, they're telling me the second victim was a female."

"Really?" My pent-up breath released in a rush.

"Guess that pretty well rules out Willie. Now I got a job finding out who she was."

"And I guess we go on looking elsewhere for Willie," I said. "Any more details about Rory Daniels's involvement with the drug materials?"

"Piecing that together slowly, I'm afraid. Can't say for sure, but it ain't uncommon for these little labs to pop up out in the sticks, finished product destined for the big cities like Albuquerque or El Paso. Rory traveled a lot 'on business.' Maybe we're about to find out what kind of business."

"Good luck with it," I said.

I mulled over the possibilities after saying goodbye. I'd forgotten to ask just where Willie's pack had been found but assumed it was close enough to the scene of the explosion that they found it in the course of processing that crime. Had Willie been hiding out in that same mineshaft? Maybe witnessed the drug dealers coming and going? Maybe they'd caught him spying and decided to do away with him.

If so, was Rory Daniels directly involved? He sure hadn't acted guilty when I'd overheard his conversation at the café. But maybe he hadn't attended Bud Tucker's funeral just to see Bud safely buried. Maybe he'd been there to see if Willie would turn up. Maybe Rory's deadlier business associates had threatened Rory, and he had to get a possible witness out of the way. Maybe I was going to drive myself crazy with all this speculation.

I heard Ron hang up his phone.

"Pow-wow?" I suggested, sticking my head in his doorway. He motioned me to a chair.

"Were you able to find out anything about Felix?" I

asked after sharing the phone call I'd just gotten.

"Some interesting stuff, actually," he said, taking a sip from his coffee and frowning at it. "Cold. Anyway, Felix McBride is a little more than just a professor of geology at New Mexico Tech. He's head of the department. Tenured. Been there close to thirty years."

He made a scribble on his notepad.

"He told me he taught Geology 101."

"The interesting part is that he *has* been checking on mineral rights in the north valley. A contact in the county clerk's office told me there'd been an inquiry within the past six months, specifically on William McBride's property. She took the call personally; there could have been others. It struck her as unusual because in her fifteen years in that office she can't remember a single other call about mineral rights on land within the city limits. Odd, huh?"

"What was the caller asking, what kind of minerals they might find?"

"County clerk's office wouldn't know that. This person wanted to know who owned the mineral rights on this piece of land. She told them it would be the property owner unless the mineral rights had specifically been deeded to someone else. She confirmed that McBride held the deed, including all rights, and that no other deeds had been filed at that time."

"Is that still true now?"

"I had her check it. Still in Willie's name."

"So Felix hasn't tried, so far anyway, to get Willie to sell or give him just the mineral rights," I said.

"Well, we don't know what he's *tried*. We just know he hasn't recorded a deed."

That brought up some unpleasant images. I pictured Felix with his strong, tan face, unnaturally black hair and pencil-thin mustache—the cruel glint in his eyes. I told Ron about how Felix had been arguing about something with Dorothy that day in the hospital. Maybe Felix knew Willie was already dead because he'd done it himself. Maybe he was trying to convince Dorothy to call off the investigators and forge a signature on the will. If she didn't know her father was dead, his request may have seemed strange to her. But if, say yesterday, he'd convinced her to fire me it could certainly account for her tirade.

And what kind of minerals could Felix possibly hope to find on Willie's land? From what I knew about the natural resources in the state, we had rich deposits of coal along with oil and natural gas but they were concentrated in the northwestern and southeastern corners of the state. The gold, silver, and copper mines had mostly played out by the early 1900s. I'd never heard of any mineral exploration at all in the Albuquerque area. The big issue these days was water shortages, with the city imposing a myriad of rules about its use and turning neighbor against neighbor with the lawn sprinkler police. But water rights were another issue entirely. What was Felix up to?

"Any of it sounds plausible," he agreed. "People have been known to take drastic measures to get a will changed in their favor."

"But how on earth will we prove it?"

He jounced a pencil between his fingers, tapping it on the desk. "Okay, let's backtrack a little. You told me Willie's truck was found in Las Cruces?"

"Parking lot of the bus station."

"And his ATM card was used twice after that."

"Once in Las Cruces, once in Phoenix. Or maybe it was the Phoenix area," I said.

"Hmmm, I'm wondering . . . Old people don't tend to go for the modern technology of ATM cards," he mused. "I wonder if this was a regular habit with McBride. Do you know if Buckman's office got his banking records, whether the bank was able to provide a video camera image of the person actually using the card?"

"He was checking on it, but I don't know what he found out," I said.

Another call to Buckman's office. He was on another line and Deputy Montoya answered. He remembered me and was willing to pull the file.

"Looks like that's a loose end we haven't gotten to yet," he said. "Sheriff Buckman is running pretty ragged there days, with this explosion and the drug thing and all."

"Well, this really is a minor detail," I agreed. "I doubt it has anything to do with your case, but I'm still treating McBride as a missing person. Do you think Randy would mind if I made a few calls directly to the banking people? I'll fax over anything they send me."

"Well . . . it's not normal. Civilians aren't usually privy to that kind of thing."

"I understand. And you guys are so busy. . . ."

"Hold on," he said. He put me on silent hold for what seemed like ages.

"Tell you what," Montoya said, coming back on the line. "Sheriff Buckman authorizes you to call them and tell 'em you're calling on behalf of our office. Ask them to fax the information to our office. I'll send you a copy." He

gave me the fax number, along with the dates and loca-
tions of the transactions.

"Well, now we have official authorization to work on
this," I told Ron on the intercom a minute later.

"I'll call them if you'd like. I have a contact at First
Albuquerque who might help move it through a little
faster."

"Any luck?" I said, peeking into Ron's office a few minutes later when I realized he was off the phone.

"Yep. Told you it pays to have contacts. Vivian personally looked up the information. She's put in the request for
the video images to be faxed to the Sheriff's office, and a
second set faxed to us."

I narrowed my eyes. "Are we going to get in trouble for
that?"

"Nah. They probably won't even know. If it ever comes
up, you gave me the instructions correctly but I misun-
derstood them. What's the harm?"

"And the bank statements? If McBride never used that
ATM card before those two times, I'm willing to bet it was
stolen from him."

"Viv says the local branch is only able to access a customer's statement for sixty days. Earlier than that and they
have to go to some archive and it takes a couple of weeks."

"Sixty days isn't going to help us a whole lot," I muttered. "That's about when Willie disappeared."

I turned toward my own office, then spun around.

"Wait—I have an idea," I told Ron. "I still have the key
to Willie's house, heh-heh."

SEVENTEEN

I grabbed my purse and keys. Rusty rose from his spot on the rug. "Yes, you can go too," I told him.

It looked like spring had finally arrived. The late April day was clear and warm. Fruit trees were in full bloom, forsythia sent sprays of brilliant yellow skyward. Along Rio Grande Boulevard the overhead deciduous trees were filling in their bare winter branches with pale green shoots. I pulled into the dirt turnaround area on McBride's property.

It was hard to tell whether anyone had been here since my last visit. We'd had enough wind that any tire tracks in the dust had been swept clean. Inside the house, the gas odor was gone. Apparently Dorothy had followed through and called the gas company. I glanced casually through the rooms but nothing looked different. I made my way to the bathroom where I'd previously found the drawers full of check duplicates.

I pulled out a handful of the small bound packets. The dates didn't appear to be in any certain order. A few inches into the pile, I came across an old bank statement, postmarked November of the previous year. It had never been opened. More checks, another statement for December, also unopened. Lower into the drawer, a January statement. None of them opened, so obviously he'd never balanced them. In fact, I'd not come across a checkbook or register where he would record his transactions. My accountant mindset went into spasms at the thought.

How could a person *never* balance a bank account? Wouldn't he worry that he was running out of money? It made me twitchy to think about it. While I might not know to the very dollar how much I have in my accounts, I certainly know if one of them is getting low enough to worry about. I certainly don't start writing checks until I know what I have to draw upon. Sheesh.

I located and set aside statements going back six months, except for the two months since Willie'd disappeared. What had happened to them? Although the bank would be faxing us copies, I was curious about what had happened to the original ones they would have mailed. I remembered finding several bills on my first visit. I'd turned them over to Dorothy to handle. But there hadn't been any bank statements. I set aside the statements and piled all the check duplicates back into the drawer.

"C'mon kid, let's go," I called to Rusty.

At my Jeep, I set the paperwork on the front passenger seat and let Rusty into the back. A large metal mailbox stood on a wooden post at the road, just outside the haphazard barbed wire fence circling the property. I walked over to it and pulled the door open. A few pieces, probably not more than what would collect in a day or two. Hmm. I decided to ask Dorothy if one of the family members had been gathering the mail regularly.

For the first time I paid attention to the stand of trees near the back of the property, large cottonwoods and shorter, brushier cedar. Willie's fence ran along the edge of a low dip in the earth, following it until it disappeared into the foliage. It was one area I hadn't checked out yet.

The temperature was quite a bit cooler in the shade and last autumn's fallen leaves carpeted the ground with a brown pad that was almost mushy in places. I stepped gingerly around a massive spider web that hung between the branches of a scrub oak and the low-hanging limbs of a cottonwood. Ahead I caught the faint odor of sulfur blended in with the smell of damp leaves and general mold.

A clearing opened before me and in its center was a small rock outcrop with water trickling from its center. Brilliant yellow and orange coated the rocks, along with a smooth white substance that reminded me of white chocolate poured over a mound of ice cream. A mineral spring. I knelt beside the gently bubbling water.

"What do you think you're doing here?" a male voice demanded.

My stomach did a massive bounce down to the bottom of my feet and back to my throat. I spun toward the sound.

"Felix! You just about scared the shit out of me!" I hadn't heard a vehicle arrive.

He wrinkled his brow, unable to place me.

"Charlie Parker. I came to the hospital to see Dorothy," I reminded.

"Oh, yes." His tone was cool. He stood with his hands in the pockets of his twill slacks, a casual pose with a somehow threatening undertone. "What are you doing here?" he repeated.

"I came by to get some information on your father's

bank accounts. Dorothy gave me a key."

"I seriously doubt you'll find any bank records out here," he said, with a pointed look at the surrounding trees.

I didn't have a very good reply to that so I started to leave the clearing.

"Ms. Parker, I don't know what you think you're going to find. Obviously, my father isn't hiding out here at the back of the property. I suggest that you confine your searches to the places he might reasonably be found."

"And where might that be, Felix?"

"For a start, you might search the mines where he said he was going prospecting. And you might question those people in White Oaks. Someone there knows more than they're saying."

He stepped aside, practically ushering me out. I felt his eyes on my back as I walked the length of the property, back to my vehicle. When I got in, I looked back to see him standing at the edge of the treeline, hands still in pockets, staring at me. I pulled out, past his white Lincoln, and drove back to my office.

"I don't think anyone's been collecting Dad's mail," Dorothy told me later. I'd called Melanie's house as soon as I got back to the office. As luck would have it, she wasn't home and Dorothy answered the phone. "I'd forgotten to ask anyone to do it."

"You might ask around," I suggested. "Some bank statements are unaccounted for and perhaps some other bills."

"I went ahead and had the gas and electricity and phone shut off," she told me. "No reason to run them until he comes back."

I thanked her and hung up. I didn't mention my encounter with Felix. Thought I'd see where our other inquiries might lead us before bringing the rest of the family into it.

"Anything from the bank yet?" I asked Ron. He was seated at his desk, a half-eaten cheeseburger in a Styrofoam container at his side, reminding me that it was well past noon and I hadn't eaten anything since my one slice of toast with coffee at home this morning.

"Not yet," he said, not noticing that the smell of the burger was practically making me drool.

"Has Sally gone for the day?" I asked.

"Yeah. Said she was taking some typing home with her."

"Good. I think we'll get along just fine without Tammy," I said.

"I know I will," he grinned. "That girl was driving me crazy, making me keep my desk neat."

"I thought you liked the new, neater you," I said.

He rolled his eyes. "Sorry, Charlie, I'm just not cut out to do things that way."

Now that he mentioned it, I noticed that his usual clutter was creeping its way across the desk. Just since this morning a stack of file folders had appeared and yellow sticky-back notes dotted the lampshade, telephone, and calendar.

I held up the few bank statements I'd pilfered from McBride's house. "I'll see what I can get from these," I told him. I went down to the kitchen and scrounged up a handful of Wheat Thins and a yogurt whose expiration date wasn't too far past.

Back in my own office I neatened a pile of papers and

placed the newly delivered mail to one side. I aligned my stapler, tape dispenser, and calculator precisely across the front edge of the desk, as if they were some kind of voodoo icons that could protect me from the encroaching clutter across the hall.

An hour later, I'd come to the conclusion that McBride's finances were probably doing just fine, although no one might ever really know. His small pension check and Social Security were automatically deposited each month and he wrote all the checks he wanted to, apparently without having to keep any record of them. And somehow it all worked out. The only thing of probable significance I learned was that Willie McBride apparently did know how to use an ATM card.

While withdrawals were few, there were some. It could also explain how he knew he wasn't overspending—simply by frequently checking his balance at the ATM machine. Maybe Willie McBride wasn't as close to senile as his daughter wanted me to believe.

"I need to get going," Ron said. He stuck his head in my doorway. He had on his spring straw Stetson and his cell phone was jutting out of his shirt pocket. "Got to get some groceries and do a few things before I head home. No fax from the bank yet, but it will probably take some time. I'll come in early the next few days and over the weekend to get some of my work caught up. Will you be here?"

"I don't know. Probably, unless Drake gets released from this fire. Which is doubtful—it sounded like it was still blazing away when he told me about it last night."

"Okay. See you tomorrow."

I didn't stay too much longer either. While I'd gleaned a bit of interesting information from Willie's old bank statements, it was nothing that could point me toward his current location. I switched off my computer and the lights, set the answering machine downstairs and left our one night lamp burning before Rusty and I headed home.

By eight o'clock that evening I found myself dozing on the sofa, unable to keep my eyes open. It had been a long week and I'd given in to my emotions a bit too much in the past couple of days. I fell into bed and didn't awaken until bars of sunlight began to infiltrate the bedroom.

Although I'd told Ron I might come into the office, when the weekend came I found myself uninspired to do so and spent the time putting the McBride case out of my mind by cleaning house, airing linens, and all that other spring stuff that domesticated creatures tend to do. By Monday morning I was refreshed and ready to face Dorothy Schwartzman or whatever else the office might deal me.

I was the first to arrive so I started coffee then checked the fax machine. Nothing from the bank, although that wasn't really a surprise. I was deep into profit and loss statements for last month when Ron and Sally arrived, each popping in to say good morning before going on to other work.

"Doesn't look like this is going to tell us much," Ron commented an hour later, stepping into my office with a sheet of fax paper in hand. "Can you identify your man from this?"

I took the page and looked at the dark image. The face was too much in shadow for me to tell whether it was

Willie. Neither the posture nor the hands, usually good indicators of a person's age, told me anything either. The figure was in shadow, backlit by harsh light that cast the main image even deeper into darkness. He wore a ball cap whose bill blocked any hope of seeing facial detail. I thought a western hat was probably more Willie's style, but couldn't say for sure.

"That's from the bank in Cruces," Ron said. "Maybe the Phoenix bank will have a better one."

I stared at the fax a bit longer but didn't come to any conclusions.

"Maybe I'll see something more in it later," I told Ron, sticking the page up on my bulletin board with a tack.

"Shirley Mason on line one," Sally's voice announced.

My Realtor friend. "Hey, Shirley," I greeted.

"Hi, Charlie. I apologize for not getting back to you on that north valley property. It completely slipped my mind until I came across a note on my desk. Give me that address again?"

I suppressed a sigh and told her Willie McBride's address.

"Hold on a sec, I'm entering it into my database. I should be able to get you some comparables."

Computer keys clicked in the background.

"Okay, something's coming up," Shirley said. "Looks like a piece of acreage down the road recently sold for $400,000. That was vacant land, so yours might be similar."

Four hundred K wasn't exactly a huge fortune, but it wasn't peanuts either. And if Dorothy managed to get it all, rather than splitting with three other siblings, it might hold her over tidily.

"Oh, wait a second, Charlie," Shirley said. "I'm getting some additional information here. It looks like . . . um, let's see . . . yes this is in the same neighborhood. Another piece of property nearby just brought a much higher price because of its mineral rights."

"You mentioned that once before—what kind of mineral rights?"

"No details, so I don't know what kind of rights they are. I'll tell you though, the selling price was nearly triple that other one."

Whoa. Now that might be worth killing for.

I hung up the phone, pondering just how Dorothy or Felix might be involved in all this.

It was three in the afternoon before the second bank fax came in and this one revealed little more than the first. The one thing I could say with relative certainty was that it was the same person. Same cap, same posture. This one had more light on the figure itself, but again the bill of the cap hid any features.

"I wonder if this is always a problem with these video cameras," I said to Ron. "Seems like anybody who didn't want to be recognized would know to just wear a cap like this."

"You might be right," he said. "Makes you wonder if someone like McBride would have the savvy to figure out how to disguise himself this way."

"I doubt it. From what everyone tells me about him, and judging by his lifestyle at home, I picture him as a simple old man, happy to prowl around outdoors a bit and dig in the dirt in hopes of finding a treasure."

"Yeah. Doesn't seem like he'd be into outwitting the banking system."

"So, what do you think? Did someone else use his card?"

"Could be, but look at this." He pointed to the left hand of the figure in the Phoenix picture. "I'd say this is an old man's hand. Seems kind of gnarled, a little out of shape."

"You're right."

"Now, if McBride was abducted and killed it seems like the attacker would have had to be someone young and fit enough to overpower him. The odds are against one old man abducting another, I would think."

"Most likely, although stranger things have happened."

"Yeah, well, that's why we never rule out anything in this business."

"I think I'll touch base with Melanie again," I said. "I hope she's surviving all right with Dorothy under her roof. Maybe I'll drive over to her place." If I phoned, I might get Dorothy on the line, like last time, and if she chose not to hand over the phone I'd be out of luck. At least in person, I'd have better luck getting Melanie first if it came down to a sprint for the front door.

I closed out my work for the day and backed up my files. I'd never been to Melanie's house, but thought I could find it easily enough from the address in the phone book. She was in the area off Academy Road that had been heavily developed in the seventies. A previous case had taken me into the area several times.

On the way I stopped at a supermarket and bought a small bouquet of mixed flowers. Maybe Dorothy would act a little more kindly toward me if I came bearing gifts.

Melanie and Bob's home was a cream stuccoed, tile

roofed, squared pillared place in a neighborhood filled with the same. Albuquerque developers tend to find a look they like and do it to death. The homes in this section were old enough now that the landscaping was past the baby stage, but not much. Trees were just beginning to top the rooflines of the second stories and shrubs had reached the point where they might actually be in need of a trim now and then. Melanie's tan Nissan sat in the driveway.

"Charlie! What a surprise," she greeted. "Come on in."

She stepped aside and waved me into a small foyer that opened into a formal living room.

"Did you bring the flowers for Mother?"

"Oh. Yes, how is she doing?"

A tiny grimace tightened one corner of her mouth momentarily. "All right, I think. She's napping at the moment. Come on in the kitchen and I'll find a vase for these."

I followed her through the living area, which was beautifully decorated in Southwestern shades of tan, gold, and brown with accents of turquoise. The kitchen looked like a chef's dream, with stainless steel appliances, cherry cabinetry, and massive granite counter tops.

"Bob's deal," she explained when she caught me gaping. "He may be an orthopedist by day but his weekend passion is cooking. Once we got him through school and could afford it, we splurged on a kitchen to die for."

"It's absolutely beautiful," I said. Like I would know what half this equipment was for, me who does nothing more complicated than frozen or packaged foods that can be microwaved.

I told Melanie about the faxes from the banks. "Did your grandfather ever wear ball caps?" I asked.

"Well, not really," she said. "His very favorite hat was a beat up old straw western thing. But I guess he did own a couple of ball caps. Does! Does own ball caps. I can't believe I referred to him in the past tense, Charlie." Her lower lids filled with moisture. "I'm sorry," she said, reaching for a box of tissues.

"It's okay. I know what you meant." I turned to look at a poster on the wall that showed glass jars full of pasta. "I didn't mean to upset you. I'm just trying to figure out what's happened."

"I know you are. And I really appreciate it."

"Would you recognize this cap?" I pulled out the better of the two faxes. "I know it's dark, but there's something written on the front of the cap. Does it look familiar?"

"Hmmm, not really. The cap, anyway. But there's something about the posture. The slope of the shoulder or something—I can't really pin it down. But it could be him." She handed me back the page. "I just don't know for sure."

"Hey, what you've told me is really helpful," I assured her. "This is the first positive news I've had in days."

I left a few minutes later, thanking Melanie again. Dorothy had not awakened from her nap during my visit—I was secretly glad.

It was after four when I left Melanie's and I still had to traverse the horrid construction zone of the interchange or figure out a way to zigzag through town and avoid it. With rush hour traffic, I opted for the latter.

I phoned Ron at home as soon as I'd settled in and popped my frozen low-fat dinner into the microwave. His answering machine picked up.

"I think I'll drive back to Phoenix tomorrow," I said to the tape. "Melanie thinks the fax photo is her grandfather, so I'm going to see what I can do."

The drive would take about eight hours and this time I decided I'd be ready for the great outdoors. I ate my microwaved chicken and rice dinner then started gathering my provisions. Into a soft duffle bag went all my previous gear plus a warm coat with hood, gloves, and several military-style Meals Ready to Eat, left over from one of Drake's flight jobs. Somehow in the back of my mind I didn't think I'd actually eat any of the MREs—being a city kid born and bred, I had a vision of hopping back in the car and running out to the nearest McDonald's when I got hungry. But common sense and Drake's voice in my head warned me that I better be ready. I set the duffle near the front door and added a sleeping bag and Drake's lightweight tent to the pile.

Although the most direct route to Phoenix from Albuquerque is to take Interstate 40 to Flagstaff and make a left on I-17, it would put me at the opposite end of the city from where I needed to be. And, if I took the southern route I could make a couple of stops on the way. I set my bedside alarm for six.

The sky was already light the next morning as I loaded my gear into the back of my Jeep. The early air was crisp and cool, with the smell of lilacs blooming overlaid by someone's newly mowed lawn. I'd eaten a bowl of cereal, some heavy granola that would stick with me awhile, and poured a travel mug of coffee. Rusty stayed right with me, making sure he was invited.

It was thirty minutes later, after we'd cleared most of

the early morning traffic, that I got the chance for the first sip of my coffee. An hour after that, we were entering the town of Socorro. I'd never spent much time here, usually just buzzing through on my way somewhere else. About all I knew about the town was that it housed the university and that the Very Large Array, those dozens of huge satellite dishes aimed outward in hopes of making contact with life outside our solar system, was somewhere near here. I'd never been to either place.

But the town wasn't that large and I located the school without much trouble. Signs pointed me toward the right department and I wandered into a large building that was stuccoed to look like adobe. The corridors looked a lot like any college corridors and I followed my instincts until I located a door with DR. FELIX MCBRIDE painted on the wavy glass upper panel.

A secretary with a pair of bright red reading glasses perched on her nose typed rapidly at a computer keyboard. Her super-short dark hair lay close to her head like a feather cap, accentuating a prominent chin and petite ski-slope nose. She finished typing a sentence before turning to look at me over the tops of the glasses.

"I'm looking for Felix McBride," I told her.

"Doctor McBride is in a meeting," she said pointedly. "Do you have an appointment?"

She knew perfectly well that I didn't. She was that kind of secretary. She probably scheduled his time to go to the bathroom.

"I just need a few minutes. When will he be free?"

She made a production of flipping the page on an appointment calendar that she kept on the credenza behind her, well away from prying eyes like mine.

"He has a few minutes free at three-thirty this afternoon," she said with a satisfied smile. Teach me to walk in here unannounced. "Shall I pencil you in?" She tapped a yellow pencil against the desktop.

Voices approached the door to the hall, which I'd left standing open when I walked in. One was definitely Felix's. He turned to shake hands with another man at the doorway, just as I turned toward him. The other man continued down the hall and Felix walked in.

"Ms. Parker." He looked surprised to see me.

"May I have a word?" I asked smoothly.

He shot his secretary a look and ushered me past her into his private office. I could just about feel her poison darts in my back.

Felix's private office was the antithesis of the standard cliché for a college professor. A large cherry desk stood in the center of the room, its surface clear except for a leather bound blotter and matching pen and pencil set, a carved wooden name plate, and an IN basket. The basket had one sheet of paper in it. The back wall was lined in bookcases filled with leather bound sets, most of which seemed to contain "minerals" or "geology" in the title. Atop the cherry shelves sat a single geode, more than a foot in diameter, displayed to reveal its crystalline purple center. Felix dropped into his high-backed leather executive chair and indicated a wingback side chair for me.

"What can I do for you, Ms. Parker?" he asked, resting one elbow on the arm of his chair and smoothing his black mustache.

"I should have thought to ask you a few questions yesterday, when I saw you at your father's place," I began. "It's just that you startled me."

He tilted his head slightly.

"Dorothy threatened to fire me on Friday. She felt I'd made some inappropriate judgments about your father's character."

"Had you?" he asked without moving.

"I don't think so. Have you heard about the explosion in one of the mine shafts at White Oaks?"

"Recently?"

"Last weekend."

"No, I guess I hadn't." His left elbow remained on the armrest, his fingers now petting the black sideburn that ran just a touch below his earlobe.

"Someone was apparently storing chemicals used to manufacture drugs in one of the mines up there. During the police investigation, they found a pack of outdoor gear that belonged to your father. Dorothy became upset, thinking I was insinuating that your father was involved with the drugs."

"Was he?" Felix asked the question so matter-of-factly it took me by surprise.

"Well, I certainly don't think so," I said. "And I wasn't saying anything of the kind to Dorothy."

"Ah, I think I understand. Dorothy inferred something that wasn't there and blew up."

"Well, yes."

"You have to understand that Dorothy places a lot of importance on appearances," he said, shifting his weight, switching chair arms and elbows.

And you don't? I thought, glancing around the room.

"Appearances in the sense of how people act. It's always eaten away at her that her own father was so, shall we say, so uncouth as to go stomping about in the dirt, grubbing for bits of gold. My own interest in metals, conducted from within the walls of a university, wasn't nearly as unpalatable to her."

"I talked to Bea afterward," I said. "She told me to keep searching for your father. Said she'd cover expenses if Dorothy refused."

His eyes hardened just a touch. "Search all you want," he said. "I think we all want to know my father's where-abouts."

He glanced at his watch just a fraction of a second before the intercom buzzed. He raised an index finger toward me as he reached for the handset. A prearranged escape route from his secretary.

"All right, Miss Adams," he said into the phone. He raised his eyes to me. "You'll have to excuse me now."

I walked out past Miss Adams and traced my way back to my car. While I hadn't expected a miracle confession or anything I'd hoped for something a bit more factual from Felix. But I felt okay about it. I'd learned a lot about his character.

EIGHTEEN

My timing was perfect as I pulled into White Oaks right at lunchtime. Randel's parking lot had two other cars in it, both local I guessed by the amount of dust on them.

"Hey there, Charlie," Keith greeted. "More of them chicken enchiladas for ya today?"

"Um, I think I better go a little lighter than that. How about a turkey sandwich?"

"You got it." He poured me a glass of iced tea and headed toward the kitchen.

The other two people occupied a single table behind where I sat at the counter. They'd opted for breakfast food, I noticed, one with pancakes, the other a plate of huevos rancheros smothered in red chile. Their conversation had lagged when I walked in but picked up again after I'd placed my order.

"So, is the latest excitement over with?" I asked Keith as he set my sandwich down on the counter.

"Guess so," he said. "Big city boys all went home. Even Buckman ain't been in since yesterday." He straightened salt and pepper shakers and wiped the counter slowly. "Sure was good for business though," he said wistfully.

"Now don't you go blowing up anything or starting any

fires just to boost your business," I joked. I took a big bite from my sandwich. He'd made it with smoked turkey and thinly sliced Swiss cheese, just the way I like it.

"No, guess I couldn't do that," he chuckled. "We'll be into the tourist season pretty soon. Things get pretty busy in the summer."

The other two men began scraping their chairs back, ready to leave. One of them handed some cash over the counter to Randel and wished him a good day. I worked on my sandwich until the door closed behind them.

"So, Keith, any new gossip about that explosion?"

"Oh, plenty. Rumors fly around little towns worse than a swarm of mosquitoes."

"Sheriff Buckman told me the second body was a woman."

"Yeah—you didn't hear? It was Sophie Tucker."

"Oh my gosh." I could feel the blood drain from my face. I set my sandwich down. "Was she mixed up with the drug thing? I can't believe it."

"They don't think so, but people are sayin' Rory was. Nobody really knows for sure. And the scuttlebutt is that maybe she was out there because she and Rory were 'involved.' "

"Like, sleeping together?" I was having a hard time getting my mind around any of this. "Rory, the man who hated Sophie's father because of some long ago banking scandal? Now he's sleeping with Bud's daughter?"

"Crazy, ain't it?" Keith started wiping the counter even harder. "Course I don't know how much truth there is to it. People start talkin' and next thing you know, they're treatin' it like fact."

Sophie dead. And if she was involved with Rory Daniels, she sure hadn't given the slightest hint about it. I should have picked up some little clue when I'd mentioned him to her. Skepticism crept in.

But if Sophie wasn't involved with Rory sexually, and she wasn't involved in the drugs, then what was she doing in the mine with him when the explosion happened?

Keith moved behind me to clear the recently vacated table. He carried the dishes to the kitchen while I chewed thoughtfully on my sandwich.

"Keith?" I asked, taking a last bite and saving a few pieces of the bread for Rusty.

"I'm right here," he answered, bringing two wrapped sets of flatware to reset the table.

"You mentioned something to me once about geology."

He raised his head and gave me a lazy grin. "Yeah."

"Well, I got the feeling that you've got a lot more education than you let on around here."

"Ahh . . . that."

"Yeah. Want to let me in on it?"

He shrugged. "Book learnin's okay," he said. "Got me a fair amount of it. But your quality of life is more important. I chose this life. Lot more fun than what I left behind."

"Know much about the geology of New Mexico?" I asked.

"Some. Ain't the same as in East Texas, but I know a little."

"Are there any valuable mineral resources in the Albuquerque area?"

"Albuquerque? Gosh, I don't think so." He went behind the counter and picked up the pitcher to refill my tea. "There are significant oil and gas deposits in the state. In fact New Mexico is first in coal production for the country. Most people don't know that. But those things are all located in other parts of the state. I don't know of anything like that in the Albuquerque area."

I noticed that he had slipped back out of his down-home hillbilly accent when he talked about his area of expertise.

"What could there be, down in the north valley of Albuquerque, that would make a piece of land really valuable?" I pondered.

"Well, the valley areas lie along the Rio Grande Rift," he said. "Now, up north a bit, and even into Colorado, you'll find these little pockets of thermal heat that come near the surface here and there."

"Thermal heat?"

"You know, like in those hot springs places like Ojo Caliente and such."

"And this would be valuable?"

"Maybe. Could open a nice mineral spa and get rich people to drop a lot of money there. If there was enough pressure, someone might be able to harness the energy for a thermo power plant."

"Really." I placed my leftover bread crusts in the center of my paper napkin and twisted the edges of it together. Someone who knew a lot about geology, someone who might have government money behind him for the development.

A pickup truck pulled up outside and two ranchers got out.

"Thanks, Keith, you may have just given me a motive."

The bells on the door jingled as the two men walked in.

"Hey, fellas," Randel greeted. "You betcha, Charlie-girl," he said to me. "Ain't no problem."

I walked out to the car, carrying my small napkin-wrapped gift for Rusty. He gobbled the bread crusts as if they were the last ones in the world. As I pulled out of the dirt parking area I could see Keith inside, fingers snagged into the edges of his red suspenders, joking with his two new customers. Interesting man.

I hadn't planned on spending this much time being sidetracked on my way to Phoenix, but as long as I was, I decided to stop in at Sheriff Buckman's office to learn more about Sophie's death. His car was parked out front when I arrived.

"You didn't tell me the woman killed in the mine was Sophie," I accused once I was standing across from his desk.

"Yeah, I did," he answered, not looking up from the folder he was writing in. "Left a message on your machine this morning." He looked up at me. "What—you didn't get it? I thought that's why you were here."

I didn't go into details about my planned trip to Phoenix.

"No, I was just having lunch at Keith's place and he told me."

"Bet he also told you that the rumor's all over town that she and Rory Daniels were having a fling."

"Well, yes, he did."

"Dammit! It's so frustrating the way these things get going. Worse than a damn wildfire."

"So they weren't?" I knew my instincts weren't totally off.

"Look," he said, coming around the desk and closing

the door to his private office. "Only a couple people in this office even know this. No, Sophie and Rory weren't involved—not in that way—trust me on that."

He rubbed his temples gingerly. "We're close to having some answers, and I just hope that's the end of it." He lifted his head. "I can't tell you anything more now, but I don't want you saying nothin' around town."

I still wasn't satisfied but I assured him I wouldn't.

I walked out to my car feeling down. Poor Sophie. Despite the fact that for one brief period I'd considered her a suspect in her father's death, I'd liked her. She'd still had that independent cowgirl spirit that's been completely bred out of city kids, bred out of a lot of country kids today too, unfortunately. I started the Jeep and hit the road.

Three people dead in White Oaks and I still didn't have Willie McBride.

When I came to a stop at the four-way intersection in Carrizozo I glanced in my rearview mirror. A midnight-blue sedan had stopped behind me. I couldn't put my finger on it but something was off. The pair in the front seats certainly weren't from around here. Even at a glance her heavy makeup and his shoulder length wavy hair told me they didn't fit with the cowboy set I'd become acquainted with here in southern New Mexico. And the car was shiny clean—one short drive down any of our dirt roads would have fixed that.

Tourists, probably. I pulled through the intersection and when they didn't turn off I reduced my speed so they could pass me before the road narrowed to two lanes again. They didn't and I eventually sped up to my own comfortable pace.

It was mid afternoon by the time I reached Las Cruces and I realized I had hours to go yet before I'd reach Phoenix. I stopped to grab a quick burger and place a call to the motel where we'd stayed before, guaranteeing a room for late arrival.

"Ready?" I said to Rusty, tugging at his leash. I'd walked him to a dirt lot beside the hamburger place and he was completely entranced with all the new smells he discovered there.

It was already way past my bedtime when I reached the outskirts of Apache Junction. I spotted the exit to my hiking trail and whizzed on past it. A decent night's rest was in order before I started anything strenuous. In Mesa I exited at Power Road and pulled into the same parking spot I'd used the last time I was here. Rusty waited in the car while I checked in and followed me excitedly as I carried our things into the room.

"Yeah, it's fine for *you* to jump around with all that energy," I told him. "You slept on the back seat the whole way."

I pulled out my notes with phone numbers of the places that might rent me a horse but it was too late to call anyone tonight. I'd spent the past six hours thinking about my plans for finding Willie, so there wasn't much else to do now but brush my teeth and go to sleep.

The sun shone as a brilliant outline against the blackout drapes when I opened my eyes. Rusty sat at my bedside, resting his large head on the sheets.

"What?" I groaned. "Do I have to take you out before I'm even awake?"

He danced toward the door, verifying that his urge to pee was more desperate than mine.

"Okay, okay." I pulled on the clothes I'd taken off the night before and slid my feet into my walking shoes without benefit of socks.

Clipping the leash to his collar I let him pull me down the hall to the outside entrance and we dashed across the sidewalk and the chipped-rock landscaping. Thank goodness he'd given me time to put on my shoes.

The air was warm already, promising a hot day ahead. I glanced at my watch and saw that it was already after eight. I better get started.

"C'mon," I urged Rusty, tugging him away from a fascinating oleander bush.

Back in the room I dialed one of the stables Dick Chambers had recommended. Line busy. Dialed the second one and a man with a rusted voice answered. I explained that I wanted to rent one of his horses to go up into the Superstitions.

"Much ridin' experience?" he asked.

"Some, but not very recent." I didn't admit that I hadn't been on a horse since my high school days. I'd been a reasonably decent horsewoman then; surely it would come back to me.

"Then I'll have to send a guide with you," he said.

"Guide?" I hadn't counted on having another person along.

"Can't have you getting thrown and my horse running loose out there in the rocks. She'd die of heat stroke, for sure."

"I'd planned on spending a night or two out, and I really don't want to spend them with a strange man. Do you have any women guides?"

"Well, no. My cowboys are all real gentlemen, though."

I finally convinced him to let me go alone, provided I left him a credit card number and authorized him to charge it for the value of the horse if I didn't bring her back. I didn't mention that he'd also have my vehicle as hostage. Surely a nearly new Jeep was worth more than his precious horse.

I got directions to his place and told him I'd be there within an hour.

"Sheesh," I said to Rusty after I hung up the phone.

I showered and re-dressed, putting on my hiking boots and smearing sunscreen on everything that was left exposed. I rechecked my equipment and fit everything except the sleeping bag inside the duffle. I hoped Mr. Cowboy's horse could handle a person plus a little bit of gear. I made sure my maps and GPS were near the top of the bag.

Rusty trotted along beside me to the parking lot. I wrestled the duffle and sleeping bag while I used my key to open the back hatch of the Jeep.

"Okay, hop in," I told the dog, opening his back door once I had the gear stowed.

For some reason I glanced across the parking lot as I was opening my own door. One row over and four or five cars down from mine sat a midnight-blue sedan. The bright yellow and red New Mexico plate caught my eye. An electric shock of fear shot through me. The odds of a couple of tourists being at the same intersection at the same time in Carrizozo then ending up at the same motel as mine in another state in a metropolitan area of three and a half million people were staggering. Impossible, I'd say.

I scanned the windows facing the parking lot. Sheer drapes covered them all, revealing nothing.

My mind shot back over the trip. How many stops had I made along the way? How had they followed me without my seeing them? Especially once I hit city traffic after dark. Paranoia crept in. A transmitter of some kind. They could have attached it when I stopped for food in Las Cruces, perhaps. I reached into my glove compartment for a tire gauge.

Pretending to check tires, I ran my hand around the wheel well of each. Behind the right rear I found it—a tiny black plastic thing with a strong magnet on the back. I pulled it loose and noticed that a small red light on it was blinking with slow regularity, like an evil eye winking. Without thinking, I reached out and stuck it to the underside of the car next to mine, a white Cadillac.

Deal with that, suckers.

I got back into the Jeep and started it. I was backing out of my slot when I looked up and saw the man with the long wavy hair walking toward the blue car. Our eyes met for a fraction of a second. Oh, shit. Had he seen me move the transmitter? I thrust the Jeep in gear and raced out of the driveway without looking either way. In my rearview I could see him running for his car.

Rush hour traffic was well under way. I caught up with a pack of cars that were doing nearly sixty on the forty-five-limit boulevard. A couple of rash moves later I was well within their midst. It isn't easy making unsafe lane changes, speeding, and keeping your eyes on the rearview mirror at the same time. I took a couple of unnecessary turns, winding my way through a small residential area, watching behind me all the time. After I was pretty sure I'd lost him I consulted my map again and took a course that would lead me east past Apache Junction.

The stable consisted of a rustic wooden building and a couple of corrals containing a dozen or so horses that appeared content to chew on the wisps of hay sticking out of the wooden trough at one end of the pen. A shiny blue pickup truck with a white horse trailer hitched to it was parked at the right hand edge of the dirt parking area.

"Hi, you must be Charlie," said the man who came out of the wooden building. He looked like his voice had sounded on the phone, kind of rusted out in places. "I'm Bert."

"Okay if I leave my car there?" I asked. I'd backed into a spot where the vehicle would be shielded by the building from anyone driving down the road. I hoped my pursuers were good and lost by now but that paranoid feeling had tracked me all the way from the motel. What if they'd been able to listen to my phone calls—they could know exactly where I was headed.

Bert nodded assent and we went inside and transacted a little paperwork. "I'll let you take Molly. She's a nice gentle mare, but not so old that it'd take you forever to get there. And she's good around dogs. Smart to take you a dog along."

"Thanks." I showed him on the map roughly where I was going and told him I had a cell phone with me.

"That's fine if you can get it to work," he said. "Half the time them things don't do so good in the mountains. Might have to find yourself a high spot."

"Now this is where you say you started before?" he said,

indicating the trailhead I'd shown him on the topo map. "Okay, here's where you are now. You'll want to take the trail from our place, right to here." He drew a thick line on my map with a pencil. "That's gonna tie you in with the one you were on."

I studied the map for a minute. Today's route was longer than the original one but not by much. And it tied in to the main trail before the point where I'd need to be watching for Willie's markers.

We went out to the Jeep, where I retrieved my duffle and sleeping bag while Bert singled out Molly, a trim palomino, from the crowd of horses and led her out of the corral. She nudged at me with her velvety nose and I stroked her forehead.

"Don't look she'll have no trouble makin' friends," Bert said. "She's a good 'un."

I reached into the duffle and pulled out an apple I'd snagged from the motel's free continental breakfast and cut a chunk off it with my pocketknife. Mollie took it gently with her teeth and crunched at it. Just to keep peace I cut a smaller chunk and gave it to Rusty. Each of them got one more piece before the apple was gone.

Wiping the juice off my hands and knife onto my jeans, I stashed the knife and pulled out the GPS. The horse turned her head to look at it, hoping for more treats, and I showed her it wasn't edible.

"Whatcha got there?" Bert asked.

I showed him how I programmed in our current location. "Now I can find my way back here from anywhere."

"Well, I'll be danged. Heard of them things but never seen one before."

He helped me strap my pack behind the saddle and he seemed a bit more at ease with our deal when I swung my leg over Mollie's back.

"I'm hoping to be back by tomorrow evening," I told him. "But I may decide to stay out an extra day or so. I've got food for four days."

"Okay," he said, turning to go back inside.

"Bert?"

He turned around.

"Listen, some guy and this lady with way too much makeup were hassling me at my motel this morning. I don't think they could've followed me here, but if anybody comes around asking where I've gone, don't let them know you've seen me, okay?"

"Sure thing," he replied easily.

"Long as he's got that credit card, he probably doesn't care what I do," I said to the horse and dog after Bert had disappeared.

I was right about my riding abilities coming back quickly. It felt a little awkward for the first few minutes but Molly was compliant and easygoing. From the stables we headed down a short dip through an old wash. The trail was clear as it came up the other side and within thirty minutes or so we'd connected to the main Forest Service trail.

Overhead, a thin layer of clouds filtered the sun's hot rays, cooling the temperature just a little. Willie's markers were easier to spot this time, since I knew what I was looking for, and by noon we'd reached the point where I'd decided to turn around the last time.

"Let's stop for some lunch." I needed to get down and

stretch my legs as much as I needed food.

My hip joints creaked as I swung down off the horse. "Oh, yeah, I'm gonna be feeling this tomorrow," I said to Rusty as I looped Molly's reins around a branch in the shade of a tree with widespread lacy leaves.

I pulled a little can of stew and one of my water bottles from my provisions, along with Willie's map.

"Okay, our next marker is a rock cairn about fifty yards down the next gully." I looked at the dog. "Do they say people who talk to animals are crazy? What do you think?"

He looked back at me like this was the most normal thing in the world. That was good enough for me.

I peeled back the pull-tab on my stew and ate it cold with the spoon on the pocketknife. I was feeling decidedly like a real outdoorsperson now. Tonight I'd have a hot dinner, I decided. One of those MREs, maybe. They even came with little desserts. Using a tiny bit of my precious water, I rinsed my spoon and dried it on the leg of my jeans. Boy, would they be ripe before this trip was over. The empty can and lid went into a plastic bag I'd brought along for the purpose, believing that hikers should always pack all trash out with them. I stuffed everything back into the duffle on Molly's back and did a couple of leg stretches before climbing back on.

"Westward, ho-oh!" I yelled to Rusty, pointing down the trail. Being alone in the desert with two animals for company was helping me drop all my inhibitions, obviously.

The terrain was becoming rockier now, and I had to watch carefully for the very faint path. Rusty loped ahead, nose to the ground occasionally. He seemed to have a pretty good idea of where to go and I wondered if he might be catching a scent, animal or human. If it was human, I hoped it was Willie McBride.

We came upon the wash indicated on Willie's map sooner than I expected. The rocky ground dropped away thirty or forty feet below us. I pulled the map out to verify. Sure enough, there was Weaver's Needle on our left. According to the topo map this gully would lead us into a sort of canyon with pretty steep sides. Looking to my right—that appeared to be true. A mountain covered with boulders rose sharply to the east of us.

"Okay," I said. "Let's see how we're going to get down there."

Rusty trotted back and forth, sniffing the ground. I turned Molly to my left, toward ground that seemed a little less steep. The dog found a place where a winding route appeared, a narrow opening of sand between the rocks. I guided Molly toward it. She hesitated at first. But Rusty, seeing that this is what I wanted to do, led the way. He bounded downward with no reservations. The horse picked her way delicately through the openings, following him. I simply hung on and tried not to throw her off balance.

At the bottom was a smooth highway of sand, easy to follow. Molly wanted a little more freedom now and I let her trot happily for a short while. Then I saw a hoofprint in the sand.

NINETEEN

"Whoa, there girl," I said, pulling her up. I stared hard at the sandy surface.

There, clearly, where the wind had been unable to blow them away were two sets of prints. One was either a small horse or, more likely, a donkey and the other was human. I slipped down from my saddle to look closer.

The human tracks looked like western boots, smooth bottoms, deeper heel. Now I'd like to be able to say that I could tell it was a male, slender and probably in his eighties—but I couldn't. I stared at the prints a long time. I traced the outline of one boot print with my finger. Then I looked up at the canyon sides that rose on either side of me.

The only sound was the rhythmic chirping of cicadas and the occasional screech of a bird. Even the wind was silent down here. I stood up slowly and looked around.

"Come on," I whispered to my companions.

I gathered Molly's reins in and led her behind me. Rusty stayed near my heel, obviously sensing something in my tone. I tiptoed for awhile, then realized that was pretty silly. The tracks were clear and easy to follow, messed up only now and then as some small animal's prints brushed across the trail. I paused and pulled Willie's sketch from my back pocket with my left hand, keeping hold of Molly with the right.

The trail on the map followed this canyon for perhaps a quarter of a mile. Then the directions became less precise. There was a large X ahead and to the left. But no indication of what kind of marker I should be looking for. I let out a breath of frustration.

Willie, of course, knew what to look for. His map wasn't meant to allow anyone to walk right up to his mine and help themselves. I stuffed the map back into my pocket and continued to follow the tracks.

At least thirty minutes had passed since we'd wound our way down into the gully. I consulted the map again and decided the perspective must be off. The tracks led deeper into the canyon, whose walls now rose steeply a hundred or more feet above our heads. Now completely in shadow, the air became cooler here.

Then abruptly the tracks ended.

I stopped short, surprised.

Looked again at the steep canyon walls. An eerie feeling crept across the back of my neck. I looked at Rusty. He'd wandered to the edge of the sandy gully and sniffed casually at a rock. Molly seemed at ease. I decided I was just giving myself the creeps, imagining things that weren't there.

I scanned the edges of the wash for some sign of where the tracks might have gone. At first glance I noticed only boulders, cactus and weeds—nothing different. Then I noticed it, on my left about twenty yards ahead, a small wooden cross. The only man-made object I'd seen in hours.

A cross.

An X.

I nudged Molly's side and started walking toward it. The piles of boulders continued upward, without a break that I could see.

"C'mere," I whispered to Rusty, waving him over. "Hold on to her."

He took Molly's reins in his mouth and sat down on my command. The docile horse stood quietly.

I crept slowly toward the edge of the sand, looking up at the small cross, which stood about twenty feet above me. Gingerly testing each rock I stepped up a level, then another. When I reached the cross I noticed that it had been there a long time. It was made of weathered wood, gray now, with deep crevices outlining the grain. Crusted dirt covered the west-facing surfaces, blown there by storm winds. I stood beside it and looked around.

Below me, Rusty waited patiently, still holding the horse's reins. I turned slowly and there at my feet was an opening.

From the bottom of the gully it hadn't been apparent, but at this height I could tell that the cross actually stood on a little promontory that had formed when rushing water had hit some particularly large boulders and redirected itself downward at a different angle. The resulting formation was a bit of a mini-canyon, with an opening into the side of the large canyon. Protected from water and weather, it was probably also difficult to spot from the air. I turned in all directions.

The narrow opening could easily be a mine, I thought. At the mouth it was probably four feet high and three feet wide. I edged my way down to it, losing sight of my animals as I dropped below the wooden cross. I quickly discovered that I couldn't tell a thing by standing outside the hole, and decided I wasn't about to go in there without a light. As far as I knew, it could just as easily be a mountain lion's dwelling. I backed away, crawling back up toward the cross.

Rusty had gotten to his feet and Molly shifted with uncertainty.

"It's okay," I called out. "I'm back."

My voice echoed crazily off the multitude of rock surfaces.

A slight breeze ruffled my hair as I looked back up and down the sandy wash below me. I still hadn't answered my initial question. There were the tracks—two sets of them including mine—leading right to this spot. Then they abruptly stopped. Where had they gone? And was it Willie McBride I'd been following?

Rusty whined.

"Okay, I'm coming," I assured him. I started down the rocky incline.

About five feet from the cross I spotted the answer. Brush marks.

The person had used the classic old Indian trick of swiping out his tracks. Whether he'd used a tree branch or something else, I couldn't tell, but I could see the wide arcs sweeping across the sandy streambed. I'd missed them before because my angle wasn't quite right. It was probably only because of the sun's position right now that I could see them at all. I stayed in place and scanned ahead. The brush marks continued around the next curve in the wash.

I scrambled down to the sand.

"Come on," I whispered to Rusty, taking Molly's reins from him.

I climbed into the saddle again and we followed the brush marks. As we rounded the curve my eyes searched for traces. It was like working a difficult jigsaw puzzle, where just the faintest nuance of color is going to tell you which is the right piece. They were there but hard to spot. I walked the horse slowly, following them for perhaps another quarter mile. The canyon was becoming increasingly narrow, only about thirty feet wide at this point. I felt Molly's nervousness as her head turned, eyeing the steep rocks beside us. I found myself doing the same.

And there it was.

Tucked into a hollow behind a huge boulder was a narrow path leading toward the top. A small clearing, no more than twenty or thirty feet in diameter, stood above us about twenty feet above the sandy bottom. The path led to it then continued to wind its way through the boulders to the top of the ridge. In the middle of the clearing were the remains of a tiny campfire. A slender stream of smoke rose from its center. I dismounted and handed off the reins to Rusty once more, signaling him to wait there.

The path was narrow but well worn and not nearly as hard to follow as the one we'd taken through the desert. I walked up to the campfire and stooped over it, stretching my hand over the center. It had been hastily covered in dirt but was still warm. I glanced around the area.

The fragile desert grass had been trampled into the dusty earth. A couple of good-sized rocks with flat tops had been arranged as seats near the fire. At the far edge of the clearing, out of sight from below, stood an old-fashioned pup tent, the kind we rigged up as kids where you basically have a blanket held up at either end by a couple of little poles. They always drooped in the center and this one was no exception. Inside the tent I could see a cardboard box with the top flaps folded closed.

Beyond the tent, I realized that the little clearing extended beyond what I'd seen from below. A second clear area, this one smaller than the first, was ringed by boulders. The vegetation in this area was far greener, indicating that there must be a small spring among the boulders. Together in an aerial view the two spots would resemble a figure eight. Tethered to the ground in the second clearing was a small mule. It was nosing through the grass and didn't appear to notice me. I turned slowly, surveying the spot but didn't see any other sign of the inhabitant.

Was this Willie McBride's camp?

I called out his name. No response but the gradually increasing wind.

Hmm. Now what?

Below me Rusty and Molly waited patiently. I looked around the camp once more but still didn't see any sign of Willie. And what if it wasn't Willie's camp? What if I'd just tracked a stranger up here? The chill that tickled my bare arms wasn't entirely due to the thickening clouds. I was a trespasser here. I decided to turn around. I followed the little path back down to the sandy bottom.

"What do you think, buddy?" I asked the dog. "Nobody's up there."

I took Molly's reins and stroked the horse's neck. The wind was picking up. If I hoped to get back to civilization before nightfall I needed to head back now. Right now. If I decided to camp out I better be thinking about a spot soon. I couldn't turn back, I decided. I'd come too far to find Willie. If there was any chance this was his camp I needed to find him. I looked back up at the tent in the clearing. Maybe if I just looked through that cardboard box—I might find something that would verify whether I was near McBride or whether I'd tracked a total stranger.

Leaving the animals behind, I started up the path again.

"Hold it right there, missy."

I stared up. Right into the muzzle of a gun.

TWENTY

"Willie McBride?" I asked.

"I heard you the first time, when you shouted it out for the whole world," he growled.

He didn't look much like the photo Dorothy had given me. But he looked more like I'd pictured him. Faded Levi's, flannel shirt, beat up straw cowboy hat with wisps of thin white hair showing below. His weathered face was screwed up into a frown and looked far more at home here in this setting than in the photo, wearing his one suit and tie. One gnarled hand held a Smith and Wesson .357, the other rested dramatically on his hip.

"Who are you?" The hand holding the gun wavered, sending the barrel on a spasmodic course from my chest to my head and down to my abdomen. His finger was firmly on the trigger, I noticed.

Behind me Rusty growled and McBride swung the gun toward him.

"Rusty! No!" I ordered. "Back away."

The dog backed off two paces but didn't sit down.

McBride brought the gun back up at me. His hand still tremored like a shrub in an earthquake.

"Could you aim that thing somewhere else?" I asked.

My voice didn't come out nearly as steady as I wanted it to.

"Not till I know who you are," he said, steadying the gun with both hands and aiming it at my face. "What do you want with me?"

I took a shaky breath. "My name's Charlie Parker. Your family hired me to find you. They've been worried."

His eyes narrowed. "Which one? Who hired you?"

I had a feeling the wrong answer here would turn me into vulture food.

"Well, all of them," I hedged. "Melanie's real worried. And Bea. You know there was a big reunion at Dorothy's and they all really wanted you there."

"Dorothy, huh. She hire you?"

"Well, like I said, they all want to know you're safe." I focused for a second on the gun barrel and swallowed. "Look, you're a grown man. I can't make you go back if you don't want to."

"You can't?" For the first time the gun drifted away.

"I'm not the law." I guessed this wasn't the best time to mention that the law was looking for him too. "Look, could we maybe sit down for a little bit?"

"Better bring your horse on up here," he said. "Tether her over there by Little Bit."

Molly looked relieved when I walked back down the incline to get her. I patted her neck and spoke gently to her as I led her up the narrow path and tied her reins around a boulder in the mule's clearing. Clouds covered the sky completely now and the wind sent a distinct chill through the air. I pulled my jacket from the duffle.

McBride had stuck the gun into the waistband of his Levi's and was stirring the campfire back to life.

"Better plan on staying the night up here," he said. "Wouldn't be smart to head down that wash right now."

He got a small flame going and added a few bits of sagebrush to it. "You got your own food?" he asked.

"Yeah. I'd be happy to share, if you like MREs." I sat on one of the flat rocks and he took the other

He made a sound that came out something like a snort, something like a laugh.

The light was fading quickly now and he suggested we cook our dinner while we had a little light to work by. I retrieved one of my packeted meals and a bottle of water. Drake had showed me how these things worked once. Willie pulled the box from his tent and rummaged through it, coming up with a can of chili and a spoon. While he ratcheted the lid of the can with a tool on his pocketknife, I ripped the top off the plastic MRE bag and examined the contents. I had a main dish of macaroni and cheese, a vacuum-sealed bag claiming to contain a biscuit, a similar one with a brownie—we'd see about that—and a packet of plastic flatware. I poured water into the mac and cheese dinner packet and set it against the base of my rock. Within minutes it began to boil.

Willie had stripped the paper label from his can of chili and set the can into the coals.

While dinner cooked, I pulled plastic bowls from my duffle and gave Rusty food and water. Although Molly seemed content sharing the desert grass and spring water with the mule, I opened the feedbag of oats Bert had sent along for her.

"So Dorothy couldn't stand me going off on my own," Willie said. We sat on our respective rocks, each eating our version of gourmet fare. "Had to send somebody to look for me."

"I guess so," I said noncommittally.

"Can't believe I ever claimed that woman as my daughter. Or the boy either." He chewed on his chili slowly.

"I guess every family's got someone they'd rather not claim."

"Well, the other two's okay, I guess. Bea turned out fine and she don't bother me much. Dorothy and Felix, though, they're a pair." He'd pulled a waxed paper tube of saltine crackers out and he dipped one into the can then stuffed the whole thing into his mouth. "Once she got that law degree, whew! It was like she all of a sudden knew everything and her old man knew nothin'. I got so sick of hearing how I needed me a will. Then I needed me a new will. Course she wasn't charging me no legal fees for it. I woulda sure put my foot down about that. No sir!"

"Why'd she say you needed a new one? Seems like one will'd be good enough for anybody," I said. We were falling into a comfortable conversation and I discovered that the MRE mac and cheese wasn't so bad.

"You'd think." He scraped at the sides of the chili can. "But Felix, now he's the one's been pestering me to death. Guess a person just shouldn't college educate their kids. Their mother really pushed for it though, rest her soul."

"What was Felix pestering about?"

"My land. Place in Albuquerque, in the north valley."

I didn't want to sidetrack him again by admitting that I'd been there.

"That boy wants me to deed the place over to him. He's got him a place in Socorro. Doesn't even want to live on my land."

"So why does he want it?"

"Mineral springs. There's two of 'em on the place. Strange, I always thought. None of the neighbors got springs on their places. These are just little ones, ya know. One of 'em's got covered over by now. But that Felix, he thinks he'll get 'em running again, build some fancy spa thing there, and get rich people from all over the place to come there and soak in the water. Ain't that the funniest thing you ever heard?" He chuckled out loud, presumably at the thought of people paying money to come sit in water that had been seeping out of his land for ages.

"Maybe there's more to it than that," I said, remembering Randel's suggestion that if the thermal resources were vast enough it might be a place to build a power plant. Either plan probably explained Felix's proprietary air the day I'd run into him at the spring.

"Well Felix sure has him some fancy ideas about it. It's that college education, ya know."

"So, do you think Dorothy's new version of the will has something in it about that?" I asked, opening my vacu-packed brownie.

"Wouldn't surprise me. I read the durn thing. Couldn't make sense of it a bit. That first will, the one she had me do up a long time ago? That wasn't so bad. I knew what it was saying. This thing, it's got all kinds of clauses—I think that's what they call 'em—clauses that don't make no sense at all. I said, 'I ain't signin' that thing till I know what it means'. She said, 'Dad you better do it now, you're not getting any younger'." He mimicked Dorothy's nasal whine pretty well. He stood up and chucked the chili can out into the bushes.

I forced myself not to say anything. I'd go out there later and pick up his trash and haul it back with my own. I crumpled my little bits of packaging materials, including the remains of the brownie. I'd always thought I never met a brownie I didn't like, but I finally had.

"She wanted me to sign that new will right there on the spot. Don't think she even showed it to the other kids. And she durn sure didn't want me to take it home with me. Hell, I mighta taken it into my head to show it to another lawyer and get me a second opinion. I said that to her once—about gettin' a second opinion—and she just about hit the roof."

I didn't have any trouble picturing that.

The wind had picked up even stronger now and a few drops sprinkled out of the sky. Lightning flashed in the distance beyond Weaver's Needle. Willie wandered outside the circle of firelight, mentioning something about seeing about a tree. It reminded me that I hadn't answered nature's call myself since early afternoon. Using my flashlight to be sure I wasn't about to surprise a rattlesnake, I found myself a bush in the opposite direction from where Willie'd gone.

I decided to set my tent up while I could still handle the flapping fabric. Rusty trotted along beside me while I unsaddled Molly and rubbed her down. The tent was relatively easy to master and I had it up in about ten minutes. I put the rain flaps over it and stashed all my other gear inside. The sprinkles of rain proved to be no more than that, for now anyway.

"Got some coffee going here," Willie said. He'd watched my progress with the tent. In the back of my mind I debated whether to invite him to share it. I hadn't much doubt that his little pup tent wouldn't survive if the wind got much stronger. But I still didn't really know him very well. I decided to have some coffee and think about it.

"Is that your mine back there?" I asked as we sat on our rocks again with mugs in hand.

For a minute I thought the gun was coming back out again.

"None a your damn business," he snarled. "Who told you about any mine anyway?"

"Melanie mentioned that you liked to go prospecting," I tried. "And, well, after Bud Tucker was murdered and your truck was found abandoned, it began to look like you might have been killed too. Keith Randel at the café in White Oaks was the only one who didn't believe it. He told me you had this favorite place and that you might have come here."

"Bud Tucker was murdered?" His face registered confusion.

"Well, that's the other thing I needed to talk to you about. Bud's daughter remembered the two of you going off together in White Oaks, back in February this was. So the police assumed you were together and that whoever shot Bud might have abducted you and taken your truck."

His brows pulled together as I talked. The confusion deepened.

"Bud Tucker wasn't murdered," he said. "Hell, I should know. I shot him myself."

TWENTY ONE

I think my mouth must have actually hung open. Time seemed suspended like something tangible in the air between us. Finally I found my voice.

"You shot Bud Tucker?"

"Yep. He, he . . ." His face crumpled as he realized what he was saying. "It wadn't no murder though. It was an accident."

"What?"

The old man set his coffee mug on the ground between his feet and gripped the sides of his head with both hands. Two wet tracks trailed down his cheeks. His beaten straw hat flipped off and fell behind him. He didn't notice. His fingers worked the scalp, as if he were trying to squeeze the memory out of his brain.

"Willie," I said gently, "tell me what happened."

His mouth worked rapidly but no words came out.

"The police found a pack of your things in one of the mines," I said. "A blanket and some clothes. And Bud was wearing one of your shirts. I found him. At first we thought it was you."

He stood up and paced to the far end of the clearing, like he wanted to just walk away but didn't know where he'd go. When he paced back toward me I noticed his eyes were bright with moisture. I patted the rock where he'd been sitting.

"Come tell me about it. Why was Bud wearing your shirt?"

He flopped down a little too hard on the rock seat and winced. He rubbed his lower back and said, "Shouldn't be doin' that, I guess." He stared into the fire.

"Whew—where to start," he said, wagging his head side to side. "Well, Bud and me went up to look around a little. We used to go prospecting together a lot. All over New Mexico and Arizona. Thought we'd found us the Lost Dutchman Mine once. Turned out to be nothin'. Anyway, I hadn't seen Bud in awhile so I called him up and said how about let's go find a few nuggets and he said okay, so I went down there in February and we were just gonna look around a little.

"Went into one of them mines, the two of us did, and we were pokin' around a little, goin' deeper and deeper, into a shaft we'd never been to before. Just lookin' at stuff. Well, it was the weirdest thing, what we found. Bunch of big cans of stuff, like five gallon buckets. Some of 'em had labels with real scientific names on 'em. Hell, I didn't know what any of it said really. Bud was moving a couple of the cans around to get a better look and I guess his arm brushed against one that had some spilled on the outside.

"Well, he starts shaking his arm like this—" he demonstrated "—and yelling 'ouch, ouch, this stuff's burnin' me,' and I didn't know what he'd gotten himself into so I just says, 'get the shirt off!' He did. He peeled that shirt off and sure enough that stuff'd eaten through the material and made his arm red in a little place. He threw the shirt on the ground and I got him a clean one out of my pack. We rinsed off his arm with some canteen water and he put my shirt on."

He got up and added more wood to the fire.

"When did the gun come into it?" I asked.

"I'm gettin' to that," he said. "Well, he'd just finished buttoning up the clean shirt when we heard a car drive up. It stopped right near my truck, where the road ends and the trail starts. So Bud and me says to each other, 'We better get outta here.' So we run out the mineshaft and decide to hide out in one of them old buildings. There's only one that ain't about ready to fall down so we choose that one. And we see these two guys walk up this path to the mine we'd just left. One of 'em's a local guy. Bud knew him by name but I can't remember what it was. And the other guy was some greasy-looking city dude. Long hair down to his ass—in a *braid*, if you can believe that.

"They head for the mine and about two minutes later they're sneaking back out and we know that they found Bud's shirt and are out looking for us. I mean, with my truck parked there and all it must have been pretty clear that we were still around. We're scared. That city guy's got a gun that he's pointing around so I pull out my little sidearm here just to be ready."

His voice wavered and he scrubbed at his face with his hands.

"Guess I wasn't too steady with her that day," he continued, "cause the next thing I know, she fires. Just like that. I didn't even know I'd put my finger on the trigger but *blam*, there went a shot. And I looked over and there was Bud, lyin' on the floor, just still as de—" His voice cracked.

He stood up and paced the length of the clearing again. Took a deep, ragged breath.

"I didn't know what to do. It was gonna be a matter of seconds before those two guys found me. No way they didn't hear that shot. Only thing I could think was, run. So I did. Hid behind some bushes while they searched the buildings. Soon as they saw Bud, they left. Got in this dark blue car and hightailed it outta there. Well, I did the same. Drove and drove."

"Until you got to Las Cruces."

He nodded.

"Then you remembered that they'd seen your truck and could easily identify it, so you got some money at the ATM and bought a bus ticket to Phoenix."

"You figured all that out?" he asked, wide-eyed.

"It wasn't difficult. The police traced the vehicle right away after we started looking for you." I shifted position on the rock. The seat was starting to get hard. "After you got to Phoenix, you got more money out of your account. Then they lost track of you."

"Yep. Took some more money outta the bank and bought Little Bit from this guy I knew here a long time ago. Got me a few supplies and came up here. Are the police still after me?"

I didn't tell him that they never had been, except for questioning. "I don't think so, Willie. But what about your family?"

"Let me think about that." He stared into the fire for ten minutes or so, then announced, "I'm hittin' the sack now." He poured the dregs of his coffee cup onto the ground and edged into his tent, placing the cardboard carton across the entrance.

I looked over at Rusty who was lying contentedly on the ground behind my rock seat. I pulled my jacket tighter around my shoulders, eased off the rock and sat on the earth in front of it, using the rock as a backrest. I stared up at the briskly moving clouds until the fire had almost completely died away.

Sometime during the night the storm intensified, whipping the flaps of my tent wildly a couple of times then dying down. I heard thunder in the distance but the rain never materialized here. I burrowed down into my sleeping bag and Rusty posted himself just inside the tent's zipped door.

By daylight my body was so stiff I could hardly crawl from my little cocoon. I rummaged through my things and swallowed three ibuprofin with some of my bottled water. I'd slept soundly, considering the rough conditions and everything I had on my mind.

Today I had to decide what to do about Willie.

While I wasn't particularly eager to return him to the loving arms of either Felix or Dorothy, I did feel the rest of the family needed to know that he was alive and well. And if it became known that he was okay, the police just might want to ask some more questions. And I couldn't deny the fact that he'd confessed to shooting Bud Tucker.

All this was running through my mind as I debated whether to slip back into the somewhat crusty jeans I'd removed the night before, which would leave me without a clean pair to wear home. My shirt wasn't in much better shape, but I decided I'd rather come back from the trail ride filthy so I could shower and change into clean clothes back in my unused motel room.

I pulled on the smelly set and emerged from the tent. The air was fresh with the scent of moisture on sage. I took a deep breath and was astounded to see that the sandy wash I'd traversed the day before was now a rushing stream. I quickly checked to be sure the animals were still with us.

Little Bit and Molly grazed happily in their little area and Rusty was, as always, at my side hoping food would soon appear.

"Can you believe this runoff?" I said to Willie as he emerged from his tent. It looked little the worse for wear through the windy night. I wondered if he'd gotten up to reset it at some point.

He noticed the rushing water for the first time. "Hell fire!" he shouted. "My mining gear!" He started to rush down the path toward the water.

"Willie! No! That water's got to be—" I was about to say ten feet deep, but it was too late. He'd run right into it and was already five yards downstream.

Without thinking I raced after him and plunged in.

TWENTY TWO

The first dunk took my breath away. The silty brown torrent was ice cold. I came up with a gasp and looked around for Willie. He was ahead by ten yards now, paddling as he rode the current, working his way across to the side where his mine was. I bobbed again, touched the bottom and slung water from my eyes.

I spat foamy water and tried to paddle after Willie. My feet touched bottom for an instant. I tried to kick off and propel myself across but succeeded only in sending myself downstream facing backward.

Anyone who thinks they can battle Mother Nature and win needs a lesson like this one. I managed to get myself facing forward again, but after only a couple of minutes struggling against the current I gave in and rode it down. I could vaguely hear Rusty barking behind me but couldn't turn my head to look. I kept my eyes on Willie's bobbing head. He was making progress to the far side and I did my best to follow his path.

Muddy water filled my eyes again and again.

Willie began to slow, reaching out for tree branches along the bank. I came up behind him, almost close enough to grab for him. Missed. He sped ahead again, turning his head as he passed his wooden cross marker.

"Help—" His words were taken away as he went under.

My feet hit the bottom and I tried to dig them in. Bad idea. The water rolled me over and threw me up butt-first. I righted myself, choking and swiping at the long strands of wet hair pasted over my face, looking around to get my bearings. Rusty was behind me, paddling furiously. Willie's head bounced like a cork as he popped above the surface ahead of me. I lifted my feet and rode the current after him.

Straining, I reached out and got a fistful of shirt collar. I gripped the shirt and the nearly weightless man in it. My right hand full of shirt, I tried to paddle with my left. When my feet hit the bottom for a second, I pushed toward the bank, wondering what I'd do if we both hit the rocks. The canyon walls were much lower now, but we'd drifted back to centerstream. I watched for any opening. Ahead on the left, a good-sized sandbar. I focused all my energy there. With burning arms and legs that had gone numb, I pushed.

Willie had stared at me when I first grabbed him. Now he rode along, limp. The water tried to carry us around the sandbar, back to the deeper channel, but I wouldn't let it.

"No!" I shouted. I felt my knees hit bottom. Crawled, using my one free hand to pull us onto the high ground. Willie suddenly weighed a ton. I gripped him under both arms and pulled, scrambling on my knees to work his body onto firm sand.

Coming at me, I could see Rusty still free-floating. I raised one arm and waved to get his attention. It wasn't necessary. He was headed toward me with the single-mindedness that only animals have. At last his feet touched bottom and he crawled forward with everything he could muster.

A swirl of brown water rushed up onto our tiny shore. I pushed Rusty toward a high spot with one hand while I grabbed again at Willie's shirt collar with the other. The water foamed over my legs but wasn't able to grip me. I watched Willie sputter and cough

Then I collapsed.

TWENTY THREE

Hot sun blazed into my eyes when I tried to open them.

I raised one hand to shade my face. Granules of sand fell into my right eye and I slammed them shut again. Rolled to my side and shook my face. My hair hung to my shoulders in muddy ropes. I shrugged a shoulder upward and wiped my face against it. On hands and knees I pushed myself up and sat on my haunches.

Willie lay facedown on the sandbar, his feet extended into the water. Rusty was higher, on dry ground. He shook himself vigorously then cocked his head toward me.

"Oh, god," I groaned, brushing my hands against my pant legs to remove some of the sand.

Rusty barked sharply twice to let me know he was all right. He trotted over to me and licked my face. Decided sand didn't taste all that great and backed away. I reached out and draped my hand over his shoulders.

"You scared me back there," I said. "Why'd you jump in, you silly thing."

He barked again.

Willie moaned. I crawled to him and rolled him onto his side. His eyes were wide open, his mouth working. He reached up to wipe sand off his lips, only to discover that his hands were even more coated.

"Hell of a thing," he grumbled.

"Are you all right?" I asked, watching him carefully.

"Hell, yes. Been through worse than this," he growled.

Maybe so, I thought, but not at the age of eighty-four.

He raised himself to his knees then used my shoulder to brace himself while he stood. It took a few seconds but he soon stood upright, shaking out his limbs in the human version of what Rusty had just done. I followed his example, brushing off as much sand as I could.

Considering that we'd only lain there a few minutes the water had receded remarkably. What had been a gushing torrent earlier was now just a steady flow.

"Flash flood," Willie said.

"No kidding. Why on earth did you jump in there?"

"Why'd you?"

"To save your sorry ass. You were headed downstream fast."

"Hell, I've survived worse in my day. Woulda done just fine here too."

There was no point in arguing with him. I jammed my hands into my back pockets and stared upstream. Not a cloud remained in the sky. Last night's storm that skipped our campsite entirely and dumped its fury in the mountains had dissipated and blown away in tatters of harmless vapor.

"Water's down quite a bit," I said. "I think it'll be simpler to wait here until we can walk back up the wash than to try to make it across country."

Especially without a compass. It would be too easy to

get off course dodging the huge boulders above. The streambed was our best bet. I sat down beside Rusty and put an arm around him.

"Got any food with you?" Willie asked. "I'm gettin' hungry."

I shot him a look and he closed his mouth.

He paced the sandbar restlessly. I kept an eye on him, worried that he'd set off again into the water. The sun beat down, drying our clothes quickly. A mosquito discovered me and wouldn't stop buzzing around my face. I waved it away for several minutes until it finally landed on the exposed skin of my forearm and I dispensed with it with a slap. I wanted nothing more at this moment than a hot shower and clean clothes. Preferably in my own shower at home.

An hour went by, according to my dirty but waterproof watch. The rushing water receded from the edges of the wash, running now in a ribbon about ten feet wide down the center.

"Let's try it," I said. "Stay close to the edges."

I soon discovered that the earth at the edges was dense clay that stuck to the bottoms of shoes in a thick muck. We moved onto the sandier portion, scuffing the clay off as we walked. Rusty trotted ahead. I noticed that his fur had dried now in crusty pointed tufts. He'd need a bath too as soon as we got home. Willie and I walked separately, neither of us speaking. All I could think about was getting packed up and getting home.

"Want to see my gold mine?" Willie asked. He pointed across the wash at the wooden cross on the hillside.

The stream of water in the center of the wash was now

no more than five feet wide and probably only ankle deep.

"I want to check on things up there," he said. "Make sure none of my stuff washed out. You can come if you want to."

I knew it was his way of saying he trusted me and hoped I wasn't still mad at him.

"Thanks, Willie, but I think I'll start packing up my stuff. You go ahead." I watched him approach the running water. "Be careful there. Make sure you have a firm footing."

He stepped into the water with a lot more respect than he'd shown the first time. It only took him three steps to cross to the dry side and he turned to wave at me. I waved and continued until I came to the narrow path that led to our campsite.

The small clearings looked as though nothing had happened. Both tents stood in place; the horse and mule were standing contentedly at their tethers. Last night's fire was long gone, so I poked around in the ashes, laid out some brush and kindling, and struck a match to it. Soon I had enough flame to heat a coffeepot.

Last night Willie had made some strong concoction full of coffee grounds but I didn't have his recipe. I decided to just heat clean water in Willie's battered pot and use my little packet of instant coffee from last night's MRE. While the water heated I disassembled my tent and rolled it into its carry bag. Among my stash of food were two more Twinkies and a packaged fruit pie, the kind loaded with fat and calories. I opted for that.

I rinsed my hands with a little of my drinking water, wishing for soap but there was none. With most of my gear stowed in the duffle and my pot of water boiling, I sat on my rock and drank my instant coffee with my nutritious breakfast.

Call it delayed reaction, call it post-traumatic something . . . I don't know. I just know that as I sat there on that rock seat by a campfire somewhere in the mountains of Arizona I was hit by a sudden case of the shakes. The morning's harrowing ride down the rapids came back at me full-force. My hands began shaking first, sloshing coffee out of the mug and onto my already-crusty jeans leg. I set the mug in the dirt and hugged myself. My shoulders picked up the shiver and it traveled throughout my body.

Rusty came over to me and I hugged him while he licked my hands generously.

The tremor passed finally, leaving me feeling wrung out and depleted.

I wondered if I could reach Drake by phone. We hadn't touched base in three days and he'd probably tried to call me. He would be worried by now. I pulled the cell phone from my bag and turned it on. No service, the little symbol read. I looked around. I was fairly well surrounded by rocky mountains. I'd try it again when I reached higher ground.

Willie came walking up the path as I was putting my phone away.

"Want to see what gold mining's all about?" he asked, holding out something in the palm of his hand.

It was a small bag made from an old sock with the top cut off and a drawstring added. He gently loosened the string and dumped the contents into his hand. There were four gold nuggets, the largest about the size of a lima bean.

"This here's my little stash," he grinned. "My rainy day money."

Unfortunate choice of words, I thought, considering the last rainy day could have well ended his life.

"Those are pretty neat, Willie," I said. "They come from your mine here?"

"Yep. Don't tell nobody though." He tucked the nuggets back into the bag and the bag into his pants pocket.

"I wouldn't do that," I assured him.

He started to pour from the coffeepot into his mug. "What the hell's this?" he asked when the liquid came out clear.

I explained what I'd done. "You'll have to do your magic to make it coffee," I told him.

He rummaged through his box of supplies muttering something that contained the word "women."

"I ain't goin' back with you, ya know," he said once we were seated again on our rocks with real coffee to drink.

"I didn't expect you would," I told him. "Had a feeling about that."

"Well, you expected right."

"What shall I tell them?" I hadn't yet thought through a good way to explain this to Dorothy.

"Tell 'em you never found me," he said.

"What about Melanie? And Bea? They're both really worried."

He set his mug down and fidgeted with the fire. I watched him for a good five minutes, giving him the raised-eyebrow question whenever he glanced my way.

"Well, all right. You can tell them two. But do you have to tell 'em where I am?"

"What am I going to say? That I found you but I didn't know where I was at the time?"

He looked all around. "Well, that's pretty close to true, ain't it?"

He had a point. In fact, with his little sketch of a map now nothing more than a wad of pulp in my back jeans pocket, I wasn't sure I could find the place again no matter how much time I had.

"What about the law?" I asked. "You confessed to me that you'd killed a man."

For a minute he looked almost panicky.

"Willie, it sounds like it was an accident." I rinsed my mug and packed it away. "I'll have to think about it."

I saddled Molly and strapped the duffle and sleeping bag behind the saddle. Willie watched but didn't move from his seat by the fire.

"What about your place in Albuquerque?" I asked. "Don't you ever plan to go back there?"

"Back to the loving arms of my family?" He grinned and adopted the same tone I'd just used. "I don't know. I'll have to think about it."

TWENTY FOUR

From my purse down in the bottom of my duffle I
scrounged up a business card and handed it to Willie.

"Next time you go to town for supplies, call me," I told
him. "I'll let you know how things worked out."

I thought he'd want to know what I ended up telling
his family and how they took it, but he simply shrugged
and stuck the card into his pocket. I rechecked my saddle
cinch and mounted.

"Now that I've lost my map to get myself out of here,
refresh my memory for me," I asked.

"Down the wash to the white rock," he said. "You didn't
see it on the way up here, cause it's only visible from this
side."

"I go past the wooden cross . . ."

" 'Nother half mile or so. On your left you'll see a big
rock with a white heart painted on it. Under the heart is
W+C."

I opened my mouth but he interrupted.

"Right there's where your trail leads you up the canyon
side."

He reviewed the other markers. I remembered them
anyway.

"What's the significance of the white heart?" I asked.

He grinned widely, his grizzled face crinkling into a roadmap of wrinkles. "Hunh-uh, ain't telling that story."

He slapped Molly on the rump and I guided her carefully down to the sandy wash. The water flow had stopped now, leaving only a damp strip down the center of the gully. The sand at the edges was completely dry where there had been a rushing torrent scarcely two hours ago. No wonder people don't believe stories about flash floods.

I spotted the white heart easily enough and followed the trail. The other markers weren't difficult to find and by mid-afternoon I was approaching the horse's home stable. She knew we were getting close and her gait picked up to an all-out gallop in the last quarter mile. I reined her in, not wanting to return her to Bert all coated with lather. She trotted peacefully the final few hundred feet.

There sat my Jeep in the parking area and there came Bert to greet us. Everything looked absolutely normal.

"Have yourself a good time?" Bert asked, coming to take Molly's reins as I unstrapped my pack.

"Sure did. Quite an adventure, the desert."

He eyed my muddy clothing and Rusty's caked fur, then inspected Molly's clean legs and coat. He didn't say a word.

I stowed my gear in the Jeep, assured myself that my bill was settled with Bert, and opened the back door for Rusty. My hands were a little shaky as I inserted my key in the ignition. Back in my room it was all I could do to peel off my crusty clothing and stuff it into the freebie plastic laundry bag before turning on the hot water tap and indulging myself in a steamy shower. I shampooed my hair twice then decided I might as well get the other fun chore over with. I called Rusty into the shower with me—not a difficult task since he loves water—and dumped half the remaining shampoo on him. After a good scrubbing and thorough rinse we both felt better. We indulged ourselves by using every one of the room's towels. I even re-rinsed the tub twice to remove all traces of the sand we'd brought back with us. I slipped into my last set of clean clothes and debated whether to call Drake.

Knowing the firefighter's schedule I guessed he wouldn't be in his room for another couple of hours at least. I decided that meanwhile I'd get some food and try to unwind. After two days of packaged, powdered, non-tasty grub on the trail I wanted something substantial, but I couldn't make myself face going out in the traffic. I ended up calling a pizza delivery place and lounging back on the bed with the television on until my dinner arrived.

Once I finished eating I found myself fighting the drowsies but knew I better call Drake before I was completely out of it for the night.

"Where have you been?" he demanded when he heard my voice.

"Didn't you get my message that I was coming back to Arizona?"

"Yeah, but you didn't say where you were staying or what you were doing there."

"I found Willie McBride," I said, not wanting to get into the minutiae of reporting every little detail. I related the story, skipping over the scarier details, making it sound more like I'd just ridden out to Willie's camp and had a nice little visit with him.

"I don't know what I'll tell Dorothy. He really doesn't want to face her again," I said. "And I can't really blame him, knowing that she really didn't care about whether he made it to the reunion or not. She's really just after his money."

"What about the other situation, back in White Oaks?" he asked.

"Well, that's changed a bit too," I told him. "I told you about the explosion at the mine? Turns out one victim was involved with drug dealers—Willie and his friend Bud saw them—and the other victim was Bud's daughter, Sophie. Rumors are flying all over town that Sophie was romantically involved with Rory Daniels. Sheriff Buckman says they're close to solving all three deaths out there but he won't say how. I tried to warn Willie that he's probably still a suspect as far as Buckman is concerned."

He filled me in on his adventures for the day, which almost sounded tame compared to mine. Everything was catching up with me and by the time we hung up I was blinking to stay awake. I pulled my jeans off and crawled between the sheets wearing my T-shirt and undies.

By the next morning I was feeling much better—clean and refreshed. My thighs were still tender from the unaccustomed time on horseback but the other adventure seemed well behind me. After helping myself to a bagel and coffee from the continental breakfast spread and feeding Rusty his usual nuggets in the room, we were ready to head for home.

The morning air was warm already. Within a month or less, Phoenix would probably be hitting the hundreds during the day. Good time to head back to our much cooler elevation. The desert flora was crisp and green this early in the morning as we passed through the little towns of Globe and Superior.

Rusty settled into the back seat and I leaned back in my seat getting comfortable for the long drive. At Show Low, a small town in a pretty mountain setting with lots of pine trees, I stopped to top off the tank before starting into the long stretch where it would be eighty or more miles between stations. The small town buzzed with everyday activity, pickup trucks parked in front of the feed store, women with small children walking across the parking lot at the grocery. I clipped Rusty's leash to him and led him to a dirt lot at the back of the station. As we came around the side of the building, after he'd done his business, I caught a glimpse of a dark blue car cruising slowly past the station. My muscles tensed. I hung to the side of the building and peered toward the street. The road curved so the car was out of sight by the time I might have gotten a look at the license plate. I stood there a minute, unsure what to do.

Rusty had reached the end of the leash now and my arm yanked forward as his weight pulled at me. He turned a questioning look my way.

Probably wasn't the same car at all, I rationalized. What were the odds?

Rusty climbed back into his seat. On an impulse I pulled out my cell phone and dialed Randy Buckman's number.

"Know a guy with long wavy hair, sometimes wears it braided, who might have a reason to be following me?" I asked without preamble when he came on the line.

"Charlie? Where are you?"

I explained that I'd come to Arizona looking for Willie McBride and told him about my encounters with the dark blue car.

"Normally I wouldn't have thought much of it, but it was way too coincidental that these people would have taken the same route to Arizona and then ended up at the same motel where I was. That's when I decided to check my vehicle."

He let out a sharp *Whew* when I told him about finding the transmitter.

"Well, I don't know about the dark blue car," he said. "But by your description of the man he could be Geraldo Rodriquez. He's a known drug dealer out of El Paso. We've suspected that he might've been involved with Rory and whatever lab he was supplying the chemicals to. Did he have a real thin mustache?"

"I think so. Didn't really get close enough to tell."

"This guy does—or he did in his mug shot. Guess he could have shaved it. But he's pretty proud of that thick, wavy hair. Doubt he'd change that." He backed away from the phone and cleared his throat. "Watch out for him, Charlie. This guy's bad, bad news. The kind who'd probably kill you just for the fun of it."

"Why would he be after me?" I shuffled the cell phone to my other ear, staring at the streets around me.

"My guess is that he's really after McBride. We think he and Bud must've seen the druggies up there at the mine. It's probably what got Bud shot and the reason they'd want to silence McBride too. Just be careful and don't let this guy get near you, especially alone."

I clicked off and locked all my car doors.

Thin mustache. I knew someone else with a thin mustache who definitely wanted to know where Willie McBride was. Someone who could have worn a wig as a disguise. The thought flitted through my head, even though I felt sure Buckman was right. Felix drove a light colored car, anyway.

Anyone can rent a car, Charlie.

And Felix had a lot more reason to want to find his father.

I shook off the feeling and started the Jeep. Drove slowly through town, watching every parking lot and intersection for a dark blue car with a bright yellow plate. Nothing.

North of Show Low the road straightened out, through the little town of Snowflake, where I saw signs for a turnoff to Heber, where Drake was fighting the fire. A big part of me wanted to turn off and find him and allow myself to be enfolded into his comforting arms. It only took a minute to get back to the reality that he wasn't in snuggling position, flying over a raging fire with all his powers of concentration needed there. I drove through, eager now just to cover the miles and get home. There was about fifty miles of two-lane empty road ahead before I'd come to Interstate 40, then a good four hours among eighteen-wheeler traffic before I'd reach Albuquerque. And, I still had to figure out what I was going to tell Dorothy about her father's whereabouts.

It was about twenty miles into the fifty-mile stretch of nothingness that the blue car caught up with me.

TWENTY FIVE

I hadn't even seen him coming.

He'd done a good job of staying out of sight while sticking right with me. I was probably forty miles out of Show Low, where I thought I'd spotted the car, and although I was still checking my mirrors regularly I had to admit I'd relaxed just a touch. An oldies station on the radio was right in the middle of a favorite Fleetwood Mac song and my head had probably even started bobbing in time to it when I glanced back and there was that distinctive blue, filling my rearview. I actually jumped and, with my move, swerved just a touch.

When I looked back in the mirror the man was grinning at his little victory.

I steadied my course and looked back again. The car was only inches from my bumper. This definitely wasn't Felix. The thin mustache was there, all right, but the face was thinner and slightly darker. Buckman was right, Rodriquez was proud of his flowing head of hair. He grinned again, showing a gap between his two front teeth. The woman was still with him, laughing with that bright red mouth.

I returned my attention to the road ahead.

Rodriquez bumped me.

I looked again. He had drifted back a few feet but I could still see the grin.

Buckman had said this guy would kill without a second thought and I believed it.

I heard his horn, just a friendly toot, right before he bumped me a second time. He'd gotten more of a run at it and this one came with enough force to send me to the shoulder. Gripping the wheel I righted my course again.

Bam!

The third bump would have been enough to send me off the side if I hadn't had a strong grip on the wheel and been ready for it. I was already doing seventy but sped up in hopes of getting some distance between us.

He matched his speed to mine.

How far was it to the nearest town? At least thirty miles, I guessed, and I didn't see another sign of civilization. The road stretched ahead in an almost perfectly straight line. He was right in my mirror again. I debated a couple of plans. A mile or so ahead I spotted a dirt pull-out, hardly a rest area, but large enough for a vehicle to get off the road. Some kind of guardrail flanked the road just beyond it.

Obviously I wasn't going to outrun him. The sedan was every bit as fast as my Jeep, probably faster. I did have one advantage, though—height. I looked back at him again. He was backing away to make another run at me. I sped up, putting more distance between us than he probably wanted. I was almost to the dirt pullout.

He floored it, racing forward to bash me. When he was less than ten feet away I slammed on my brakes with both feet hard on the pedal. The Jeep fishtailed and I pulled hard to keep her straight. The blue sedan slammed my left rear bumper, taking the corner of it right through his grille. I whipped back onto the road and gave it all the speed I dared. The sedan came at me again.

He pulled close once more and I repeated my last maneuver, braking and swerving. This time I wasn't so lucky. I veered off the left edge of the road, kicking up a plume of dust and gravel as the Jeep swerved precariously on two wheels, missing the guardrail by inches. My eyes slammed shut as I wondered where Rusty was at the moment. In slow motion, the car settled back onto all four tires and I wrenched the steering wheel back to guide her straight onto the road. Checked my mirror once more.

The sedan had slid sideways down the left lane and now sat with its passenger door wrapped around the thick wood abutment of the guardrail. White vapor billowed ominously from its front end. I slowed to a stop and looked back. Rusty had leaped over the seat into the cargo compartment and was barking furiously at the other car. My heart pounded as I shushed him.

Rodriquez was climbing out the driver's door, reaching inside for his passenger. He had a smear of red across his cheek. He looked at me and started to reach toward his belt. I didn't wait. I let two more mile markers go by before I slowed down. At the next wide spot I pulled over and got out my cell phone. I had to wipe my sweaty palms on my jeans before I could punch in the numbers. Dialed 911 and got a county dispatcher from somewhere I wasn't familiar with. I told him there was a wrecked car at the abutment and gave the highway and mile marker number.

I also told him the man in the car was wanted on drug charges in southern New Mexico and that he was armed and dangerous. I was guessing about the armed part—I hadn't actually seen a weapon—but better to report it that way than to send an unsuspecting officer to face Rodriquez.

A howling, flashing squad car zoomed by me heading south as I was entering Holbrook a few minutes later. I pulled off at the first McDonald's I came to, got out and stood on quaking legs, resting my forehead on the doorsill of the Jeep. The shakes set in then. I opened Rusty's door and put my arms around his neck, letting him lick my face as much as he wanted. He was content with about five licks before he became more interested in the smells emanating from the restaurant.

"Wait here," I said. "We're both getting treats after that ordeal."

I closed his door, grabbed my purse from the floor of the front seat, and walked back to survey the damage. It wasn't as bad as I'd expected. My left bumper was bent slightly upward at the corner and the metal quarter panel had a little wave in it. Most people wouldn't even notice it and it certainly didn't affect the way the car handled. With body shop prices what they are today it was probably only about a thousand dollars worth.

With a much lighter mind and a heart that was nearing its normal rate, I strode into McDonald's and ordered a Big Mac and two cheeseburgers with fries all around—Supersize, please. I sat on a stump of the petrified wood the area is known for, with Rusty at my side and we ate our sumptuous lunch. I watched the highway constantly, the irrational fear nagging that Rodriquez could somehow get back into his car and come after me. He didn't and we were soon back on the road.

Home never looks quite so good as when you've had a close call. In my case, make it two within twenty-four hours. I was ready to lock myself in and not come out for a week. But I still had Dorothy to face. Tomorrow, I decided. I climbed into bed and was asleep within moments.

I was back in court with Dorothy, this time in my underwear. She stood again behind her table; I sat behind mine trying to hunch down in my seat.

"Your Honor," she was saying, "I submit that the defendant knows my father's whereabouts and refuses to tell me."

The judge, who had been smiling indulgently at her, turned and glared at me.

"I hired her to find him and to give me the results of her investigation." Her gray curls dipped dramatically as she spoke in her characteristic slur.

All eyes in the courtroom turned to me. I crossed my arms over my chest, wishing I'd at least put on a lacy bra instead of the utilitarian white one I wore.

"Well?" the judge said. "How do you answer the allegation?"

I opened my mouth but nothing came out.

"As I told the court," Dorothy butted in, "she refuses to answer."

"So I see," said the judge. He slammed his gavel down. "Bailiff! Lock her up and figure out a way to make her talk."

This time when the bailiff grabbed me I fought back. I

swung around and caught him in the face with my right fist. He flinched backward and I seized the moment and ran, giving Dorothy a final "so there" parting stare before I hit the swinging door leading to the corridor.

I ran and ran, but couldn't reach the elevators. My legs were mired in something like Jell-O and I couldn't breathe. I could hear shouts behind me. Dorothy and my pursuers were catching up. I reached for the elevator button but it was way beyond my grasp. My legs pulled harder and harder, trying to get me there but I wasn't moving fast enough. The crowd was about to reach me. I felt a hand on my shoulder.

"No!" My scream woke me.

I lay there for a full minute, gripped in the paralysis of the after-dream. My face was buried in my pillow. Gradually I turned my head to get some air. Movement returned slowly to my limbs, like frost receding from a tree once the sun hits it. I stretched to break free from the last of it and sat up in bed, pulling the covers around me and running my hands through my hair.

Could Dorothy really force me to tell Willie's whereabouts?

I got up and went into the bathroom where I ran cool water in the basin and splashed it onto my face. Felt my way to a towel and patted dry. Took a few deep breaths to rid myself of that suffocating feeling.

Could she?

I slipped back into the warmth of my blankets and noticed the bedside clock said it was only two-fifteen. Not exactly a decent hour to call anyone for advice. Huddled in bed wearing nothing but a pair of panties I felt vulnerable. I got up again and slipped on my terry robe and slippers.

One thing about living in a city is that you're never in total darkness, not the same kind of deep velvet black you find in the country. By the light of the streetlights I padded my way through the house to the kitchen without turning on lights. I poured a mug of milk and set it in the microwave to warm. The back yard was bathed in moonlight, the same moon that had shone over a tiny campsite in Arizona the night before. The same moon that was now watching over Willie and his little mule tonight.

"Why should I tell her?" I whispered aloud.

Only Willie and I knew his exact location. Drake was the only other person who knew I'd actually located him. I didn't have to tell Dorothy anything. I stood up straighter. No, I didn't have to tell her anything at all.

I pulled the mug of hot milk from the microwave and added a packet of hot chocolate mix.

But *should* I tell her? I stirred the hot chocolate slowly. If I told her I hadn't found him, would she simply hire another detective?

I sipped at my cocoa and stared out into the yard. If I told her I'd located her father, that he was alive and well and didn't wish to come back, would she accept that? How far would Dorothy and Felix go to get those papers signed? The whole thing rattled around in my head but I decided I couldn't stay up all night thinking about it.

I yawned deeply, rinsed my mug and went back to bed. Rusty hadn't budged from his rug, a testament to the depth of his sleep. I fell asleep eventually, still without answers.

The phone startled me awake while I was still in that peaceful no-dream state a few hours later. The clock said it was six-thirteen.

"Charlie? Randy Buckman here."

"Geez, don't you ever sleep?" I grumbled.

"Sorry, I apologize for the early hour. Just wanted to bring you up to speed and give you a big thanks."

"What'd I do?" I mumbled, still only half awake.

"Caught Rodriquez for us, that's all," he said. I could hear his big smile at the other end of the line.

"I guess the Arizona police brought him in then?" I asked.

"From what I hear, he wasn't going anywhere with whatever you did to his car."

"Hey, I didn't touch his car—well, only a little bit. Would it be fair if I yelled, 'He started it!'?"

He actually chuckled out loud that time. "There's more good news," he said. "We came across evidence that Rory is the one who murdered Bud Tucker. We'd just about put together a case good enough to take to the DA. Somehow, information about the evidence leaked out of this office— and I could kill the person who did it, if I just knew for sure—and Sophie found out. Looks like she decided not to wait for the courts. Looks like she followed Rory up to the mine and tracked him inside. There was a Smith and Wesson .357 beside her body. And a bullet in his. Burned as they were, we at least got that much. Chances are her shot is what set off the explosion."

"Oh geez," I said, sitting up on the edge of the bed. My mind flitted back to Willie's confession.

"Then things really started to get sticky."

This wasn't sticky enough?

"When it came out that it was their two bodies in the mine, people just started to build this story about an affair between them." He sighed deeply. "It ain't the real situation, but the real one ain't any better so I'm just letting the rumors fly. I can only hope it all dies down pretty soon. Her funeral was yesterday and she's buried right beside her dad. Rory's got no people here so he's been taken to west Texas where some cousins live."

"And why was Rodriquez tailing me?"

"He'd seen your Jeep several times near the mines and knew you'd been snooping around up there. Assumed you'd found the drug stuff and he was keeping an eye on you. He told us he knew you'd met with me several times and thought we were planning to use you as a witness against him in court."

"That's ridiculous!" I sputtered. "I didn't know about the drug stuff and I certainly couldn't have tied him to it."

"But he didn't know that," he pointed out. "Let's just say this guy isn't the brightest bulb in the chandelier. He focused on you and that was that."

"Well, I can't say I'm too unhappy about wrapping his car around that bridge abutment then," I said. "So, does that tie up all three of your cases now?"

"Looks like it does," he said. "You got any news about Willie McBride for his family?"

"I'm . . . I'm still working on that one," I said. He didn't exactly ask whether I'd found Willie, did he?

"Well, guess that's about it. Except that there's a friend of yours here in my office who wants to say hello."

I heard the phone being shuffled around. Buckman's

voice in the background said something about getting some coffee.

"Hey there, Charlie-gal!"

"Keith?"

"That's me."

"What are you doing there?" I asked. "You didn't get dragged into this whole drug-dealer arrest thing, did you?"

"What? Aw, hell no. I just come by with some fresh donuts for the guys and heard Randy say you was on the phone. Just wanted to say hi."

"Well, I'm glad you did. Looks like things in White Oaks are all wrapped up now," I said. I hesitated. "Keith?"

"Yeah?"

"Know that item from your cash drawer?"

"Yeah."

"I found the X. What you thought would be there, it was."

"Gotcha."

"I haven't decided yet whether to tell his family yet. So don't say anything."

"You bet. You stop in now if you ever get back out this way," he said. "And drop me a card at Christmas."

"I will."

TWENTY SIX

I spent most of that day wondering exactly what I'd tell the McBride family members. In the end I decided that Dorothy and Felix would have to work harder to realize their selfish dreams. I wasn't going to hand anything to them. Dorothy threw a fit when I gave her my final report and refused to pay our bill, but Bea held true to *her* word. I called Bea in Seattle and told her the full truth, including Willie's and my wild ride in the flash flood. She'd followed through on having a notarized statement added to the new unsigned will, proving that it had never been validated by her father. She would let Melanie know that her grandfather was alive and well, nothing more.

Willie had told me he didn't want anything more to do with his family, but I had managed to persuade him to do one little thing. If he sent a Christmas card to Bea each year, it would prove he was still alive, which would leave Dorothy and Felix fuming if they tried to have him declared legally dead after he'd been missing seven years. That little clock couldn't begin ticking until seven years after the last card came.

Bea called me about a month later to let me know that her father had actually called her. She'd convinced him that if he planned on never moving back to Albuquerque he should sell his north valley property. The money could be banked and would leave him financially set for the rest of his life and preclude any dirty tricks by Felix. He'd agreed and she wondered if I could recommend a good Realtor in Albuquerque. Of course, I did.

Drake had a busy fire season, which put his fledgling company on much firmer financial ground, although I didn't get to see much of him until the seasonal monsoon rains began in August.

Willie's confessing to shooting Bud Tucker bothered me from time to time. It was the only part I'd never told another soul, except Drake. I had a nagging feeling I should have told Randy Buckman about it. But since I didn't do it right away, the opportunity just sort of slipped away. It wasn't really a murder, I justified. From Willie's account of it, I was sure it had been an accidental shooting. Buckman had wrapped up his case file anyway. Sophie was the only one to whom it might have made a difference and she, bless her heart, was gone now too. Even if she'd lived, that bit of news couldn't have made her life happier. So I couldn't see much point in bringing it out.

It's a secret I'll just have to live with.